WILLIAM TELL

JENSEN TANNER

Based on the play 'Wilhelm Tell' by Friedrich Schiller

TIMELINE
BOOKS

Cast of Characters

Hermann Gessler, *Governor of the Schwyz and Uri cantons*

Baron Von Attinghausen, *free noble of the Swiss cantons.*

Ulrich Von Rudenz, *his nephew.*

Landenberg, *Governor of Unterwalden*

Bertha Von Bruneck, *Austrian heiress and ward of Gessler*

People of Schwyz

Werner Stauffacher, *farmer, landowner*

Gertrude Stauffacher *(Werner's wife)*

People of Uri

Daniel Furst, *(father of Hedy Tell)*

William Tell, *huntsman, archer*

Hedwig (Hedy) Tell, *wife of William*

Walter and Tristan Tell, *sons of William and Hedy*

Jakob Muller, *farmer*

Rosselman, *the Priest*

Kuoni, *shepherd*

Werni, *huntsman*

Ruodi, *Fisherman*

People of Unterwalden

Arnold of Melchthal, *farmer*

Conrad Baumgarten, *woodcutter*

Anna Baumgarten, *(Conrad's wife)*

Other characters

Pfieffer of Lucerne, *traveller*

Johann, *Fisherman's Son.*

Seppi, *Shepherd's Assistant.*

Armgart Mechthild, *peasant woman* |

Friesshardt, *Soldier*

Leuthold, *soldier*

Rudolph De Harras, *soldier and lead guardsman of Gessler*

Duke John of Swabia

Stussi, *ranger*

Elsi, *girl in Altdorf*

Preface

Switzerland in the Medieval Age

In the 13th century, the country we now know as Switzerland consisted of a series of mountainous territories and cantons – a far-flung part of the Holy Roman Empire – which were largely autonomous. The cantons had a traditional, medieval feudal system, comprising wealthy noble families, their serfs, and the common peasants.

However, this began to change with the rise of the Habsburg family dynasty in neighbouring Austria.

As dukes, archdukes, and emperors, the Habsburgs ruled Austria for centuries. They commanded armies and spread their power and influence throughout central Europe.

By the early 14th century, they had embedded their rule in the Swiss cantons, imposing tax-collecting bailiffs. The brutal Austrian Emperor, Albert, installed local governors, who in turn instigated oppressive laws, harsh penalties, and acts of injustice against the Swiss people.

Prologue

Elsi squirmed between the legs of adults, ignoring her mother's shrill calls from somewhere in the crowd. Her heart thumped as she pushed forward, ducking under elbows and around skirts. She had never seen so many people stopped in the Altdorf town square, pressing against each other like sheep in a storm. The voices above merged into a drone of worry and fear, but she caught fragments that made her stomach twist.

'They can't really mean to—'

'The poor boy—'

She broke through to the front. There, across the square, before the linden tree, stood Walter Tell, straight-backed against the rough bark. An apple as red as a sunset was perched on his curly hair, and he was so still he might have been carved from stone. But Elsi saw the slight tremor in his hands, his fingers digging into his palms. She knew Walter from church, where they'd shared honeyed bread after services and played tag in the graveyard. Just last Sunday he'd shown her a nest of baby thrushes hidden in the bell tower.

Walter's face held no trace of his usual mischievous grin. His jaw was set, eyes fixed ahead with a determination that made him look older than his ten years. Elsi had seen that same look during Christmas service when he'd insisted on holding his own candle despite his mother's protests.

The ring of soldiers cast long shadows across the square. Sunlight glinted off their swords, sharp points aimed inward like a cage of steel.

Their faces were hard, unmoved by the crowd's fearful murmurs. A woman behind Elsi sobbed. Another whispered a prayer.

'He's just a child,' someone said.

'Silence!' A soldier barked, striking his sword against the cobblestones. The crowd flinched at the metallic clang, but Walter didn't move. The apple remained perfectly still on his head.

Elsi watched Governor Gessler shift on his black stallion, his thin lips curled into a cruel smile. His velvet cloak caught the breeze, revealing the gleaming sword at his hip. He raised a gloved hand, silencing the crowd's pleas with a dismissive flick of his wrist.

'The boy seems braver than his father,' Gessler called out, his voice carrying across the square. 'Perhaps we should have him shoot the apple instead.'

The crowd's fearful gasps made Elsi's chest tighten. She caught sight of Walter's father, William Tell, stepping forward, his chiselled cheekbones lined with anguish. His broad shoulders, built from years of hunting in the mountains, were tense beneath his leather vest. The crossbow in his hands trembled as he checked the bolt and then he raked his fingers through his clipped beard.

'This is madness,' someone said above her. 'To make a father shoot an apple off his son's head. One slip…'

Tell's eyes, sharp as a hawk's, darted between the apple and his son. A strand of dark hair fell across his furrowed brow as he raised the crossbow. Elsi had seen him at church, always standing tall and proud, but now his hands shook as he took aim. Elsi had always thought Walter's father looked like a giant, but now he seemed smaller, hunched over his crossbow as if it were suddenly too heavy to hold.

'Father!' Walter's clear voice rang out. 'Don't worry about me. You never miss. I trust you!'

The simple words seemed to steady Tell. His hands stopped shaking, and he drew himself up straighter. Elsi saw the look that passed between father and son, a moment of pure understanding that made her eyes shimmer with tears.

She watched Tell's hands move to his quiver. Her breath caught as he drew two arrows, the metal tips catching the sunlight. The first he tucked away with deliberate care into his belt, partly covered by his leather jerkin. The second he nocked to his bow.

Gessler's eyes narrowed at the motion, his fingers tightening on the reins so much his knuckles looked as though they'd poke through his gloves. His horse stirred beneath him, sensing the tension.

A woman near Elsi dropped to her knees, her prayer beads clicking together as she began to whisper. Others joined her, their voices rising in a desperate chorus. 'Holy Mother, protect the child...' The words spread through the crowd like ripples in a pond, growing louder with each passing moment.

'Shoot now, Tell,' Gessler commanded, raising his hand. His cold smile never reached his eyes. 'Or shall I have my men string up both you and the boy?'

Elsi's hands trembled as she clasped them together, adding her own silent prayer to the chorus around her. Why was this happening? What if the arrow struck Walter's head? The crowd's pleas seemed to bounce off Gessler like rain from stone, his expression remaining as hard and unmoved as the mountains in the distance.

The little girl's heart pounded as Tell raised the crossbow, his powerful arms shaking. She'd seen him carry deer across the mountain paths after successful hunts, yet now his strength seemed to falter. The weapon wavered, pointing first too high, then too low.

The square fell silent. Elsi felt the press of bodies around her, adults leaning forward, their breaths caught in their throats. The only sound was the soft creak of Tell's leather vest as he adjusted his stance.

She wanted to squeeze her eyes shut, to block out what might happen next. But her gaze remained fixed on Walter, standing so still beneath the apple. His face showed complete trust in his father, and something about that trust kept her eyes open, even as her stomach churned with fear.

Tell's finger tightened on the crossbow's trigger. Elsi saw his chest rise with one final breath, saw his eyes squint with the same focus she'd witnessed during archery demonstrations after church. The crossbow steadied.

The snap of the release cracked across the square like summer lightning. Elsi jumped at the sound, her heart seeming to stop as the dark bolt streaked through the air and the crowd pushed forward, past her.

A collective gasp rose from the people. Elsi felt herself rising on her tiptoes, straining to see past the shoulders of those in front of her, desperate to know if Walter survived.

Chapter One

Anna Baumgarten pushed another log beneath the steaming bucket of water, her slim fingers shaky as she stoked the flames. Her dark hair fell loose around her shoulders, having come undone from its neat braid during her rushed preparations. The fire's glow caught the sheen of sweat on her high cheekbones and flushed face.

Through the cottage window, she watched the Imperial Seneschal cross her yard. The man's very presence made her skin crawl. Known as the Wolfshot - a term for young noblemen that the servants whispered behind cupped hands - he carried himself with the swagger of someone who knew his position granted him power over common folk like her.

He had appeared at her door not an hour past, demanding a hot bath be prepared. Anna assumed it was for his own use after a long day of carrying out his duties at nearby Rossberg castle. As Imperial Seneschal, he wielded considerable influence, overseeing the castle's labourers and servants while currying favour with Governor Gessler himself.

The late afternoon sun cast long shadows across the yard as he approached. Anna's hands shook harder as she fed another stick to the hungry flames beneath the bucket. The water bubbled and steamed, almost ready for use.

Anna's breath caught in her chest as the Seneschal's footsteps crossed her threshold. At barely twenty-five, he carried himself like a seasoned lord - back straight, chin lifted, pale blue eyes cold with entitlement. His

11

fine velvet doublet and polished boots spoke of wealth that far exceeded his station, likely gained through extortion rather than honest service.

'The water better be ready, woman.' He yanked at his collar, revealing a pale throat marked with a duelling scar. The recent wound still looked angry and red - a reminder of his quick temper and quicker sword.

'It needs more time to heat properly, my lord, before I empty it to the tub.' Anna kept her voice steady despite her racing pulse. This was the second bucket and it would complete the bath. The whispers of other village women echoed in her mind - tales of his unwanted advances, of cornered maids and tearful confessions behind closed doors.

'I'll be the judge of that.' He strode to the bucket, steam rising around his angular face. A lock of dark hair fell across his forehead as he peered into the water, his lip curling. 'You've had plenty of time. Or perhaps you're being deliberately slow?'

Anna lifted her chin, meeting his gaze. 'The water will be hot when it's ready, as befits your lordship's station.' The words tasted bitter on her tongue, but she forced them out with feigned deference.

His eyes tracked her movements as she added another log to the fire. The way he watched her made her skin crawl, like a predator sizing up its prey.

All of a sudden his hand shot out, gripping Anna's wrist. His fingers pressed into her flesh, thumb tracing across her pulse point. The touch sent ice through her veins.

'Such a pretty thing, wasted on a common woodcutter.' His breath carried the sour tang of wine. 'You deserve better than chopping logs and washing linens.'

Anna wrenched her arm free, backing away from his towering form. 'My husband provides well enough.' The wedding band on her finger caught the firelight. 'I want nothing more than what Conrad gives me.'

The Seneschal's face hardened, his earlier facade of nobility cracking to reveal something darker underneath. He advanced, forcing Anna to retreat until her back hit the rough wall.

'Your husband serves at my pleasure.' His voice dropped low, menacing. 'One word from me to Governor Gessler about suspected disloyalty, and he'll rot in chains. Perhaps you'd prefer to ensure that doesn't happen?'

Anna's heart thundered against her ribs, but she kept her voice steady. 'Conrad is loyal to the crown. You'll find no cause against him.'

'Loyalty can be... questioned.' He planted his hands on either side of her head, caging her between his arms. 'Smart women know how to protect their husbands. Are you smart, Anna?'

Anna was alongside the kitchen bench and she reached out her right hand, her fingers closing around her wooden ladle on pure instinct. The smooth handle felt solid in her grip as she swung with all her might, catching the Seneschal across his scarred jaw. The crack of wood against bone filled her ears.

She didn't wait to watch him stagger. Her legs carried her through the door and into the fading daylight, heart pounding. The path to the forest stretched before her. She ran, her skirts hitched high, breath coming in ragged gasps. Branches whipped at her face as she followed the familiar route to Conrad's clearing.

She knew these paths like her own heartbeat - every root, every stone, every twist that led to where Conrad worked. The trees thinned ahead, revealing glimpses of the timber yard.

'Conrad!' The name tore from her throat.

Through tear-blurred vision, she saw him at his work, his short but powerful frame silhouetted against the trees. His axe rose high, catching the last rays of sunlight on its blade.

'Conrad!' she cried again.

The axe stopped mid-arc. It slipped from Conrad's grip, thudding into the earth beside a half-split log as he turned toward her voice.

Anna stumbled into Conrad's arms, her chest heaving from the run. The words spilled from her in fragments. 'The Seneschal - he came for a bath - his hands on me -' She clutched Conrad's rough shirt, breathing in his familiar scent. 'He threatened you, said he'd tell Gessler -'

Conrad pulled her closer. He ground his teeth as understanding darkened his features. Without a word, he released her and strode to where his axe lay embedded in the stump. The muscles in his back tensed as he wrenched it free.

'No!' Anna grabbed his sleeve, her fingers digging into the coarse fabric. 'He's the Imperial Seneschal. They'll hang you if you raise a hand against him.'

'Let them try.' Conrad gently but firmly removed her hand from his arm. 'Stay here, Anna. Don't move until I return.'

'Please.' Her voice cracked. 'He's not worth your life.'

Conrad cupped her face with his palm. 'No man threatens my wife.' His eyes, usually soft with tenderness, blazed with a fury she'd never seen. 'Stay hidden. Promise me.'

Anna's protest died in her throat as Conrad turned away, axe gripped tight in his hand. She watched him disappear down the path toward their cottage, leaving her alone among the scattered wood chips and half-split logs. He was acting out of character, and she knew he'd come to regret it. Her legs gave way, and she sank to her knees, trembling with fear - not for herself, but for what awaited her husband at the end of that path.

***

The fisherman, who had worked the waters of Lake Lucerne his whole life, felt the sudden chill as a powerful wind sprang from seemingly nowhere and whipped across the steel-gray surface of the lake. Just an hour before, Ruodi had watched when the first rays of dawn painted the Swiss sky in hues of amber and rose, casting a golden sheen across that very same surface. A gloriously calm morning. He liked nothing more on these mornings than to watch his boy, Johann, out on the lake in his small boat, checking the nets that had been set the night before, with Johann's youthful voice carrying across the water as he sang an old Swiss melody.

But now Ruodi felt a piercing stab of concern.

He knew better than anyone how unpredictable the weather was but even he was stunned by how suddenly the day turned dark. His weathered face creased with rising unease as black clouds spread out rapidly from behind the jagged peaks of the mountain that overlooked the lake, a strong wind springing up in their wake.

14

'Johann!' His voice rang out across the water. 'Storm! Bring her in, boy. Now.'

The boy's song faltered, his gaze following his father's outstretched arm. He'd been totally absorbed in scanning the nets and had taken little notice of the turn in the weather. Disappointment crossed his features, but he nodded and called back, 'Yes, papa. I see it.'

As Johann guided his boat back to shore, the wind grew wilder, and the rumble of distant thunder became a roar, carrying with it the scent of rain. On the shore, Ruodi worked swiftly, securing loose equipment and tying down the larger fishing vessel.

'Ruodi.' A call came from the dirt path further back and Ruodi turned to see Kuoni, the shepherd, who was carrying a wooden milk pail across his broad shoulders, his young assistant Seppi trailing behind him. 'Good morrow, my friend.' Kuoni tipped his head upwards, indicating the thick layer of clouds. 'But perhaps not as good as we would normally hope for.'

'No "perhaps" about it,' said Ruodi. 'Do you seek shelter for your pail?'

'Yes. I was on my way to Gottfried's farm when...' He shrugged, tipping his head to the sky again.

Ruodi gestured to his hut. 'Set it down in there. The heavens are about to burst, I can feel it in my bones now. And yet fifteen minutes ago there was no sign this was coming.'

Kuoni strode toward the hut. 'I've not seen a tempest brew this fierce this quick since the year of the Great Storm.'

Seppi, eager to prove his worth, chimed in. 'The sheep were restless all night, Master. They sensed it coming.'

The shepherd, his beard flecked with dew, nodded approvingly at his apprentice. He placed the pail of milk inside the door of the hut. 'The animals have a way of knowing. They are smart – smarter than many men I know.'

Seppi's eyebrows raised in wonder. 'There are animals smarter than men?'

Ruodi and Kuoni both laughed. 'As you become a man, young Seppi, you will learn this for yourself,' Kuoni said.

Ruodi's wife appeared in the doorway, telling Kuoni she would make certain the milk was kept safe, and asking if he and Seppi would be taking shelter with them.

'I need to go and herd my flock to the stables,' Kuoni said.

The woman looked to the sky as rain began spitting, the wind whistling through the window of her modest home. 'You'll not make it before they scatter.'

'I must try,' Kuoni said. 'I cannot afford to have any of them die in this. And this looks like no ordinary storm.'

'It feels anything but ordinary,' the woman agreed.

As Johann's small boat scraped against the pebbly shore, Ruodi moved to help the boy secure it. Kuoni and Seppi were about to leave when another figure approached along the path. Ruodi looked around and saw that it was another neighbour, this time the farmer, Werni. Like a couple of the other farmers, Werni was also a huntsman, who took to the mountains in the early morning to seek out the chamois that were plentiful throughout the Alps. 'I was nearby,' he called out. 'Can I help secure your boats, Ruodi?'

'We are fine,' Ruodi said, 'but it would make sense for you to take shelter until this thing passes.'

Werni nodded his head in thanks as he came closer. 'As you know, my father also fished these waters for many years,' his eyes lifted to the rapidly darkening sky, 'and despite his age, he still has an unnatural sense when it comes to these forces of nature. He told me just yesterday that there will be many of these fierce tempests in the days to come. He says the Dark Talkers are angrier than they have ever been.'

Seppi's eyes widened in curiosity. 'Master Werni, who are the Dark Talkers?'

'Legend says they are spirits who can bring storms and end them. It is said that when the people of the land are oppressed, the Dark Talkers become more and more agitated and their fury knows no bounds.'

The men exchanged knowing glances, their unspoken thoughts giving voice to a very different storm, one they feared far more than the tempest that was coming down on them now.

As Kuoni and Seppi headed off, Ruodi heard a muffled cry and his breath caught in his throat as another figure came, not from the path, but bursting through the undergrowth of the forest that skirted the other side of the hut. Squinting through the rain that had begun to fall, Ruodi recognized that it was one of the men from the neighbouring Unterwalden canton, Conrad Baumgarten, although he had never seen the man looking like this, his clothes torn and muddied, his face stricken with terror. Blood trickling from a gash on his forehead.

'Conrad Baumgarten?' Werni stepped forward, his hand instinctively reaching for the knife at his belt. 'What in heaven's name has happened to you?'

Kuoni and Seppi turned back, drawn by Baumgarten's cry and his ragged appearance.

Baumgarten's eyes darted wildly, scanning the treeline behind him, his chest heaving. 'Please, I need safe passage.' His eyes fixed on Ruodi. 'Can you get me across the lake?'

'What's happened?' Ruodi repeated Werni's question. Even as he spoke, he heard something in the distance, other than the howl of the wind. The hooves of horses.

'Wolfshot. The Imperial Seneschal of Rossberg,' Baumgarten said, his voice ragged, 'late yesterday he marched into my home with his guardsmen waiting outside, as if he owned it. Demanded that my poor wife prepare him a bath…can you believe it? When she refused his advances, he tried to force himself on her.' His voice shook. 'She fled to warn me in the woods. I returned to find him…' His fingers closed around his axe handle. 'He was tearing through our home, shouting he'd have her arrested. When he saw me, he drew his sword.'

Kuoni crossed himself. 'Lord have mercy.'

'I struck before he could swing and my axe caught him in the chest.' Baumgarten's eyes glazed with the memory. 'His blood soaked into our floorboards.'

Ruodi felt ice on his spine that had nothing to do with the cold wind. 'He's dead?'

'God help me, yes.' His shoulders slumped. 'I ran, but his imperial guard, waiting outside, saw me, gave chase. I lost them in the forest but I

17

fear that this morning they have reinforcements with them and have guessed I'd make for your ferry, Ruodi.'

'Christ give us strength,' Ruodi said.

Kuoni glanced at Ruodi and Werni. 'He did what any of us would have done to protect our wives. But the consequences—'

'And your wife?' Kuoni asked.

'I told Anna to go to her sister's house in Steinem and wait.' His voice was a rasp, struggling for breath, his body wracked by sheer terror, his arms gesticulating wildly. 'Please. I fear the horsemen are only minutes away.'

Ruodi looked into the desperate man's face and felt the weight of the decision before him. To aid a fugitive was to risk everything – his livelihood, his freedom, perhaps even his life. Yet to turn away a countryman in need went against everything he and the others believed in as Swiss men.

Swiss. The very name made his heart beam with pride. It had been used increasingly by the locals for their people and their lands, derived from the Schwyz canton, one of the founding cantons of their forested region.

The rain grew heavier, and Ruodi looked out on the lake. The normally placid waters were choppy, transformed into waves becoming higher by the minute, swept by winds that it was not hard to believe reflected the fury of the so-called Dark Talkers. 'It's already too late,' he said to Baumgarten. 'It would be madness to attempt a crossing, we'd both be drowned.'

Baumgarten fell to his knees. 'Then I am a dead man.'

'Your best bet is to run, man, take to the hills again,' said Werni.

'Even in this storm, they will not turn back. They will outrun me, if not on horseback, then on foot. What have I done? *What have I done?*'

Ruodi felt a pang in his chest. He knew Baumgarten was right. The soldiers would not return empty-handed to face the wrath of their viceroy, the governor, Gessler. He looked with distress to the path, expecting to see the horsemen thunder in through the veil of the rain, but instead, his brow furrowed and his eyes widened. Another figure on the path.

Ruodi motioned to the others and they turned their attention to a man striding purposely toward them, his tall, imposing frame silhouetted like a ghost in the dim light. As the figure came into clearer view, Ruodi knew instinctively from the man's gait who it was, the piercing eyes and grave expression beneath the weather-worn leather cap a look he had seen many times before, as was the crossbow strung across this man's back. 'Tell,' he called out. The man strode down the shore path, his strapping build evident beneath his leather hunting vest. His eyes took in the scene with swift assessment. Even through the strengthening wind, his presence seemed to calm the chaos around him.

'William Tell, the archer?' Seppi asked, breathlessly.

'The very same,' young Johann answered him.

Chapter Two

Reaching them, William Tell, adjusting his crossbow, said, 'I was on the rise and saw horsemen across the valley, heading this way despite this oncoming storm.' His gaze took in their faces, puzzled by the despair he saw there, and the villager who was on his knees. 'Ruodi, old friend, what's happened?'

'Baumgarten's killed the Imperial Seneschal and wants to take flight across the lake,' Ruodi said.

'What?' Tell's gaze locked onto Baumgarten, assessing him. 'Why?'

Baumgarten blurted out what he'd told the others.

Tell listened to the man's story, and then spoke quietly. 'So you defended your wife's honour, perhaps even her life.'

'Yes.'

'I am sorry to hear you were put in that position.'

'Gessler's men are animals,' Baumgarten managed, his whole body shaking, 'they think themselves above the law, above decency. They will see me swing from the gallows.'

The sound of horses' hooves grew louder and they all looked to the path.

Tell's mind raced. He thought of his own family – his sons Walter and Tristan and his wife, Hedwig, affectionately known as Hedy to William and their friends. He could only imagine the lengths he'd go to protect them. The Habsburg lords of Austria were tightening their grip on the forested Swiss cantons of Uri, Schwyz, and Unterwalden, sending more men like their governor, Hermann Gessler to rule with increasingly cruel authority. This time it had been Baumgarten and his wife that Gessler's man had attacked. Tomorrow it might be Tell's own wife or any other honest person in the mountains. The injustice of the Austrian rule had been burning a hole in his chest for a long time now – since the death of his father – and was something he'd forced himself to suppress, purely for the safety of his loved ones. He was, after all, a simple huntsman. Not a warrior.

His gaze went to the lake. He had seen those waters roiling in bad weather before, but there was no doubt this storm was building up to be worse than any seen in many years.

He turned to Ruodi, his voice firm despite the doubt that was gnawing at him. 'If you can lend us your boat, I'll take him.'

'You can't be serious, Tell. Look at those waves.'

'If we go now, there's a good chance we can make it across before the full force of this storm hits.'

Ruodi shrugged. 'I won't stand in your way of trying to help this man. But Tell, think of your own family…'

The archer looked out on the lake. 'We can make it if we go now.'

'Then God go with you,' Ruodi said, hurrying to untether the larger of the boats. 'You'll need His favour out there today.'

'Tell,' said Werni, 'my father warns of storms worse than any we've seen. The Dark Talkers are showing their wrath for what is happening in our country.'

'I'm not one for superstition, Werni,' Tell gestured at the skies, 'but I have nothing but respect for the power of Mother Nature. I can only pray that she is on our side.' He checked the hull for weak spots, and then, satisfied, he and Ruodi pushed the vessel into the water.

'Into the boat,' Tell commanded Baumgarten.

Baumgarten stumbled forward, his eyes wide with a mixture of fear and gratitude. 'I don't know how to thank you, Tell—'

'Save your breath, you'll need it for prayers once we're out on the lake.'

As Baumgarten settled in the boat, Ruodi pushed them off and Tell's powerful arms took over, driving the oars through the seething waves.

21

Tell knew this storm was moving in faster than most but as he rowed, he found the increase in the wind was even more rapid than he anticipated. He had been rowing only a short time when the power in the wind lifted, more than tripling in its intensity, every gust slamming against the boat like a battering ram. It was like a creature in unimaginable pain, Tell thought, writhing, tossing, lashing out, and the boat rocked violently and rose and fell with the crashing swells, the rain now coming down in a torrent.

His face hardened, his eyes squinting against the rain.

Have I made a grave miscalculation?

As the wind raged against the small craft, he leaned into it, using his body weight to keep them upright, his muscles burning with the effort as the water smashed down over them. 'Baumgarten,' he shouted to be heard above the roar of the elements, 'bail water as fast as you can or we'll sink before we're halfway across.'

Baumgarten scrambled to scoop water into the boat's bucket and cast it out but Tell feared that for every attempt three times as much surged in, coming from every direction.

He rowed and rowed, and time lost all meaning, every second seeming an eternity. It started to feel as though they'd been out on the lake forever. As he tried to keep his vision on the far shore, Tell imagined for one crazy moment that he saw the face of his father in the ghost-like mist that the rain had imprinted on the air.

He knew these waters as well as he knew the back of his hand, as well as he knew the mountains where he hunted. Lake Lucerne was twenty-four miles in length and a maximum of two miles in width, ringed by steep limestone mountains. It flowed into four basins, Uri and Kussnacht Lakes among them, with enormous rocky promontories giving the waters of Lucerne a twisting, star-shaped appearance when viewed from on high. Tell had been out on this lake in a storm once before, although a storm not nearly as ferocious as this one, his father teaching him to row. Father and son had been taken by surprise when the weather turned and a thunderstorm struck, the depth of the lake giving rise to huge waves as though they were out on an ocean.

'Feel the water, William,' his father's voice echoed in his mind. 'It's alive, son. Respect it, work with it, treat it as your friend, not your enemy.'

Tell hoped his father was watching now. He recalled his father showing him how to grip the oars when everything was slick with the water, and how to find the rhythm in the wind, however erratic it might seem, and to adjust, and continually readjust, to go with the storm's flow, not against it, to use its movements to his advantage.

But despite his strength, his experience on the lake, and his determination, Tell was tiring, gasping for breath as the waves slammed over the boat. It was half full of water, with Baumgarten's efforts barely keeping them from submerging. Tell knew the most important thing was to prevent them from overturning, he'd managed that so far, but try as he might to squint through the veil of rain and mist he could no longer see the opposite shore. He was no longer certain he was making any headway at all, despite the pure adrenaline behind every stroke of the oars, despite his focus on staying on course.

And then a wave more monstrous than the others crashed into them, a crescendo of force and sound, and the boat tipped sharply and one of the oars was wrenched out of Tell's grasp.

***

On the shore, Ruodi paced frantically, his eyes straining against the rainstorm. He'd sent the boys inside the hut with his wife. Kuoni and Werni stood like statues behind him, drenched, their faces set like granite.

'Do you see anything?' Werni asked, his voice barely audible above the wind.

Kuoni shook his head. 'Nothing. I fear that your Dark Talkers have taken them.'

Suddenly, the pounding of hooves cut through the crescendo of the storm. Ruodi whirled around, his heart sinking as he saw a group of soldiers thundering towards them.

'Halt!' the lead horseman bellowed, reining in his mount. He cast his gaze over the three men. 'What are you doing standing outside in this storm?'

'We've just secured my boats,' Ruodi said, 'and then we heard your approach, sir.'

'You are a bad liar, fisherman. Where is the murderer, Conrad Baumgarten?'

Ruodi raised his hands. 'We've seen no one, sir. The storm —'

'Liar!' the soldier spat, dismounting. He grabbed Ruodi by the collar. 'We know he came this way and I expect he hoped to flee across the lake. Do you not also ferry people across these Godforsaken Swiss waters?'

'Yes, my lord.'

'Where are you hiding him, fisherman?'

Werni intervened, his voice steady despite his fear. 'Please, there's no one here but us. I'm a simple farmer and hunter, and Kuoni here, a shepherd. We're just waiting out the storm.'

The soldier scanned their faces. 'If I find you're harbouring a criminal, you'll all rot in a dungeon.' He turned to his soldiers. 'Search the area,' he commanded.

As the soldiers fanned out, Ruodi whispered a silent prayer for Tell and Baumgarten, hoping against hope that they had made it to safety on the far shore. His and Tell's fathers had been friends, and the boys had learned together from their fathers how to fish, how to hunt, and how to row. Tell had, of course, been the better hunter, becoming skilled with the crossbow and later the winner of several local archery tournaments. Although a hunter and not a fisherman by trade, Tell had, with his physique, also been the stronger of the two when it came to rowing. Ruodi knew that if anyone could navigate the ferocity of the storm out on that lake, it was William Tell.

He was snapped back to the present by a bellow from the lead soldier, his face contorted with rage as his men returned empty-handed from their search. But not without information. 'There appears to be a space for a third boat, which is missing,' one of the soldiers reported. 'Indications in the mud are that it was set there not long ago.'

The lead horseman turned on the three men. 'You've helped him escape.' His voice was a snarl, his spittle flying in Ruodi's face. 'You will pay for this treachery, do you hear me? You will regret your actions for the rest of your miserable lives.'

With a cruel smile, he turned to his men. 'Burn it,' he commanded, gesturing at Ruodi's modest hut. 'And then the boats. Let this be a lesson to all who defy Gessler's authority.'

'But how? The rain…,' one of the men questioned.

'Take your torches, fools, and light it from the inside. The timber will fuel it and when the rain extinguishes the flames it will be raining down on a burnt-out hull.'

Ruodi's anguished cry pierced the air as the soldiers set torches to his home and the two remaining craft. 'My family!' He ran toward the hut and embraced his wife and son, as they ran out, terrified, with Seppi right behind them.

And then they stood back helplessly, as the flames erupted from the interior, licking hungrily at the thatched roof, devouring years of memories in moments. As if to aid the oppressors, the rain lightened while the wind maintained its relentless force.

'Thank your God that I spare your lives, but when the Governor's new prison is built, we'll return to arrest you.' The lead horsemen then commanded his men to ride out.

Kuoni and Werni gasped and Kuoni sank to his knees, lashed by the rain, as the soldiers rode back along the path. The two boys held onto one another, and Ruodi's wife held onto him, shaking, tears streaming down both of their faces.

***

Unable to row, and drained of his strength, Tell clung to the sides of the boat, and made certain Baumgarten was doing the same. Another massive wave lifted the boat's bow high into the air before dropping it into a trough. But in that moment Tell caught sight of the shoreline, closer than he'd realized. A bolt of lightning lit the air around them, illuminating the sheer cliff face ahead. 'There!' Tell shouted to

Baumgarten. 'The current's pushing us to that gap in the cliffs.' The rain was stinging his eyes. 'We're not far from the shallows. When I tell you to jump, swim for that gap.'

The boat lurched sideways as another wave caught them broadside, nearly capsizing. Tell shifted his weight, somehow keeping them upright. A rocky outcrop materialized and Tell roared, 'Jump.'

Baumgarten hurled himself from the boat, went under, and then resurfaced and lashed out for the shore, able to stand within seconds as he reached the shallows, and then stumbling as he hit the slick, moss-covered rocks. Tell followed in one fluid motion, abandoning the craft as it was pulled in, splintering against the rocks moments later.

'I owe you my life,' Baumgarten said, his chest heaving as he lay panting on the gravel of the shore.

Tell squatted alongside him, catching his breath. 'My father once told me,' he spoke softly, more to himself than his companion, 'that a man's true measure is found not in how he weathers the storm but in how he helps others through it.'

'A wise man,' Baumgarten said.

Tell motioned to the forest slope beyond the rocky shore. 'Take that deer track, it leads to a cave where we can take shelter.'

Baumgarten coughed and wheezed. 'And what becomes of me after that?'

'When the storm has passed, I have a friend who may be able to help.'

Baumgarten's face showed relief, and then he scrambled up the slope.

Before he followed, Tell glanced back across the lake, his eyes fixed on the distant shore. Even through the rain and mist, he could see the orange glow of fire. His heart constricted, knowing all too well what this meant. The horsemen had taken out their rage on Ruodi and the others. In the act of saving one man, had he condemned three others?

He choked back his anger and then he set off up the slope.

Chapter Three

The late afternoon sun cast long shadows through the branches of the ancient lime tree that stood before Werner Stauffacher's house in Steinen. The house itself was impressive, newly built of the finest timber, its windows gleaming, its walls decorated with painted coats of arms and proverbs that caught the eye of passing travellers. It stood within sight of the bridge that crossed the nearby river, a testament to its owner's hard work and prosperity on lands that had been in his family for generations.

It was hard to believe that just hours before, the region had been battered by the worst storm in years, but in its wake, the sun shone and the birds twittered. In the front garden, Pfeiffer of Lucerne, a merchant whose travels gave him a keen sense of political winds, was preparing to take his leave after a brief visit, his cloak billowing behind him as he strode towards the front gate, his lean frame taut with urgency. Werner Stauffacher, a well-built man with greying temples and the leathery hands of one who worked his own lands, followed, his face creased with concern.

'I implore you again, old friend,' Pfieffer said, turning as he reached the gate, to face Stauffacher. 'Do not bend your knee to Austria. Our ancient freedoms hang by a thread.'

Stauffacher's hand unconsciously rose to rub his chin. 'What choice do we have with the Habsburgs' reach growing stronger by the day?'

Pfeiffer's eyes flashed. 'There is always choice, Werner. Our forefathers did not wrest these lands from the wilderness only to have them stolen by foreign tyrants. I know you think the same.'

A breeze ruffled the leaves of the nearby Linden tree, its broad, gnarled trunk one that Stauffacher's forebears had also looked upon, and he felt the presence of those generations. He tried to persuade his friend to stay and talk longer, but Pfieffer shook his head. 'I must reach Gersau by nightfall. But remember – whatever these new rulers inflict on us with their pride and their greed, bide your time, don't swear allegiance to them as some of our noble class have done, do not do their bidding.'

'You speak of rebellion,' Stauffacher said, his voice low. 'It's a dangerous word.'

'Not as dangerous a word as complacency,' Pfieffer said. He gripped Stauffacher's shoulder. 'Remember the charters that our forebears created years ago to proclaim our rights. Remember who we are, Werner.' He embraced his friend and then, with a final, piercing look, he turned and strode away, his figure soon swallowed by the gathering dusk.

Stauffacher watched him go, rooted to the spot, his mind conflicted. The Austrian Empire had always been there, a distant but ever-present authority, its power and influence now a shadow across all of the cantons. To defy it seemed madness. And yet…Stauffacher's gaze drifted to his home, to the skilfully tended fields beyond, while his mind thrust forth the memory of his encounter the day before with Gessler. This land, this life…it was theirs, not Austria's to command. What was it Pfieffer had said?

Remember who we are.

As he stood lost in thought, a gentle hand touched his arm. He turned to find Gertrude, his wife of thirty years, her gaze apprehensive, her eyes searching his face. 'Werner, what has been said that Pfieffer's visit has left you so…agitated. Is this about Gessler, again?'

He saw in his wife the strength and wisdom that had been his anchor through so many personal challenges. 'It's not just one of Gessler's acts,' he said, 'but a thousand of the man's small tyrannies, merging it seems into something far worse. The new taxes, the arbitrary arrests, the way

Gessler parades through the streets as if we were conquered foes rather than fellow countrymen.' Stauffacher's tone grew bitter. 'Pfieffer tells me that Gessler has a prison under construction in Althof, a fortress to cow us into submission.'

Gertrude took a deep breath. 'A prison?'

'And he intends to fill it. Another way to rule by fear.'

Gertrude led him to the bench under the tree and they sat. She took both of his hands in hers and squeezed them with reassurance but her face was marked with worry.

'Pfieffer sees the growing unrest,' Stauffacher said, 'and the need for organized resistance given that the path of negotiation has only ever gone around in circles. He believes with my connections I'm the best one to speak out against Austrian injustice, to address a gathering of like minds.'

'And, of course, he's right,' Gertrude said. 'The people of these cantons know your honour and your heart.'

'Gessler rode by our house yesterday afternoon,' Stauffacher said. 'The arrogant peacock lingered with his horsemen, sneering at the fine stonework and the painted proverbs. Said it was unseemly for mere peasants to live so well, that we forget our place. *Mere peasants.* As though I have not for decades played a part in building our community here. As though the words of the old Swiss charters mean nothing.'

'You didn't tell me this last night.'

'No.' He shrugged.

'My dear, dear husband. Do you think I haven't been aware that you've been holding back on your thoughts for months?'

'Always more perceptive than the rest of us. You think I would know that by now.'

She gave a gentle smile. 'Maybe in another thirty years.'

He returned the smile, if only briefly, and it occurred to him it was the first time he'd smiled in days, maybe weeks.

'I sense there's more. What else did this coward say?'

'He asked who owned this house though he knew full well,' Stauffacher confided. 'When I told him it was held in fief from the Emperor, has been for generations, his face darkened as though I'd

29

insulted him. He said that he was the law here and he would not have peasants building as they pleased, acting like lords of the land.'

Gertrude remained calm, listening intently, her nobility showing in her straight spine and lifted chin. 'My father used to host canton leaders in our hall,' she said. 'I learned much from their councils when I was a girl, I listened to them discuss the old imperial charters by the fire. I know our rights, and I know Gessler's kind.' Her voice hardened. 'Gessler hates men like you because you represent freedom and hard work and you have the respect of the villagers. And what is he? A younger son with nothing but his title who envies what men like you have achieved.'

'Even so, what can a man like me do? What can any of us do?'

'The first thing is to acknowledge that you're not alone in this. Just as Pfieffer has told you, others think as you do, not just here in our canton, but in Unterwald and Schwyz. Men who believe the ideals of the old charters need action, not just words. Perhaps it's time these men found each other. Someone needs to take the first step in uniting them.'

Stauffacher stared at her. 'You're speaking of rebellion.' His voice was a whisper, as though speaking at normal volume would give the words more credence.

'Or survival.'

'Once a spark is lit it could lead to war. Violence that does not spare people, property, or our flocks.' He gestured to the house. 'Everything could burn.'

Gertrude's response surprised him. 'Then perhaps that is the chance we must take. The alternative is to condemn our children and our children's children to an oppressive rule that never stops spreading. And I know you hold fears for our family's future, you've spoken of that on more than one occasion.'

He nodded. 'I have.'

They sat in silence for a while, listening to the rustle of the leaves in the breeze, the chatter of the birds, and watching the sun as it sank lower on the horizon, the twilight settling over the land.

'You are right,' Stauffacher said presently. 'As is Pfeiffer. We need to unite our cantons. But it will take time...'

30

'Which is running out. Either way, this needs proper, considered planning, and discretion. And you're the best man for it, not Pfeiffer, he's too much of a firebrand.'

Stauffacher nodded slowly but said nothing. He felt a great shift within his breast, an overwhelming sense of duty, a call to action that he had tried to resist for too long. He thought of Gessler's monstrous arrogance in raising taxes beyond the ability of many to pay, of having his soldiers raid properties, of building a prison to spread fear and cement his rule. But he was equally unsettled by the enormity of uniting men to rise against an enemy that wielded great power. The risk was immense.

'You'll need allies. Trusted men from each canton,' Gertrude said.

'Yes.'

'You know men in Uri. Daniel Furst, and the baron, Von Attinghausen. Intelligent men, who feel as you do.'

'Attinghausen, for all his high birth, loves our country's freedoms as much as any commoner,' Stauffacher said. 'And Furst, yes, his thoughts are known to a number of us. He's been like a brother to me. And there's Melchthal. Outspoken, but highly regarded throughout the cantons.

'You'll speak with them?'

He nodded. 'I'll make preparations to meet with them within the week.'

Gertrude leaned closer to him, her hand touching his cheek. 'Remember. You won't be alone in this.'

He gave a half smile, fighting back the doubt that was still there, nagging at him.

They might have sat there for a while longer, enjoying the calm of the twilight, given they faced an uncertain future, when Stauffacher noticed a movement at the edge of the garden. Two figures approached along the path, reaching the gate, and he immediately recognized a friend from Uri, William Tell, not someone he expected to see today, and not at this hour, so far from his home in Bürglen. Beside Tell strode a shorter man, his movements hurried and anxious, his face gaunt, his clothes muddied and torn. As were Tell's.

'William,' he called. 'What brings you here at this time of the day?'

Tell's eyes darted around the grounds of the homestead as he drew near. 'Forgive this intrusion, Werner. I'm afraid there's been an incident on the shores of the lake. I must ask your help for this man but I must also tell you he is a fugitive from Gessler's soldiers.'

Gertrude spoke up. 'Then you must come inside at once, Gessler's men have been known to ride by our property.'

Once inside, Gertrude led them to chairs in the chamber. 'I've never seen two men in such need of refreshment,' she said, 'I have soup on the stove.'

Tell's shoulders relaxed and he broke into a grin. 'You're a godsend.'

As Gertrude went to the kitchen, Tell said, 'Werner, this is Conrad Baumgarten of Unterwalden. The Imperial Seneschal invaded his home and attempted to violate his wife. Baumgarten rushed to confront the Seneschal—'

'I had no choice,' Baumgarten cut in, his words tumbling out in a rush. 'The Wolfshot swung his sword at me, and I struck the coward with my axe…'

Stauffacher rubbed his chin as he listened.

'I know you have given others refuge,' Tell said. 'If you can help—'

'I am sorry for your troubles, Baumgarten,' Stauffacher said, his voice firm. 'I can offer you sanctuary but only briefly. I'm no longer certain this home is safe from intrusion by the Austrians.' He told Tell and Baumgarten about his encounter the day before with Gessler, as Gertrude returned with the soup.

'We'll hide you in the old grain store,' Stauffacher said. He couldn't but marvel inwardly at this turn of fate – the rebellion that he, Gertrude, and Pfieffer had spoken of, unexpectedly taking shape on this very day, at his very home. He was surprised by the calm manner in which he was responding. It was not a mirror of the anxiety he felt. 'It's secluded, and I can arrange provisions to be brought discreetly. Once we've ascertained it's safe, we'll arrange safe passage for you, perhaps to the Rigi mountains where I know of a rebel camp.'

Baumgarten slurped the soup from a spoon. 'I cannot thank you enough, sir.'

Tell nodded approvingly. 'A sound plan, my friend. And another friend, the fisherman, Ruodi, will need our assistance. I saw his hut burned to the ground by the Austrians.'

Stauffacher shook his head.

'Dear Lord,' Gertrude said.

'Can you stay the night, William?' Stauffacher asked. 'There's something I need to speak to you about.'

Tell scooped up the last of his soup. 'I must get back to Bürglen,' he said. 'Hedy will be worried that I did not return from my early morning hunt, and they will have heard what's happened to the fisherman. I need to get back to her.'

'Then let me have a quick word while I walk with you to the gate.'

Tell said his goodbyes to Gertrude and Baumgarten, and as he walked out of the homestead, Stauffacher, walking alongside him, said, 'You're aware of the unrest that's taking hold across the cantons, and this incident at the lake is further proof that things are escalating. Will you join me in meeting with the canton leaders to plan for opposition to what the Habsburg rule is doing to us?'

'You know that I share your desire for freedom,' Tell said, 'but you have seen how Gessler's soldiers respond to any act of defiance. Any organized act of opposition will be met with force.'

'That is my fear, yes.'

'You're talking about a rebellion against an enemy that has weaponry and horsepower that we can't match.'

'Pfieffer, the traveller, has spoken to many throughout the cantons and he believes it's possible. Either way, I think we both know that revolt is coming, whether organized or not, and it would be better to be prepared, manned, and well-armed in advance, surely?'

The two men stood in silence at the front gate, as Tell considered his friend's words. 'I can't give you an answer right now, Werner,' Tell finally said. 'As much as I agree, my conscience reminds me I must consider every possibility. As well as the impact on Hedy and Walter and Tristan.'

'Can you return in the morning, then? Gessler has a prison under construction at Altdorf. Ride here, and I will join you on my horse, and we shall ride to see this monstrosity for ourselves. I expect it will help both of us in weighing our consciences.'

'I've heard word of this prison.'

'Gessler's forced locals to work on the construction to cover their unpaid taxes. Treating them as slaves.'

Tell clasped Stauffacher's shoulder. 'On the morrow, then,' he said before he waved and headed off along the path.

Stauffacher watched Tell's retreating figure disappear into the fading twilight. The night was falling, but it wasn't the only darkness he felt closing in.

Chapter Four

The sun beat down on the backs of the labourers as they toiled at the construction site near Altdorf. Sweat dripped from brows furrowed in concentration and exhaustion, the rhythmic clink of metal on stone punctuated by grunts of exertion. Looming over it all was the half-built fortress, its unfinished walls a stark reminder of the Austrian authority's tightening grip on their land.

Tell and Stauffacher crested the hill overlooking the construction site, bringing to a halt their horses, two fine, long-legged palfreys that boasted a magnificent sheen off their black hides. Tell cast his eyes over the scene, his body stiffening as he watched a soldier strike a worker with the flat of his sword. The man stumbled but didn't fall, forcing himself to continue hauling stones.

'Young men who couldn't meet their taxes, forced to work here when they should be tending their land,' Stauffacher said, 'and old men who should be seeing out their years in the comfort of their homes. This is worse than I feared. This is the future of the Swiss cantons, William, unless we act.'

The two men cantered their horses down the hill, for closer inspection, close enough to hear the raised voice of the Taskmaster as he strode around the perimeter of the site. 'Faster, you lazy dogs! This fortress won't build itself!'

Tell felt his nerves tighten as he suppressed his anger.

These were good, decent farmers and craftsmen, treated worse than animals.

They had barely reached the edge of the construction site when a commotion erupted near the half-finished wall. An elderly man, his face lined with exhaustion and despair, had fallen to his knees.

'I can't go on,' the old man wheezed. 'Please...'

Tell's lips twitched as he watched two soldiers approach.

'On your feet, old man!' the taller soldier barked, prodding the elder with his boot. 'The day's work isn't done until the governor says it's done.'

The old man tried to rise but collapsed again, his frail body shaking with the effort. Tell began to dismount, but Stauffacher's firm grip on his arm held him back.

'You can't interfere,' Stauffacher said. 'We can't help him if we're dead or in chains.'

Tell's mind raced, seeking a solution that wouldn't jeopardize their greater cause. He watched in horror as the soldiers roughly hauled the old man to his feet.

'Perhaps,' Tell said, his voice carrying across the site, 'the respected soldiers would allow me to assist this man? Surely Governor Gessler would prefer the work completed efficiently?'

The soldiers turned, eyeing Tell suspiciously. He forced his face into a mask of subservience.

'And who are you to make such an offer?' the shorter soldier demanded.

'William Tell, a humble huntsman,' Tell replied, dismounting and bowing. 'I have strength to spare and would gladly lend it to ensure the governor's project proceeds as planned.'

The soldiers exchanged glances, confused but clearly considering the proposal. Finally, the taller one nodded curtly. 'Very well, huntsman. But if his work slows, you'll both feel the lash.'

As Tell moved to support the elderly man, he caught Stauffacher's approving nod. It was a small victory, but Tell knew that even the smallest spark of defiance could ignite hope. And hope, Tell knew, was what these people needed most. It was the only move he could make to assist the old man that would not incite violence.

A hush fell over the construction site as the clatter of hooves and the creak of carriage wheels announced Governor Gessler's arrival. His procession came to a halt on the road that ran alongside the far side of the site. Tell's muscles tensed, his hand tightening on the elderly man's arm as he helped him lay another stone.

Gessler emerged from his ornate carriage, his dark hair slicked back, his sharp features carved like granite, his cold eyes sweeping over the workers as he strode toward the Taskmaster. His cape billowed behind him, revealing a polished silver sword strapped to his side. Tell felt a chill as the governor's gaze passed over him, lingering for a moment too long.

'My lord governor,' the Taskmaster said, bowing low. 'The work progresses as ordered.'

Gessler's thin lips curled but there was no warmth in his grin. 'Indeed. And yet, I sense an overwhelming lack of enthusiasm among these ungrateful swine.'

Tell bit back his disgust, and kept his eyes fixed on his work, acutely aware of the governor's every movement.

Gessler strode to a point where the road intersected with the corner of the site. 'Bring me the standard,' he commanded.

One of his entourage hurried forward, carrying a long pole topped with one of Gessler's caps, adorned with the Habsburg eagle. The governor commanded that the pole be planted firmly in the ground.

He then instructed his herald to make a proclamation.

The herald raised a hand, and the crowd fell silent. His voice rang out.

'By decree of His Imperial Majesty, Albert of Austria, and enforced by Governor Gessler, all who pass this place shall bow to this hat as if it were the Emperor himself, and his governor. This is the symbol of Austrian authority, and those who fail to show proper reverence will face severe punishment.'

Gessler then stepped forward, his voice adding to the proclamation. 'Those who refuse will be chained to the site's wall, to take up more comfortable residence in the cells once the prison is completed.'

Tell's heart raced as he watched the faces of his fellow Swiss. Fear and anger warred in their expressions but no one spoke out.

Gessler motioned toward several of the workers. 'You three. Pass this way and bow before the pole.'

'This is madness,' the old man beside Tell said. 'To bow to a hat?'

'Quiet,' Tell's voice was beneath a whisper, his eyes darting to Jakob Muller, one of the three men Gessler had indicated, a herdsman with whom Tell had hunted chamois many times. He knew Muller to be a stubborn man.

For God's sake Jakob, bow, Tell thought.

Muller remained upright, unmoving, his eyes locked on Gessler's.

'You there,' Gessler called out, pointing. 'Why do you not move?'

Muller's voice was steady as he replied, 'I bow to God and to just laws, Governor. Not to a hat on a pole.'

A collective gasp rose from the crowd. Tell's mind raced, searching for a way to defuse the situation before it spiralled out of control.

'My lord,' Tell called out, while maintaining his distance. 'Forgive our simple neighbour. He's addled from too much sun and hard work and has misunderstood the importance of the cap. Surely a man of your wisdom can overlook such a minor slight?'

Gessler's stare bore into Tell and a flicker of recognition passed across his features. 'You are the archer, are you not?'

'Yes, Governor.'

Gessler's eyes flickered between Tell and Muller. He spoke in a lowered voice that carried even more menace than his shouts. 'I am a fair man who will allow a second chance on this occasion.' His stare bore into Muller. 'Bow or be chained.'

Muller had looked in Tell's direction when he'd heard Tell's voice, and Tell now hardened his expression, conveying with his eyes as best he could for Muller to comply. He hoped that what passed as unspoken communication between the two men would convince Muller that this was neither the time nor the place for an act of defiance.

Muller stood unmoved.

Tell took a slow, sharp breath.

But then, Muller turned back to face Gessler. He walked forward and bowed before the cap on the pole.

Gessler glanced at the Taskmaster. 'You are to ensure better obedience from these peasants in future.'

'Yes, my lord.'

Gessler shot a glance at Tell. 'And you, archer, will be fined for your insolence in speaking out of turn.' Gessler widened his gaze to take in the crowd. 'The next act of defiance will be met with the full force of my authority, regardless of petty excuses.' And as an aside to the soldier, he said, 'See that these dogs get back to work and that they make up for the time lost while we waited for that simpleton to bow. And send collectors to Tell's house to collect the fine.'

'Yes, my lord.'

As Gessler turned away, and the soldiers moved forward, gesturing for the workers to return to their labours, a piercing cry shattered the tense silence. It was followed by the sickening thud of a body hitting the ground. Tell's head whipped around, his heart leaping into his throat as he saw a crumpled form at the base of the fortress wall.

'The tiler!' someone shouted. 'He's fallen!'

The crowd surged forward, their earlier fear forgotten in the face of tragedy. Tell pushed through, his stomach churning as he approached the broken body. The tiler's eyes stared blankly at the sky, his limbs bent at unnatural angles.

Several voices called out. 'Is he dead?'

Tell knelt, pressing his fingers to the man's neck. He closed his eyes, shaking his head. 'He's gone,' he said softly.

A collective wail rose from several of the gathered workers.

'Why are these men not working!' Gessler barked from further back.

'Back to work!' the soldiers ordered, brandishing their swords.

'Pathetic,' Gessler said as he and members of his entourage returned to the coach.

Tell's fists tensed but the anger he felt was overtaken by his grief for this man, for this man's family, for these workers, for all of his countrymen. This had gone too far, the need for action overdue. How could he have not seen it up until this point?

A flash of movement caught his eye and a woman's voice rang out. 'Help him.' She pushed through the crowd and knelt beside the fallen tiler, her eyes brimming with unshed tears.

Tell looked at her. She was not one of the workers' wives, she was a noblewoman. 'It's too late for him,' Tell said.

'This man deserves respect,' the woman said, standing and glaring at the soldiers. 'And his family deserves aid.' She reached into her purse, pulling out a handful of gold coins. 'Who here can help transport him home? I'll pay for a proper burial.'

Tell watched, amazed, as the noblewoman's compassion cut through the crowd's despair. Her actions stood in stark contrast to the cold indifference of Gessler and his men.

The Master Mason stepped forward, his sweat-lined face twisted in disgust. 'You can keep your blood money, my lady,' he said. 'We take care of our own.'

The young woman recoiled as if struck, confusion and hurt flashing across her delicate features. Tell wondered at the sincerity of her gesture. Was this truly compassion, or merely guilt from one who benefited from their oppression? He wondered what she was doing here, and then realized that she was with Gessler's procession.

'My lady,' Tell said softly to defuse the moment. 'I rode here. I can take him on my horse.'

The woman nodded. She glanced at the coins in her hand before returning them to her purse. 'Thank you. What's your name, sir?'

'William Tell, my lady.'

'Tell... You're the one the governor was just speaking with. You're the archer, aren't you?'

Tell nodded, suddenly wary. 'I am, my lady. Though these days, I'm just a simple huntsman.'

She nodded again, her gaze intense as if she could see right through him. 'No man deserves a death like that of this poor man.' Without another word, she retreated, striding after Gessler's entourage. Tell watched her as she reached the carriage. A frown creased his brow as he watched her exchange hushed words with one of Gessler's advisors, before being helped into the carriage by the soldiers. Her presence here was a puzzle, one that didn't quite fit.

Stauffacher, who had been watching from the edge of the site, came forward, and helped Tell carry the body and lift it onto the back of the horse.

A moment later, Gessler's carriage passed by, and although he was not alongside the road, Tell saw the woman looking out, her eyes locking with his for just a moment.

'Strange company for a woman of compassion,' Tell said, tightening the last rope that secured the body in place.

'That's Bertha von Bruneck, the Austrian heiress,' Stauffacher said. 'Rumour has it she's Gessler's niece and his ward, but as you've seen, she's not cut from the same cloth as that tyrant.'

Tell's hands stilled on the rope. 'A wolf in sheep's clothing, perhaps?'

'Or a sheep among wolves,' Stauffacher countered. 'We should keep an eye on that one, William. Perhaps she could prove an unexpected ally.' He inclined his head back toward the construction site. 'What of the elderly man you were helping?'

'I'll tell the soldiers we need his assistance in getting this unfortunate man's body back to his family, as promised to Gessler's ward. I don't think they'll be bothered to argue with me on that.'

As he walked back to where the Taskmaster was stationed, Tell was approached by The Master Mason.

'Tell,' he said, his voice low and urgent, 'I fear what we're building here is even worse than it appears.' He glanced over his shoulder, ensuring the Taskmaster was out of earshot. 'There are dungeons... they're designed for more than just holding prisoners. There are chambers... devices...'

'What kind of devices?' Tell asked, though part of him knew the answer.

The Mason's eyes darted nervously. 'Instruments of torture, sir. The likes of which I've never seen. They mean to break more than just bodies here.' Before he could say more, the Mason saw the Taskmaster turning their way, and the Mason hurried back to his position.

41

Tell strode across the site, motioned for the elderly man to join him, and then spoke to the Taskmaster, explaining the situation. He knew that the Taskmaster had overheard the exchange between Tell and Gessler's ward, and would not want further involvement in anything that might get back to the heiress's ear. 'Then go,' was all he said, disinterested.

Tell was dreading the next task, breaking the dreadful news of the tragedy to the roof tiler's family, and then helping them to bury their loved one. He motioned for the elderly man to ride doubled-up with Stauffacher.

'I know the tiler's address,' Stauffacher said. As they rode off, he added, 'The cruelty here is beyond what even I had imagined.'

'I know that Baron von Attingausen has made representations to the Habsburgs about fairer laws and taxes,' Tell said.

'Yes. And been rebuffed each time.'

'When you meet with the leaders of the three cantons, suggest they join with the Baron, presenting a unified front, and demand Gessler lower his taxes and treat our people with the respect they deserve. They must understand that Gessler and his like are misusing their power and sowing the seeds of discontent.'

'I fear, William, that it is far too late for the canton leaders to carry any influence with the Austrians, but your suggestion is at least worth consideration.'

'What we've witnessed here today is sickening, but for the sake of our families, every attempt must be made to try and broker a peaceful outcome.' As they rode back, Tell could not shake his fear that any continued attempts at negotiation by the Swiss nobility, driven by the people, would fall on the deaf ears of an Austrian Emperor who believed that all lands were his for the taking. Whatever Tell's misgivings about the act of rebellion, whatever fears he held for his wife and his boys, Governor Gessler's oppression was like a creature from ancient folklore, screaming, charging, assaulting his senses from every direction. If the fire of rebellion was ignited, he knew there would be no turning back.

***

As Tell approached his modest cottage nestled in the shadow of towering Alpine peaks, the weight of the day's events eased from his shoulders. The soft glow of candlelight spilled from the window, a beacon of comfort in the gathering dusk. His wife, Hedy's silhouette appeared in the doorway, her graceful figure a stark contrast to the harsh realities Tell had been subjected to. Tell never ceased to be calmed by her serene nature and natural beauty, and her long, dark hair lifted in the breeze as she rushed to meet him. Her eyes, filled with warmth and concern, searched his face. 'I've been worried. The village is abuzz with rumours.'

Tell dismounted, his weary muscles protesting as he embraced her. The scent of her hair, fragrant with herbs from her garden, momentarily grounded him. 'Hedy,' he murmured, drinking in her presence, and he took her face in his hand and kissed her.

They entered the cottage and the familiar sights and smells enveloped Tell like a comforting blanket. The crackling hearth, the aroma of fresh bread, the soft furs draped over well-worn furniture – all spoke of home and safety. But safe for how long?

Hedy guided him to a chair, her gentle hands working to ease the knots from his shoulders. 'What happened at the construction site of the new prison? I've heard talk of an accident, and Gessler's cruelty.'

Tell recounted the day's events. 'A man died. Fell from the scaffolding. And Gessler…didn't flinch or offer sympathies. The poor soul's life meant nothing to him.'

Hedy's sharp intake of breath mirrored the disgust Tell felt. He told her about the cap on the pole and the order for all who passed to bow to it.

'I have hoped every day, for our sons, for our country, that things would improve,' she said, 'but it seems they're growing far worse.'

'Werner Stauffacher is planning a secret meeting with the leaders of the cantons,' Tell said. 'He's enlisting the aid of several men, I believe your father among them, to help arrange the meeting.'

Hedy sat alongside him, her eyes meeting his. 'I pray they can find a solution. I don't want to see rebellion that could lead to violence any more than you do. It's hard not to fear for our country's future, and for Walter and Tristan—'

She was cut off by their boy, Walter, bounding in from the back garden. 'Papa!' The boy threw his arms around his father. Tell hugged him back, his eyes still on Hedy, and then averted by his younger son, Tristan, rushing in. He felt the warmth enclose his heart as he relaxed, surrounded by his family.

Later, Tell stood on the back porch that he had built with his own hands and gazed at the stars that sprinkled like glowing dust mites across the night sky. Hedy's words replayed in his mind, mingling with images of the day. The tiler's broken body, Gessler's cold indifference, the cruelty of the soldiers to the workers, the fear in their eyes, the construction of a prison fortress designed to crush the spirit of the people.

Regardless of whether there was a people's revolt or not, either way, he feared for what the future held for all of them.

Chapter Five

The morning light stretched across the alpine clearing. Tell stood tall, his hands resting on his son Walter's shoulders as they gazed at the makeshift target – a knotted pine trunk scarred by countless arrows.

'Here,' Tell said, handing Walter a small yew bow. 'Do you remember what I taught you about the grip?'

'Yes, papa!' Walter's small fingers curled around the smooth wood, his eyebrows drawn together. Tell watched with pride as his ten-year-old son assumed the proper stance, feet shoulder-width apart, back straight. The boy was quick to learn, his form nearly perfect despite his tender years.

'Draw the string back to your cheek,' Tell instructed, guiding Walter's elbow. 'Feel the tension build in your arms, like a tree branch bending in the wind.'

As Walter complied, Tell's mind drifted to his own father, to lessons learned long ago in clearings much like this one.

'Your grandfather taught me to shoot in a place not unlike this,' Tell said, his eyes scanning the mist-shrouded peaks in the distance. 'He always said that to master the bow, one must first master oneself.'

Walter relaxed the string, turning to look up at his father with wide, curious eyes. 'What else did Grandfather teach you?'

Tell smiled, ruffling his son's hair. 'He taught me to read the mountain's moods, to listen to the whispers of the wind, and to respect the power of nature.' He paused, memories flooding back. 'Once, when I

45

was not much older than you, we were caught in a sudden storm high on the slopes...'

As Tell recounted the tale, he demonstrated the proper technique, nocking an arrow and drawing it back in one fluid motion. Walter watched, enraptured, as his father continued.

'The wind howled like a thousand wolves, and the rain lashed at us. Your grandfather found us shelter in a small cave, but the cold was bitter.' Tell released the arrow, watching it arc through the air to thud into the centre of the target. 'He taught me then that our greatest strength lies not in our weapons or our skills, but in our ability to endure, to adapt.'

Walter nodded solemnly, his young face set with determination. 'I want to be strong like you and Grandfather,' he said.

Tell's heart swelled with love and a touch of sorrow. He knelt beside his son, meeting those earnest eyes. 'Strength comes in many forms, Walter. The bow is but one tool. True power lies in knowing when to use it, and when to stay your hand.'

As Walter nocked his own arrow, Tell watched closely, noting the boy's steady hands and unwavering focus. He was reminded of himself as a boy, firing his first arrow, and he thought of the future –uncertain and fraught with danger for his country. He had resolved to go and meet with Stauffacher and his father-in-law after they'd had their meeting with the canton leaders, to listen to what strategies came of it, but he remained unsure to what extent he could become further involved, given the risks – risks he was not prepared to place on Hedy and the boys.

'Remember,' Tell said, 'every arrow you loose carries with it our history, our traditions. It is an extension of who we, the Tells, are.'

Walter loosed the arrow, and though it fell short of the target, Tell's pride knew no bounds. For in his son's determination, he saw the resilience of all the Swiss people.

'Papa, when can I use the crossbow, like you?'

'When you're older, and you've mastered the standard archer's bow. As I did.'

Walter lowered his bow. His brimmed with curiosity. 'Father, what happened to Grandfather? Why isn't he here to teach me too?'

Tell's hand, which had been reaching to adjust Walter's stance, froze mid-air. The morning breeze suddenly felt colder against his skin. He swallowed hard, his throat constricting around words he wasn't ready to speak.

'That's... a story for another time, Walter,' he said, his voice soft but strained. He forced a smile. 'When you're older, I promise there will be many more stories to tell.'

Walter's face fell, but he nodded, accepting his father's words with the trust of youth. 'Alright, Papa. Can we practice more?'

'Of course,' Tell said, grateful for the distraction. As Walter returned to his stance, Tell's mind drifted, the present fading as memories surged forth unbidden.

He saw his father again, proud and defiant, standing before the Habsburg soldiers. It all came rushing back and he jerked, his breath catching in his chest.

'Papa?' Walter said. 'Did I do something wrong?'

Tell blinked, forcing himself back to the present. 'No, no, you're doing well.' He watched Walter draw the bow once more.

The political unrest that simmered throughout the Swiss cantons seemed to press in around them, even here in this peaceful clearing. Tell's caution, born from the tragedy of his father's fate, was at odds with his desire to see his homeland free.

The next shot from Walter hit the target. Walter leaped for joy and Tell laughed, a wave of calm washing over him, if only for a moment.

**

The clatter of dishes filled the Tell household as Hedy wiped down the worn wooden table. Sunlight streamed through the small window, casting a warm glow. A gentle knock at the door broke the quiet rhythm of her work.

'Come in,' Hedy called, smiling as she recognized the silhouette of her neighbour.

Iris shuffled into the kitchen. Dark circles shadowed her eyes. Hedy's heart saddened at the sight of her friend, so changed since her husband's passing.

'Iris,' Hedy said softly, reaching out to clasp the other woman's hand. 'Please, sit. I'll make us something to drink.'

As Hedy busied herself boiling water over the hearth, her mind raced. Iris's unexpected visit often meant she had news from the village. And in these troubled times, that news was rarely good.

'I hope I'm not intruding,' Iris said.

Hedy shook her head, offering a reassuring smile. 'Never. You're always welcome here. You know that. You know I love to see you.' Since her husband's death, Iris's self-esteem, which had never been strong, was more fragile than ever.

Hedy poured the steaming water over fragrant herbs. She placed a cup before Iris, watching as her neighbour's unsteady hands wrapped around the warm pottery.

'There's talk in the village,' Iris began, her eyes darting to the window as if checking for unseen listeners. 'People are so angry, Hedy. The Austrian grip tightens by the day, and now, with what has happened to Ruodi, the fisherman, and Baumgarten, the woodchopper from Unterwalden...' her voice trailed away.

Hedy's stomach knotted. She hated seeing how the growing unrest further unsettled Iris, hated the haunted expression it cast in William's eyes, hated when she sensed it in the hushed conversations in the town, conversations that ceased when anyone passed by.

'What kind of talk?' she asked.

Iris leaned in, her voice dropping. 'Whispers of resistance. Some of the women say it's time for the men to fight back, to reclaim what's ours, and that they'll do whatever they must to help. Others are not so sure, they're afraid of what it might mean for their husbands and their children.'

The thought of open rebellion sent a chill through Hedy as images of William, Walter, and Tristan flashed before her eyes. Yet beneath the fear, there was a feeling of inevitability. War was on the horizon.

'And what do you think?' Hedy asked, studying her friend's face.

Iris's weary eyes met hers. 'I think... I think we can't go on like this. But the cost of standing up...' Her voice faltered, the unspoken weight of her own loss hanging between them.

Hedy reached across the table, grasping Iris's hand. 'We will find a way. Together.'

As Iris nodded, Hedy's gaze drifted to the window, to the hills beyond. William and Walter were out there, having Walter's archery lesson. Her greatest fear was that the skills her child honed would one day, before he was fully grown, be needed for more than hunting game.

Iris's fingers trembled. 'But what can I do?' she asked. 'I'm just a widow, with no power, no influence. How can someone like me make a difference?'

Hedy squeezed her friend's hand. She searched for words of comfort, drawing on the strength she'd witnessed in Iris over these past few months. 'You underestimate yourself, dear friend. I know you doubt yourself but every day, you rise and face the world. You tend your home, you help your neighbours. That resilience, that unwavering spirit, it's exactly what our people need.'

Iris's eyes glistened, but a small smile tugged at her lips. Hedy continued, 'You've shown more courage than many men I know, simply by carrying on. That strength, that determination – it inspires others. Never doubt its power.'

As Iris absorbed her words, Hedy's thoughts turned inward. She thought of William, of the quiet conversations they'd had late at night, voices low to avoid waking Walter and Tristan. The risks of resistance weighed heavily – the threat of imprisonment, or worse. Yet the alternative, a life of oppression for their sons, was the alternative.

'We all have a part to play,' Hedy said. 'Some may take up arms, but others... we keep the heart of our community beating. We tend to those in need, we preserve our traditions, we whisper hope when despair threatens to overwhelm.'

She paused, considering how much to reveal. 'I believe in our cause, Iris. I believe we must stand against tyranny. But we must also be wise, and protect those we love.'

Iris nodded. 'Have you heard the latest decree from Governor Gessler?'

'I have. He demands that we bow to his hats, one mounted on a pole where he builds his prison, and another, in the town square that the prison overlooks. As if we were servants to pieces of cloth.'

Iris shuddered. 'It's not just the hats, Hedy. Just days ago my friend Gwendolynne's, boy was flogged for speaking back to an official in the marketplace. Ten lashes. He's just a boy of seventeen for God's sake!'

Hedy's heart skipped a beat. She thought of Walter, a little older, imagining him in the place of Gwendolynne's son. The image filled her with a mixture of rage and terror. She bit back on her lip. 'Gessler's cruelty knows no bounds,' she said, running her fingertips over the grain of the wooden table. 'He seeks to break our people's spirit.'

'But how do we resist without putting our families at risk?' Iris was voicing the question that haunted them all.

Hedy gave it some thought. 'By remembering who we are, by teaching our children, by keeping our traditions alive in the safety of our homes. And we wait, Iris. We wait for the right moment, when those men who can act will do so.'

As she spoke, her thoughts drifted to her father. She prayed that his and Stauffacher's meeting with the canton leaders would bear fruit, that a path to freedom would reveal itself.

Her gaze fell upon the hearth, where a fresh loaf of bread sat cooling on the stone. The aroma of wheat and yeast filled the air, a comforting scent. Without a word, she rose and wrapped the warm loaf in a clean cloth.

'Here,' she said softly, pressing the bundle into Iris's hands. 'Take this. It's not much, but...'

Iris's eyes shone as her fingers curled around the offering. 'Oh, Hedy,' she said. 'You're too kind.'

Hedy shook her head, a gentle smile playing at her lips. 'I don't think there can be any such thing as 'too kind.' We must support each other, even in the smallest ways.'

As Iris clutched the bread to her chest, Hedy could see some of the weariness lifting from her friend's shoulders.

'Thank you.' With a nod, Iris turned to leave. Hedy followed her to the door, watching as her friend made her way down the path. As Iris's figure grew smaller in the distance, Hedy's thoughts turned inward again to William, Walter, and Tristan. She was one of the lucky ones, destiny had looked favourably on her, but how long could she rely on destiny and luck?

***

The clearing echoed with the thwack of arrows striking their target. Walter's final shot embedded itself in the tree trunk with a satisfying thud, mere inches from the makeshift bullseye his father had carved. Tell's face broke into yet another proud smile, his hand coming to rest on his son's shoulder.

'Well done, Walter,' he said. 'Your aim improves with every lesson.'

Walter beamed up at his father, chest puffing with pride. 'Do you think I'll ever be as good as you, Papa?'

Tell chuckled, gently pinching the boy's cheek. 'With practice and patience, you may well surpass me one day.' His eyes grew distant, memories of his own father's teachings flitting through his mind.

As Walter collected his arrows, Tell found himself marvelling at his son's determination. The boy's small hands worked the arrowheads free with growing confidence.

'Walter,' he called, 'come, stand with me a moment.'

The boy trotted over, bow clutched to his chest. Together, they gazed out over the vast expanse of their homeland. The mountains rose majestically in the distance, their snow-capped peaks piercing the azure sky.

'What do you see, Walter?' Tell asked.

Walter squinted. 'I see... our home. The mountains, the forests.'

A lump formed in Tell's throat. 'And it is a land worth protecting, Walter. Remember that. Our skills, our traditions – they are not merely for sport or sustenance. They are the very essence of who we are.'

"You sound very proud of our town, papa.'

Tell laughed. 'Do I now, young man? Well, perhaps I'm just getting old and full of longing.'

Walter giggled. 'You're not old, papa. What do you mean by full of longing?'

'Remembering times past.'

'I don't understand.'

'You will one day.' Tell grinned and embraced his son. His heartfelt wish had always been that his country's freedoms could be returned peacefully. But he had the unshakeable sense that his wish now seemed further away than ever.

Chapter Six

Daniel Furst's house in Uri was a solid timber structure on stone foundations, sitting on a slope that overlooked the road. Inside, the floorboards creaked beneath Arnold von Melchthal's footsteps as he paced the confines of the main room. He couldn't help but feel trapped. Shadows from the sunlight seeped through the wooden beams and danced on the rough-hewn walls, adding to his unease.

'The bailiff, that cur, he dared to take my plow oxen. Said it was "payment" for imagined slights.' Melchthal's eyes, dark with fury, met Furst's. 'Those oxen were like family. When he took them, they knew. They bellowed and fought against the ropes. When I protested, he laughed. Laughed, Furst! As if our livelihoods were mere playthings for his amusement.'

The older man watched, his face lined with concern. 'And what did you do?' he asked, dreading the answer.

Melchthal's shoulders sagged, guilt and defiance playing in equal measure across his face. 'I struck him. God help me, I couldn't stop myself.' He ran a hand through his shock of reddish hair, his voice dropping to a whisper. 'He tried to arrest me but I lashed out, hurled insults, and then ran. Foolish, I know, *foolish*.'

A flicker of movement beyond the window caught Furst's attention, and he raised a hand in warning. 'Lower your voice,' his words were barely above a whisper. 'Gessler and Landenburg have ears everywhere. Sometimes I wonder if even the walls are safe from their spies.'

His eyes flashed, and then he calmed himself, taking a slow breath.

53

'How do you keep your composure in the face of these injustices?' Melchthal said. 'Wisdom born of age, or have the years simply worn away your fire?'

Furst knew Melchthal to be an impetuous youth, who was understandably angry at the theft, so he overlooked the sleight. He stepped closer, placing a steadying hand on the young man's arm. 'You acted as many men would, faced with such injustice. But we must be cautious now, Arnold, more than ever. Talk of rebellion has spread and it's reached Gessler's ears.'

'Caution?' Melchthal forced himself to keep his voice low. 'For how long must we endure this tyranny?'

Before Furst could reply, a knock echoed through the house. Both men froze.

'Quick!' Furst gestured frantically. 'Hide yourself. The bedroom along the hall.'

As Furst moved to answer the door, he wondered if Melchthal had been followed. If the Austrians found him in the house, then Furst himself would be judged guilty of aiding a fugitive.

He opened the door and his tense posture melted into relief as he saw the familiar face of Werner Stauffacher.

'Werner, old friend.' He clasped Stauffacher's arm, drawing him inside. 'Your arrival is as welcome as it is unexpected.'

Stauffacher's eyes crinkled with a grim smile as he returned the gesture. 'I wish that I came bearing better tidings, Daniel.'

More bad tidings? Furst gestured for Stauffacher to come through. 'What news, then?'

'Is it safe to speak freely?'

Furst nodded, then called out, 'Arnold, you can come out now. It's Werner Stauffacher.'

Melchthal emerged from the room, and Stauffacher's eyes widened in recognition.

'Arnold,' Stauffacher said. 'When I set off this morning to visit Daniel, I did not know I'd find you here. I'm sorry, lad, about your father.'

Melchthal felt the blood drain from his face. 'What of him?'

'You've not heard?'

'Heard what?'

'I received news just minutes before leaving home, that Landenberg's men came for your father. When he couldn't, or wouldn't, reveal your whereabouts, they...' The words caught in his throat.

'What?' Melchthal's voice cracked. 'What did they do?'

Stauffacher met the young man's glare. 'They held him down and put out his eyes with hot irons.'

Furst's heart lurched and Melchthal staggered backward as if physically struck, his broad frame colliding with the cupboard. The young man's face drained of colour, his mouth working soundlessly at first, and then, 'Oh God, no. Father.'

The anguished cry that tore from Melchthal's throat made Furst flinch. The young man slammed his fist into the wooden wall, again and again, until his knuckles split and bled.

Furst moved to support the younger man, but Melchthal shrugged him off violently. He paced like a caged animal, his breath coming in ragged gasps. 'This is my fault,' he choked out, his voice raw. 'I should never have left him. I should have stayed, faced the penalty for my actions.'

'You could not have known the depths of these barbarians' depravity,' Stauffacher said

'I'll kill him.' Melchthal's voice trembled with barely contained fury. 'I'll tear Landenberg apart with my bare hands for what he's done.'

Furst stepped toward him. 'Arnold, I understand your pain, but—'

'You understand nothing,' Melchthal rounded on the older man. 'My father is blind because of *me*, because I dared to stand up to a bully. How can you counsel patience now?'

Furst's voice remained steady. 'Because rushing headlong into vengeance will only lead to more bloodshed, with yourself either dead or in chains. We must be smarter than that, Arnold.'

Melchthal's chest heaved as he struggled to control his breathing.

Stauffacher cleared his throat, drawing their attention. 'There may be a way to channel your anger, Arnold, into something greater than personal vengeance. There can be little doubt now that our people stand at a crossroads. The Habsburgs believe they can break our spirit through cruelty and fear. I travelled here to see you, Daniel, to propose a meeting, a gathering of like-minded men who yearn for freedom as we do. If a rebellion erupts, then it has no chance of success unless it has leadership and organization.'

Furst's eyebrows rose. 'A gathering? Where? We can hardly march into the marketplace and announce a revolt.'

'There's a remote meadow atop a hill that can be seen from the shore across Lake Lucerne. The shepherds often speak of it. Difficult to reach but easily accessible by boats that can be launched from points in each of the cantons.'

Furst nodded. 'I know of it.'

Melchthal's anger gave way to curiosity. 'Who would attend such a meeting?'

Stauffacher's gaze swept between the two men. 'I will be approaching the council leaders from Uri, Schwyz, and Unterwalden. Men I know, men who believe in the rights proclaimed in the early charters, who would be willing to risk everything for the chance at liberty.'

'The nobles among them won't help us,' Melchthal said bitterly. 'They might speak in hushed tones about rebelling but in louder voices, they curry favour with the Austrians to their own benefit.'

'Don't be so sure,' Stauffacher replied. 'Baron von Attinghausen still remembers what it means to be Swiss. And when we meet, we convince them by showing the people's fire.'

'How?' asked Furst.

'By presenting those elders with capable men who can be trusted to spearhead different groups. If each of us three selects ten men – trustworthy men who have quietly expressed their wish to see action, then we present a united front. A front that's worthy of the councillors aiding via their resources and networks.'

'It would only take one traitor to alert the Austrians,' Melchthal said. 'If they plant soldiers along the shores beneath that meadow we'd all be walking into a trap.'

Furst rubbed his chin thoughtfully. 'The Rutli meadow is remote enough that those unfamiliar with the shepherd's trails would not find it in the night. The first group to arrive can light a campfire. The glow would be seen in the night air by those who know what to look for. And we can use signals, a way to identify ourselves to our friends, to signify it is safe, but a signal that would mean nothing to anyone else.'

'Such as?'

'A series of owl calls. Three hoots, then two. It's not uncommon in these parts, but distinct enough for our purposes.'

Stauffacher nodded approvingly. 'A good plan. Now, as for spreading the word...'

Melchthal straightened, a determined glint in his eye. 'I'll go to Unterwalden. I know the paths, the people. I can rally support there.'

Furst shook his head. 'It's dangerous, Arnold. Landenberg's men will be searching for you there.'

'I know every hidden trail and cave in those mountains,' Melchthal said. 'I'll be a ghost, disguised, venturing out at night. The men of Unterwalden will listen to the son of a man they respected, a man their governor had blinded.'

Furst stroked his beard. 'If we can bring the three cantons together...it will be a reflection of the old days when our forebears swore an oath against foreign judges.'

'The first step to be suggested – and Daniel, it was your daughter, Heddy's husband, William, who raised it with me – is for an entourage of our nobles to present a stronger case than any presented before, to the emperor himself.'

'That could present an enormous risk,' Furst said, 'not immediately to the barons themselves, but in the form of retribution on the people once the nobles' actions reach the ears of Gessler and Landenberg.'

'You're not in agreement, then, on that?'

Furst pressed his lips together. 'Let us see first what comes of this meeting at the Rutli meadow.'

Stauffacher saw in Furst what he felt in himself, a moment of trepidation as the gravity of what lay ahead weighed on their minds.

It was Furst who broke the silence, his voice low. 'For the forest cantons, and for the charters first agreed by the elders of Schwyz.'

'For the forest cantons,' Stauffacher and Melchthal repeated and the three men touched their fists together in solidarity.

A distant sound pierced the solemn atmosphere and Furst moved to the window, peering out. From his house's elevated position, he could see the town square. 'Austrian troops,' he said. 'Performing a drill in the village, another display meant to cower the people into subservience.'

He watched as the soldiers began to march along the road, a beating drum and the rhythm of the soldiers' steps more a show of their strength than anything else. If he had doubts about the road he'd set off on, they dispersed at the sight of those troops. His heart beat with anger but at the same time, he wondered if the cause of the Swiss people had been left too late.

Chapter Seven

The heavy oak doors of Attinghausen Castle's great hall swung open, the seneschal announcing the arrival of Ulrich von Rudenz. He strode in, his velvet doublet and polished leather boots a stark contrast to the rough-hewn stone walls and simple wooden furnishings. The great hall stood as it had for centuries, its stone walls hung with ancient shields and helmets that caught the morning light streaming through narrow windows. The young nobleman's eyes darted about, taking in the rustic surroundings with a mixture of familiarity and growing disdain.

'Uncle?' Ulrich called out, his voice echoing in the cavernous space. The scent of woodsmoke and fresh bread hung in the air, reminding him of simpler times. Times he cherished, but times he was now eager to leave behind.

Baron Von Attinghausen emerged from a side chamber. Despite his frailty at eighty-five years, he cut an imposing figure in his fur-lined robe as he walked forward with his chamois-horn staff. The lines that crisscrossed his face betrayed his age but his eyes remained as clear as those of a younger man and his commanding presence could still fill the old hall. Seeing his nephew, his face broke into a warm smile.

'Ah, Ulrich, you've arrived just in time for the morning ritual.' He clasped his nephew's shoulder. 'Come, join us.'

'Uncle, I've come to speak with you on an urgent matter.'

The Baron's bushy eyebrows furrowed. 'Whatever it is, it can wait. Our people come first, my boy.'

With that, he turned and strode towards the castle's courtyard, where a group of farm workers – serfs – had already gathered. Ulrich hesitated, torn between his desire to press his case and the ingrained respect for his uncle's traditions.

As they stepped into the crisp morning air, Ulrich watched his uncle transform. The kindly old man became a powerful figure of quiet authority, his back straightening as he addressed the assembled workers.

'My friends,' the Baron began, his voice carrying across the yard, 'another day dawns on our beloved land. Let us give thanks for the bounty it provides and the strength in our arms to tend it.'

A murmur of agreement rippled through the crowd. Ulrich observed the reverence in their eyes, the way they hung on his uncle's every word. It was a far cry from the glittering court of Austria he so yearned to join.

The Baron went on to add, 'In these troubled times, we must stand united. Our freedom, our very way of life, depends on it.'

Ulrich fidgeted, his uncle's words striking a chord he'd rather ignore. He thought of Bertha, of the life that awaited him beyond these mountains. Surely there was more to the world than this simple existence.

The Baron reached for an ornate silver cup, its surface engraved with ancient symbols of the Helvetii people, who were Celtic early settlers of the cantons along with various Roman and Germanic tribes. He filled it with amber mead and raised it high. 'Let us partake in the cup of unity, as our forefathers have done for generations.'

The cup began its journey, passing from hand to hand. Each worker took a reverent sip, their faces solemn with the legacy of tradition.

When it reached Ulrich, he hesitated, his fingers brushing against the cool metal. The expectant gazes of the workers bore into him, and he felt a flicker of shame at his own reluctance. He lifted the cup to his lips. The sweet liquid was a stark contrast to the bitterness he felt.

As the last worker drank, Baron Attinghausen dismissed them with a nod. Then he and his nephew returned to the great hall.

'You seemed... uncomfortable with our morning ritual, Ulrich,' the Baron said. 'Has something changed?'

Ulrich frowned. 'Uncle, I respect our traditions, but...' he paused, searching for the right words. 'Don't you think it's time we looked beyond these mountains? The world is changing, and we must change with it.'

A crease appeared between the Baron's eyes. 'And this is the urgent matter you wished to discuss?'

'Yes.'

'You speak of change? What kind of change?'

'Progress, Uncle. The Austrian court offers opportunities we can't even imagine here. I know the Austrians have sought your allegiance in the past and I understand your reasons for denying them. But that was then, and times are changing. Why should we limit ourselves to these valleys when there's so much more to be gained?'

Attinghausen's eyes clouded over. 'Gained? And what would be lost in the process, Ulrich? Our identity? Our freedom?'

Ulrich let out a deep sigh. 'Freedom? We're already under Austrian rule. Why not embrace it, make the most of what it offers?'

'You have been spending too much time among them,' Attinghausen said. 'This has been a point of concern to me for a while.'

'They have offered me an official role,' Ulrich said. His mind drifted to Bertha – her face swam before him, a vision of beauty and complexity that both enthralled and confounded him – and to the promise of power and influence that awaited him in the court of her uncle, Governor Hermann Gessler. Yet the Baron had always exerted an influence over him, that was why he sought his blessing, to sweep him away from the small voice inside that whispered of doubt, of the price these ambitions might exact.

The Baron's voice softened. 'My boy, I fear you're being blinded by the glitter of the Habsburgs. Remember who you are, where you come from.'

Ulrich's response caught in his throat. He was torn between the pull of his heritage and the allure of a grander destiny, and his uncle wasn't making it any easier.

Attinghausen carried on: 'Ulrich, our traditions are not chains that bind us, but roots that give us strength. Have you forgotten the price our forefathers paid for the freedoms we enjoy?'

Ulrich paced, conscious of the ancestral shields. 'I haven't forgotten, Uncle,' his voice was tight. 'But we can't live in the past forever.'

The Baron coughed and shakily went to sit in one of the ornate chairs. 'And what future do you see for our people under even more Austrian rule?'

Ulrich's mind filled with visions of marble halls and gilded thrones. But beneath it all, doubt still nagged and he was aware, as he watched the baron sit, that his uncle's health had been failing. 'A future of prosperity, of... of progress.'

Attinghausen's eyes flashed. 'Progress? Is that what you call bowing to tyrants? Trading our dignity for a few scraps from their table? I treat our serfs here with respect. That is *not* the way of the Habsburg ruling class under Emperor Albert.'

The young nobleman felt his cheeks burn with shame and defiance in equal measure. 'It's not like that, Uncle. You don't understand—'

'I understand all too well. I see a young man so eager to prove himself that he's willing to sell his birthright for a moment's glory.' The Baron coughed again, the hack like a rattle in his chest. 'This is not something of which your parents, God bless them, would have approved.'

Ulrich was torn between frustration at his uncle's position and a genuine concern for the older man's wellbeing. He squared his shoulders, drawing himself up to his full height. 'You speak of birthright, Uncle, but what of opportunity? The Austrian court offers more than just glory – it offers a chance to shape the future.' His voice rang with a youthful arrogance that made Attinghausen wince. 'We can't remain isolated forever. The world is moving on, and we must move with it or be left behind.'

'And at what cost, Ulrich?'

'We can have both, Uncle. We can retain our identity while embracing progress. The court—'

'The court,' Attinghausen interrupted again, 'is not what you think it is. You must have heard of the cruelties being imposed on our people.'

'Tall tales.'

'Is that what your new friends tell you? I fear your life as a noble has cocooned you from too many harsh realities – truths you would see with your own eyes if you spent more time on the land and less in those fancy establishments. And what of Bertha von Bruneck? Does she factor into these grand plans of yours?'

The young nobleman froze, his heart skipping a beat at the mention of Bertha's name. How did his uncle know? He struggled to keep his face impassive, but a telltale flush crept up his neck.

Attinghausen's eyes softened. 'Ah, I see. The heart often leads us down treacherous paths, my boy. But be wary. The court's intentions – and Bertha's position within it – may not be as clear as you believe.'

Ulrich's hands balled into fists at his sides, suppressing his irritation. He spoke slowly. 'You speak of things you don't understand, Uncle. Bertha is not some pawn in the court's game. She sees the potential for a united future, just as I do.'

The Baron's eyes took on a distant look as he gazed past Ulrich to some unseen point in the past. 'When I was not much older than you, Ulrich,' he said, his tone reflective, 'I too faced a choice between power and principle.'

Ulrich's curiosity was piqued and he cocked his head, waiting for what it was his uncle was about to impart.

'There was a time,' the Baron said, 'when I was offered a position at the Habsburg's Imperial Palace in Vienna. It would have meant wealth, influence, everything a young nobleman could desire.' He paused, a rueful smile playing at the corners of his mouth. 'And I was sorely tempted.'

'What happened?'

'I accepted,' Attinghausen said. 'For a brief time, I revelled in the glitter and pageantry of court life. But soon, I saw the true cost of my decision.'

The Baron's eyes met Ulrich's, filled with a mixture of sorrow and hard-won wisdom. 'I was asked to support unjust laws upon our people, to turn a blind eye to the suffering it would cause. Even then, the Habsburg's intentions were to spread their power and influence further into the forest cantons. Each day, I felt a piece of myself slip away, replaced by a stranger I no longer recognized.'

Ulrich swallowed hard, his mind racing. How many times had he imagined himself in Gessler's court, basking in the glow of power and prestige? 'How did you find your way back?'

'It was the voice of my own uncle, much as I speak to you now, that called me home. He reminded me of who I was, the privilege of my Swiss nobility, of the people I had sworn to protect. I came to realize that all the riches of Austria could not compare to the wealth of a clear conscience and the love of one's people. It is why I have always held in such high regard our morning ritual, drinking from the ceremonial cup with the people who work my land and tend to this residence.'

'I never knew,' Ulrich said. 'But uncle, much has changed since that era.'

'But not for the better. Ulrich, you stand at a crossroads. The path you choose now will shape not only your future but the fate of our people. Let me guide you, as I was once guided.'

'I don't know. There is a chance to make a real difference in Gessler's court.'

Attinghausen rose from his chair, his movements slow. He crossed the room to stand before his nephew, placing a hand on Ulrich's shoulder. 'My boy, I have watched you grow from a child into a man. I know the fire that burns within you, the desire to make your mark on the world. But I beg you to reconsider the path you're choosing.'

Ulrich felt his resolve waver. For a moment, he saw himself as a boy again, listening wide-eyed to tales of Swiss courage and independence. 'I only want what's best for our people,' he said.

'Then stand with us, Ulrich. Our strength lies in our unity, in the bonds we share with our fellow Swiss. The court may offer gold and titles, but it's not worth the cost to your soul.'

Ulrich stepped back, breaking his uncle's grip. 'I'm sorry, Uncle, but I cannot stay. We can continue this another time. I've been asked to attend a meeting of Gessler's officials in Altdorf so I must be on my way.'

He strode towards the wide oak doors. As he reached for the iron handle, he hesitated, turning back one last time. 'I do not abandon our people, Uncle. I seek a different path to protect them.'

Attinghausen's face fell. 'May you find wisdom on your journey but remember, our history and the roots of our land run deep.'

With a final nod, Ulrich pulled open the door and was gone.

Attinghausen's gaze drifted to the weathered shields adorning the walls. He murmured to himself, addressing the painted visage of his long-dead father, 'What would you make of this world we've inherited? My nephew chooses the glitter of foreign courts over the solid stone of our mountains.'

His thoughts were interrupted by the seneschal, the manager of the castle's staff and affairs. 'My Lord Baron, you have a visitor.'

'Who is it?'

'Werner Stauffacher, of Steinen. He seeks your wise counsel on an important matter.'

'Send him in,' said Attinghausen, 'With the unrest that ripples through our canton, I feel I know what it is he has come to say.'

Chapter Eight

Fingers of silver light stretched across the jagged peaks above as Arnold von Melchthal led his men up the treacherous path.

'Watch your footing,' he said to the others. They had come this far without incident and he didn't want anyone slipping and injuring themselves.

The men from Underwalden had come across the lake in two small boats, five men in each, with only the moonlight as their guide. Melchthal had breathed a sigh of relief when he saw that there was only a light breeze and that the lake was placid. If the waters had been rough they would have had to abandon their mission.

As they crested the final ridge, the Rutli meadow spread before them, a luminous expanse under a low-hanging moon.

They were the first to arrive. 'We must signal the others,' he said.

The men gathered kindling and struck flint. Soon, a small flame flickered to life, shielded by a ring of stones.

'Melchthal,' came a hushed voice. It was the fugitive, Baumgarten, the man who'd axed one of Gessler's seneschals to death – and whom Stauffacher had arranged to hide with rebels in the Rigi Mountains. His short frame was coiled with nervous energy as he approached. 'Listen.'

In the distance, barely audible, came the faint tolling of a chapel bell across Lake Lucerne. 'It's midnight,' Baumgarten said. 'The others should be here soon.'

Melchthal nodded, feeling the burden of leadership. It was a role he was not comfortable with but had thrust himself into after the blinding of his father. 'Keep watch,' he instructed. 'We must be vigilant.' Although he'd enlisted the aid of men he trusted implicitly, Melchthal was well aware that there were traitors hidden among the people of the cantons – weak men who had been seduced by the promises of the governors.

'Do you think they'll come?' Baumgarten asked.

'They'll come,' Melchthal said with quiet conviction. 'We've all suffered too much to turn back now.'

The crackling of the fire filled the tense silence as they waited, each man lost in his own thoughts. Melchthal's mind drifted to the risks they faced, the families they had left behind. But as he looked at the determined faces of his companions, he felt a surge of resolve. Stauffacher had told him he should constantly offer encouraging words to inspire others, as even the strongest of men would be plagued by doubts at the enormity of their mission.

'We're doing the right thing,' he said to the men. 'For our homes, for our children. For the Swiss people.'

The men nodded solemnly.

It was then that they heard the owl hoots, delivered as per the pre-arranged signal. Another group, approaching from another direction, seeking reassurance that the way to the firelight was safe.

Melchthal cupped his mouth and mimicked the sound.

There was silence again.

Minutes later a rustle in the undergrowth made Melchthal tense, his hand instinctively reaching for his blade. But as the shadows parted, relief washed over him. Werner Stauffacher emerged, leading the Schwyz contingent. Close behind, Daniel Furst and the priest Rosselmann guided the Uri men into the firelit clearing.

No words were spoken as the newcomers joined the circle, only nods of acknowledgment and clasped forearms. Melchthal studied their faces, seeing his own resolve mirrored in their eyes.

Stauffacher stepped forward, his presence commanding attention without a word, the firelight casting shadows across his face. When he spoke, his voice was low but carried easily to every ear.

'Brothers,' he began, 'we stand here tonight in reverence to our forefathers, renewing an alliance forged in the blood and sweat of those who came before us when they settled these lands.' His gaze swept the circle, making eye contact with each man in turn. 'They sought for the right to govern themselves, to live free from the yoke of foreign rule. And now, we find ourselves facing that very struggle.'

Melchthal felt a surge of emotion at Stauffacher's words. The anguished, stricken face of his father filled his mind.

Stauffacher continued. 'The bailiffs sent by Austria treat us not as men, but as chattel. They mock our traditions, trample our rights, and seek to break our spirit.' A murmur of agreement rippled through the gathering. 'But they do not know the strength that flows through Swiss veins. They do not understand that our love for this land, for our way of life, cannot be extinguished by their decrees or their swords.'

Daniel Furst interjected, his normally gentle face hardened with resolve. 'We do not wish for violence nor are we seeking to overturn the natural order. We ask only for what is rightfully ours – the freedom to govern ourselves as we have done for centuries.'

Melchthal spoke up. 'This is the crux of it. We're not revolutionaries; we're defenders of our birthright.'

Stauffacher raised his voice. 'The path ahead is fraught with danger. But I ask you, what is the alternative? To bow our heads and accept the chains they would place upon us? To watch as our children grow up knowing nothing but servitude to unjust laws?'

A chorus of denials answered him. Melchthal felt his heart swell. This was why they had come, not just to plot and plan, but to reaffirm their commitment to a cause greater than themselves.

Stauffacher cleared his throat. 'So,' he said quietly, but with steel in his voice, 'our cantons must unite and decide on how best to proceed. What do we do now?'

Daniel Furst spoke up. 'We must tread with care. Our goal should be to preserve our ancient rights, not to ignite a revolution that could destroy everything we hold dear.'

Melchthal bit down on his lip but forced himself to listen patiently. Furst went on to say, 'Let us not forget the wisdom of our forefathers who secured these liberties through a mix of action and diplomacy.'

The gathered men murmured among themselves, some nodding in agreement, others frowning in contemplation. Melchthal's fingers curled into fists at his sides.

'I have met with those who are leaders in our communities,' Stauffacher addressed the group again, 'including Baron von Attinghausen, who has much influence with the other nobles. Some of the representatives of those barons are here tonight and can attest to the outcome of those talks. They have all had audiences in the past with the Emperor in Vienna to no avail. But now the Habsburg's reach throughout the cantons is much greater, and the barons believe that even if they were to join together as a delegation to attend the Emperor's court, they would be dismissed, even laughed at. They fear that such an impassioned approach now would only raise suspicion that an organized revolt was in the wings. So, our decision on how to proceed is made all the more difficult.'

Unable to contain himself any longer, Melchthal raised his voice, his words tumbling out with barely restrained emotion. 'My oxen were taken, my father blinded, Baumgarten here saw his wife attacked by an official of the court. Many of us have seen the cruelty inflicted on those forcibly enlisted to build a fortress that will imprison those who speak out.' All eyes turned to him as he continued. He gestured toward Ruodi, the fisherman. 'Ruodi from Uri had his home burned and is under the imminent threat of arrest for committing no crime, as are Kuoni, a shepherd, and the huntsman, Werni. He paced, his arms flailing. 'Gessler and Landenburg revel in their power, treating our people like cattle, and the Emperor merely affords them greater authority, and sends more governors to oversee more of our lands.'

The men listened in grim silence. Melchthal could see the conflict in their eyes – the desire for justice warring with the fear of consequence. 'But Furst is right,' he admitted. 'To act rashly means certain defeat. Our strength must lay in our unity and planning.'

The tension in the circle eased, and Melchthal saw approving nods.

It was then that a new voice cut through the night. 'I may have a solution,' said a young man, stepping into the firelight. Melchthal recognized him as Baron Attinghausen's nephew, Winkelried. 'My uncle, the baron, wanted to be here tonight but his age and ill health said otherwise.'

The gathering murmured amongst themselves while they waited for him to continue. 'During Christmas,' he said, 'the castle guards will be distracted by festivities. We could use that to our advantage.'

A hushed silence fell over the group as they considered his words. Melchthal felt a spark of hope. 'Go on,' he urged.

'The servants bring their annual gifts to the castle halls at Christmas. At the three castles in which the governors now reside, ten or twelve men could enter alongside those servants, bearing more gifts but with our blades concealed beneath our robes.' Winkelried outlined the rest of his plan, detailing how others could simultaneously create diversions in the towns. Messengers would be appointed, he said, to travel among the cantons with further instructions for the people in the weeks leading up to the event. As Winkelreid spoke, Melchthal found himself nodding along, seeing the potential in such a plan. 'These organised groups could wrest control of the castles with only limited combat and very little bloodshed.'

'It's risky,' Furst said. 'If even one of the three incursions fails the consequences would be severe.'

'And if we do nothing?' Melchthal countered, unable to keep the edge from his voice. He took a breath, steadying himself. 'Forgive me. But surely we must weigh the risk against the cost of inaction.'

The men began to debate in earnest, voices rising and falling for over two hours as they considered the plan from all angles. Melchthal listened intently, his mind racing.

Eventually, Stauffacher's voice cut through the murmur of debate, silencing the group. 'We've heard all sides. Now, we must decide. Those in favor of Winkelried's Christmas plan, raise your hands.'

Melchthal lifted his hand, his eyes darting around the circle. One by one, hands rose, some quickly, others with hesitation. He counted silently, his breath catching as the majority became clear.

'It's decided then,' Stauffacher announced. 'We move on Christmas.'

Melchthal studied the faces of his compatriots, noting the steely resolve in their eyes. Even those who had voted against the plan now nodded in acceptance, their expressions hardening with commitment.

Rosselmann, the priest, stepped forward. 'Brothers,' he said, his voice low but carrying clearly in the night air, 'first, let us pray. For each of us. And for every man, woman, and child throughout the cantons.' Silence fell again as Rosselmann began. 'Form a circle,' he instructed, 'and raise your hands to the heavens.'

As Melchthal took his place in the circle, he found himself standing between Winkelried and Furst. He raised his hand, feeling the cool mountain air on his palm.

The priest intoned his prayer, concluding with, 'We put our trust in God Most High, and fear no human power.'

'We have chosen our path,' Stauffacher said. 'But before we part, I suggest we seal this pact with an oath.'

A murmur of agreement rippled through the group and Melchthal felt the importance of the moment.

'Keep your hands held high in solidarity, and Furst, Melchthal, you two, and I, representing our cantons, will join our hands.' As they did, Stauffacher's voice rose, 'We pledge our lives, our fortunes, and our sacred honour to the cause of freedom, to this new Confederacy…for our homes, for our families…for our cantons unified as one country…'

As the last words of the oath faded into the crisp mountain air, Melchthal looked around at his compatriots, seeing the same mix of determination and trepidation that he felt.

'Remember,' Stauffacher called out as the group began to disperse, 'patience and discretion. We must each return to our valleys as if nothing has changed.'

Melchthal took one last look around the meadow and saw that Furst and Stauffacher were doing the same. The challenges ahead were daunting, but the memory of this night would sustain him. He gestured to the Unterwalden men and set off, leading them back down the slope to their boats.

Chapter Nine

Bertha von Bruneck stood on the balcony of her quarters, her hands clasped tightly behind her back as she looked down on the castle courtyard. Her thoughts, though, were in the past – weeks earlier, when she had stood in the same manner, hands clasped behind her, at the edge of the prison construction site. She'd surveyed a scene thick with dust, the air filled with the rhythmic clang of hammers, and the sun unforgiving on the backs of labourers straining under the weight of the stone slabs they carried.

With her tall stature and elegant presence, Bertha stood out from the soldiers and workers nearby, her blonde hair swept back in a neat bun, her tailored black dress a symbol of her nobility. A lump had formed in her throat as she watched a young man, no older than seventeen, still a boy in many respects, struggle to carry a bucket of mortar across the uneven ground. His thin arms trembled with the effort, and she felt an overwhelming urge to rush to his aid. But she remained rooted in place, acutely aware of the gulf that separated her world from his. The gold bracelet on her wrist, and the fine velvet of her dress, had suddenly felt like shackles, reminders of her complicity in these people's oppression.

As she wrestled with those thoughts, two Habsburg officials strode past, engrossed in conversation, tipping their heads to acknowledge her as they went.

'The new measures are working well,' the taller of the two men said, his voice low and satisfied. 'These Swiss dogs are finally learning their place.'

His companion chuckled, a sound devoid of mirth. 'Indeed. Gessler's idea to confiscate these workers' weapons was particularly effective. They can't very well rebel without swords and bows, can they?'

Bertha's breath caught in her throat, her eyes widening at the casual cruelty of their words. She had known of the oppressive policies, of course, but to hear them discussed so callously made her skin crawl.

'And what of the new taxes?' the first official inquired. 'Have they been implemented?'

'Oh yes,' came the smug reply. 'The governor's doubled the levy on grain. They'll be lucky to have bread on their tables come winter.' The two men laughed.

As they moved out of earshot, Bertha sagged against the wall, her mind reeling. Although she was of noble Austrian birth, she had spent much time here when younger. The Swiss cantons she had known and loved as a child seemed to be vanishing before her eyes, a land instead of fear and suffering. And she, with her noble blood and Habsburg connections, was part of the system that had brought this about.

Bertha's gaze swept once more over the construction site, seeing it now with new eyes. Each labourer was not just a faceless worker, but a person with hopes, dreams, and a right to freedom. The prison they were building was more than just a prison, it was a symbol of the chains that bound all of them to the Austrian Emperor, Albert's, rule.

She watched as her uncle, Gessler, marched before the workers and addressed them as the pole adorned with a cap was placed on the ground.

As Bertha turned to leave, and return to the same carriage that Gessler strode back toward, she paused, her eyes meeting those of an older man whose arms trembled with exertion.

She stepped toward him. 'Allow me,' she said softly, reaching for her water skin. The man's eyes widened in surprise as she offered it to him.

'My lady,' he rasped, hesitating before accepting the drink. 'You shouldn't—'

'Please,' Bertha insisted, her voice gentle but firm. 'You need it more than I.'

As the labourer drank gratefully, Bertha glanced around, noting the quiet determination in those working on the same team as this older man. 'Your strength is admirable,' she murmured, loud enough for the small group to hear. 'The canton of Uri is fortunate to have such resilient sons.'

A flicker of pride passed through their eyes, quickly masked but not before Bertha caught it. There was something else there, beneath the surface. Anger.

Before she could say anything else there was a sudden commotion. Her gaze snapped upward, following the sound to the half-finished roof where a lone figure teetered precariously on the edge.

'Watch out!' someone called out, but it was too late.

Time seemed to slow as the roof tiler lost his footing, his body twisting in a desperate attempt to regain balance. Bertha didn't breathe as she watched the man plummet through the air.

The sickening thud of flesh meeting stone echoed across the site, followed by an eerie silence. For a moment, no one moved, the horror of the scene freezing them in place.

Then, as if a spell had been broken, chaos erupted. Workers rushed towards the fallen man, their shouts a cacophony of fear and disbelief.

Bertha found herself moving forward, her feet carrying her towards the tragedy before her mind could process what she was doing. As she neared, the crowd parted, revealing the broken body of the roof tiler.

His eyes, wide and unseeing, stared up at the scaffolding he had fallen from. Blood pooled beneath him, a stark crimson against the pale stone.

'Oh, God,' Bertha breathed, her hand flying to her mouth. The smell of copper filled her nostrils, and she felt her stomach lurch.

A rough hand grasped her arm, steadying her. 'You shouldn't see this, my lady,' a labourer said gently, his own face ashen.

But Bertha couldn't look away. This man, this life snuffed out in an instant, was more than just a casualty of construction. He was the price of ambition, of oppression, of the very system she had been born into.

'What was his name?' she asked, her voice barely above a whisper.

'Heinrich,' someone answered. 'He had three young ones at home.'

Bertha felt ill. A father. A husband. His life cut short while forced to build a prison for his own people.

As the initial shock began to fade, she became aware of the hushed conversations around her. The fear in the workers' eyes, the resignation in their slumped shoulders. This wasn't the first death they had witnessed, and they all knew it wouldn't be the last.

She recognized the man who had pleaded mercy from her uncle for one of the workers just minutes before – the archer named Tell – kneeling over the body. 'He's gone,' she heard Tell say.

Bertha had pushed forward, offering gold to anyone who could help return the man's body to his family, but the offer of gold was declined and Tell had said he would remove the body. Standing amidst the tragedy and injustice, Bertha felt something within her shift. She could no longer be a passive observer to the suffering of the Swiss people. It was time to act.

As Bertha left the construction site, her eyes caught sight of a group of women approaching, their arms laden with baskets. The scent of freshly baked bread wafted through the air.

'Who are they?' Bertha asked one of the nearby workers, her gaze fixed on the approaching women.

The man answered, 'Our wives and mothers, my lady. They bring what little food they can spare to sustain us through our toil.'

Bertha watched as the women distributed their meagre offerings among the labourers. A gentle touch here, a whispered word of encouragement there, small acts of defiance against the crush of oppression.

One woman, her face lined with age and worry, caught Bertha's eye. She approached, proffering a small loaf of bread. 'You look weary and distressed, child,' she said softly. 'Please, take this. We all must keep our strength.'

Bertha's throat choked with emotion. 'I... I cannot accept. Surely your men need this more than I.'

The old woman smiled. 'We all need nourishment, my lady. Not just for our bodies, but for our spirits.'

As Bertha accepted the bread, their hands touched briefly. In that instant, she felt a surge of something powerful. A kinship, perhaps?

'Thank you,' Bertha said, and she hurried away, choked by emotion. *How have I been so blind for so long?*

***

Bertha compared the prison site with the ordered and mannerly scene in the courtyard and in the halls of the imperial estate. She stepped from the balcony into her rooms, thinking back to her childhood, to the lessons of compassion and nobility her parents had instilled in her before their untimely deaths. Those values seemed a mockery now.

It was after their deaths that she'd been taken under Hermann Gessler's wing.

An unwelcome memory surfaced. Gessler's voice, cold and dismissive, echoed in her mind.

'My dear Bertha,' he had said, lips curled in a sneer, in response to her concerns about the stories she was hearing, 'you mustn't concern yourself with the rabble. These Swiss peasants are little more than beasts of burden, useful only for their labour.'

She had been silent then, too shocked by his casual cruelty to respond. But now, the memory of that conversation added to the spark of defiance that had been stirring within her.

She sat at her writing desk, quill poised over parchment. And then she wrote. 'My dearest Ulrich, I write to you with a heart heavy heart, full of purpose.' She dipped her quill again, her face pinched in concentration. How much could she safely reveal? How much did she dare?

'The plight of the Swiss people weighs upon my conscience,' her script flowed elegantly across the page. 'I find myself questioning the justice of our current governance. Perhaps, in your wisdom, you might offer counsel on how one might alllay such suffering?'

She sat back, reading over her words. Vague enough to avoid suspicion, yet pointed enough that Ulrich would surely understand her meaning.

As she sealed the letter with wax, Bertha's gaze drifted to the window. She and Ulrich had grown close these past months, his interest in her evident. But Ulrich had become very attached to the court, showing a growing allegiance to the Habsburg's plans for this region. What Ulrich didn't know – what no one at the court knew – was that since that day at the prison, Bertha had been sneaking out from the court, donning a peasant's robe and hood as a disguise, and frequenting the commoners' markets. She had wandered the stalls, hovering, listening to hushed conversations, presenting herself as a woman suffering from the oppressive policies. She had gained the trust of a few and had heard there'd been secret gatherings of a rebellious group.

Her heart quickened now when she thought of the next step she intended to take.

***

Night fell, the castle was quiet, and Bertha knew how to leave the grounds, avoiding the watch of the guardsmen, though every shadow in the torchlit corridors seemed to reach for her.

Once outside, she donned a plain cloak over her dress, pulling the hood low over her face, and made her way through the twisting streets of the old town.

The meeting place was a decrepit barn on the outskirts, far from prying eyes. As Bertha approached, she hesitated, fear overtaking her determination.

She steeled herself and she pushed open the creaking door.

As her eyes adjusted to the flickering candlelight, a dozen pairs of eyes turned to her, their gazes hardening with suspicion and for a moment, Bertha felt her resolve waver again.

'Who are you?' a gruff voice demanded. A tall man, his own face partly obscured by his hood, stepped forward, his hand resting on the hilt of a concealed dagger.

Bertha pulled back her hood, her blonde hair catching the light. She knew it was only through being open and honest that she had any hope of gaining the trust of these men. And she saw that there were a few women also in the gathering. 'I am Bertha von Bruneck,' she announced. 'I've come to offer my aid to your cause.'

Murmurs rippled through the group. Bertha could hear the distrust in their whispers.

'Von Bruneck?' another man said. 'Gessler's ward? How do you know of this meeting?'

'I've been spending time among you, listening to your stories of hardship, and making inquiries.'

'Why should we trust you?'

Bertha lifted her chin, meeting their gazes. 'Because I've witnessed the cruelty of the Habsburg regime firsthand. I can no longer stand idly by while such oppression continues. And you can trust me because I've revealed my identity, despite the grave danger it poses to me.'

The tall man who had first spoken narrowed his eyes. 'Pretty words, my lady. But you were raised in a gilded cage. What can you truly offer us?'

She took another step forward, her voice impassioned. 'My heart beats for your freedom, as does yours.' Her mind raced, calculating her next move. She knew this moment would define her path forward. 'I can offer information,' she said firmly. 'Access to the inner workings of Gessler's court. And resources – gold, to assist with the supplies you need to further your cause.'

A tense silence fell over the barn. Bertha could feel their judgement but there was no turning back now. 'I understand your mistrust. But I ask you to look beyond my name, beyond my upbringing. I am here, risking everything.'

The tall man exchanged glances with his comrades. Slowly, the atmosphere in the barn began to shift.

'Very well, Lady Bertha,' he said finally. 'We'll hear you out. But know this, it will take time for us to know for certain that you are not acting as a spy.'

'You don't need to impart any sensitive information to me, I do not need to be privy to your plans. But you will have from me, however small, whatever assistance I can provide.'

Arrangements were made to meet with Bertha again, but the next time, with just a couple of men, until stronger trust had been built for greater involvement.

As the rebels filed out of the barn, their hushed voices fading into the night, Bertha remained rooted to the spot, her mind awhirl with the enormity of what had just happened. She watched as they disappeared into the shadows.

The tall man who had spoken for the group lingered, his eyes studying her with curiosity. 'You've taken a great risk tonight, my lady,' he said. 'Are you certain you wish to continue? Are you prepared for what may result from this if you are discovered?'

Bertha met his gaze. 'I am,' she replied, although she could not have been less certain of anything. She hoped her voice didn't betray her nerves.

He nodded, a glimmer of respect in his eyes. 'Your support could turn the tide of this rebellion. Go safely, Lady von Bruneck.'

As he turned to leave, Bertha said, 'Wait. I have revealed myself. Are you prepared to tell me your name, sir?'

He paused, looking back over his shoulder. 'Albert. Albert von Melchthal.'

With that, he was gone, leaving Bertha alone in the barn. She stepped outside, the cool night air caressing her flushed cheeks.

She began her cautious journey back to the castle, her steps light despite the gravity of her newfound purpose. The moon cast her shadow before her, a silent companion on this first step of a grand mission her parents would have been proud of.

Chapter Ten

The thud of axe against wood echoed through the morning air. Tell's arms flexed with each swing as he split log after log in the yard. Sweat glistened on his brow despite the cool breeze.

He paused for a moment, wiping his forehead with the back of his hand as he surveyed the growing pile of firewood. His scanned the surroundings, ever alert to potential threats in these troubled times.

From the corner of his eye, he caught sight of Hedy moving between the house and garden, her graceful form a welcome distraction from his brooding thoughts. Her dark hair fell down her back in loose waves, catching the sunlight, her tunic a muted brown that blended with the earth and plants surrounding her. She knelt to gather herbs, her movements casual, yet there was a stiffness in her shoulders that spoke of underlying worry.

Tell frowned as he observed his wife. Her concern was not unfounded, given the whispered talk of rebellion that she'd heard from the neighbours and what she knew of her father's involvement. Tell longed to ease her fears, to assure her that all would be well, but any such words felt hollow even in his own mind.

'Hedy,' he called out. 'How fares the garden this morning?'

She looked up, a smile gracing her features, even if only briefly. 'Well enough. The thyme is coming in nicely, and the rosemary shows promise.'

'Your herbs have seen us through many a winter.'

'As has your strength. Though I confess, I worry more and more when you venture beyond our lands these days.'

Tell set down his axe, crossing the yard to stand before her. He took her hands in his, rough palms enveloping her delicate fingers. 'I know, my heart. But I must hunt, and trade with the villagers.'

Hedy's eyes shimmered and it seemed to Tell that she was holding back on something. 'I understand. I only ask that you be cautious. Gessler's men grow bolder by the day, and of course, you drew attention to yourself when you visited the prison.'

'I've paid the fine.' Tell's expression hardened at the thought.

Hedy nodded. As she returned to her herbs, Tell picked up his axe once more.

The air carried the lilting notes of their son Walter's song, a cheerful melody that wafted across the yard. Tristan, his younger brother, crouched beside him, eyes wide with admiration as Walter nocked an arrow to their small bow. The boys' laughter mingled with the birdsong.

'Watch this, Tristan!' Walter exclaimed, his face scrunched in concentration. He aimed at a knot in a distant tree, his small hands steady. 'I'll hit it right in the centre, just like Papa.'

As Walter drew back the string, a crack split the air. The bowstring snapped, whipping back and narrowly missing the boy's face. Walter's song died on his lips, replaced by a startled gasp.

'Oh no,' he cried, examining the broken weapon. Tristan looked on, his lower lip trembling.

Walter's heart raced as he glanced towards his father, still working in the yard. He swallowed hard, gathering his courage. 'Papa,' he called out, his voice wavering.

Tell set down his axe again, turning to face his son. His gaze fell upon the broken bow. 'What's happened, my boy?'

Walter held out the bow, his hands shaking. 'The string broke, Papa. I... I didn't mean to. Can you fix it?'

Tell gently took the bow, examining it closely. 'Walter, do you remember what I've told you about your tools?'

Walter nodded, his eyes downcast. 'That we must care for them as we care for ourselves.'

81

'That's right.' Tell knelt, bringing himself to eye level with his son. 'And what do we do when something of ours breaks?'

Walter's forehead creased in thought. 'We... we fix it ourselves?'

A smile tugged at the corner of Tell's mouth. 'Indeed. Come, I'll show you how to restring the bow. It's a skill every man should know.'

The boy's face brightened and he and his brother followed their father to the work shed.

***

Hedy paused in her gathering of herbs, her gaze drawn to her sons as they followed William. She loved William's strength, his unwavering commitment to their family and their land. Yet that same strength, that fierce independence, sent a chill of fear through her heart as the stories of their people's oppression grew with each day.

She set down her basket.

'William,' she called, her voice carrying a hint of trepidation. 'A word, please?'

Tell emerged from the workshop, his broad shoulders filling the doorway. 'Does something trouble you?'

Hedy hesitated, struggling to find the right words. 'The boys... they're so young to be learning such skills with the bow, in particular, Tristan. Is it not too soon?'

'Neither is younger than I was when my father taught me.'

'Times were less troubled then.'

Understanding dawned in his eyes. 'You fear that when they're older these skills will see them drawn into a conflict.'

'Which is what I also fear for you.'

'If anything, these troubled times are all the more reason for our boys to learn these skills.'

His gaze drifted to the workshop, where the sound of Walter's laughter drifted out. 'Our sons will forge their own paths, Hedy. We can only arm them with the tools that will serve them best whatever the future holds.'

She nodded but despite the common sense of Tell's words, her anxiety only deepened. 'You spoke yesterday of going to see my father today.'

'Yes. I'll depart for Altdorf shortly.'

Hedy's fingers twisted in her apron. 'Altdorf? Why there?'

Tell's hand found hers, gently stilling her fidgeting fingers. 'Stauffacher will also meet us there. It was a halfway point between our homes for each of us to reach.'

'Stauffacher wants you to become more involved in his and my father's plans,' she guessed, resignation in her voice.

'There was a meeting at the Rütli meadow a few weeks back,' he explained, his voice low but firm. 'Men from Uri, Schwyz, and Unterwalden met to discuss our future. Stauffacher and your father mean to update me on the progress being made.'

'I have a bad feeling about today, William.'

'Ah, that's the reason you are so unsettled. You have an inner feeling that is whispering in your ear.'

Hedy's eyes widened. 'I've heard that Gessler is jealous of your achievements in the archery tournaments.'

'He is jealous of every good Swiss man,' Tell countered. 'Not a reason for me to fear him any more than any other man. But it's contempt for his rule rather than fear that I feel for him.'

She gripped his hands. 'Please. I beg you, stay home today. Gessler's men are everywhere, and in their cowardice, they are always looking for ways to impress him with vile acts.'

Tell's thumb traced soothing circles on the back of her hand. 'That's why I must go. We can't live each day in fear of going about our business in our own land.'

Hedy felt her heart constrict. She had always had pride in her husband's principles but her sense of unease was stronger than she had ever known it to be.

She searched his face, finding no trace of doubt or fear. It was this unwavering resolve that had first drawn her to him, and now it was the very thing that worried her, as he was also a stubborn man, unprepared to listen to a voice of reason when his own mind was made up.

He cupped her cheek gently, his thumb brushing away a stray tear. 'My love, I understand your concerns. But I cannot cower in the face of tyranny.'

She leaned into his touch, her words barely above a whisper. 'Is it cowardice to protect your family? To ensure your children have a father?'

'Let me tell you something of my encounter with Gessler,' he said. 'When I spoke up and asked him to show mercy to Jakob Muller, I held his gaze, stared deeply into his eyes. And do you know what I saw in his eyes? Fear, Hedy. For all his power, all his cruelty, he is just a man. A bully who knows his rule is built on sand.'

'Even so, don't travel there today.'

'I gave my word to your father.'

Hedy's irritation and worry flared into something else, anger, and her voice rose. 'I ask of you this one thing, William. *One thing*. And you refuse, you cannot see beyond your own intents.'

Walter burst into their midst, his youthful energy cutting through the tension. 'Papa! Are you leaving for Altdorf now to see Grandpapa? Can I come with you?'

'Eager for adventure, are you?' He ruffled Walter's hair affectionately.

Walter nodded vigorously. 'I want to see the town, and perhaps I could help you with your business there.' His chest puffed out with pride. 'I'm old enough now, aren't I?'

Hedy stared hard at her husband.

'He will be safe with me, Hedy.'

She shook her head. 'Even after I've told you how strongly I feel, you'll not only go but you'll take one of our sons with you.'

'Have faith, my love.' Tell reached for her but she pushed his hand away.

'We will be safe, Mama,' Walter declared.

Hedy took a deep breath, a lone tear shimmering in the corner of her eye. 'Then promise me one thing, William.'

'Of course.'

'Bring yourself, and our son, safely home to me.'

Chapter Eleven

The alpine meadow stretched before Bertha, a patchwork of green dotted with vibrant wildflowers swaying in the gentle breeze. She paused near a cluster of edelweiss, the star-shaped flowers a stark white against the verdant grass.

She was dressed for the hunt but had managed to slip away from the clamour of the hunting party. The others, so focused on their hunting efforts, would not notice her absence for a while. Even so, her heart beat with anxiety against her ribs, each step carrying her deeper into the forest. Shafts of sunlight pierced the canopy, dappling the forest floor with golden pools that seemed to guide her path.

Her fingers skimmed along the rough bark of an ancient oak, its gnarled branches reaching skyward like beseeching arms. The tree's steadfast presence grounded her, lending strength to her resolve. She breathed in the earthy scent of moss and decaying leaves.

As she neared the secluded glade, a flicker of movement caught her eye. Ulrich von Rudenz emerged from the shadows, his ornate attire a stark contrast to the untamed wilderness surrounding him. The sunlight glinted off the golden embroidery adorning his doublet, a reminder to her of his newfound allegiance to the Austrian court.

The sight of him stirred a mix of emotions she struggled to contain. She watched as his gaze darted nervously about the clearing, searching for her.

'Bertha?' he called softly.

She stepped forward, revealing herself. 'I'm here.'

Relief washed over his features. 'I feared you wouldn't come.' He rushed toward her.

'Did you think I would abandon our people so easily? Unlike some, I haven't forgotten where my loyalties lie.'

Ulrich flinched at the barb. 'No, of course not. I worried that you might have trouble straying from the hunting party.'

'The court nobles are not that smart.'

'I long for the time when we no longer must meet in secret when we want to be alone together. Surely now that—'

'Now that you have advanced in the court of Gessler,' she cut across him. 'You think that my uncle would give his blessing between his niece – an Austrian noble who is his ward – and a junior member of the old Swiss aristocracy who has deserted his own kind? He would never sanction it.'

'But he has bestowed favours on me, and a position in the court.'

'He uses you as a pawn, as he does me. He seeks your allegiance to help him infiltrate more of the Swiss nobility who have not pledged their fidelity to him, hoping the younger ones will follow in your footsteps.'

He seemed unsettled by this and his face fell. 'And how are you his pawn?'

'Do you think Gessler's reach for power is only in these Swiss cantons? As you're aware, I inherited estates on both Swiss and Austrian land. In my heart, I am both Swiss and Austrian. My uncle would seek to marry me off to one of his Viennese sons, extend his power over all those estates, and send me off to Vienna.'

'Are you certain of that? Your uncle's courtiers sought me out, introduced me to men of influence, and Gessler himself has offered me a senior role.'

'All of it mere seduction.' She kept her voice steady. She'd been waiting for many weeks for the chance to speak openly and honestly with Ulrich, although her approach to the rebel group was something she wasn't ready to share with anyone. Not even him. Not yet. Their friendship had evolved into much stronger feelings, but she'd been disappointed by his most recent actions. 'I read your letter. I've read it several times, and each time, I was more and more troubled.'

'I meant no offense,' he said, 'I only wished to share my aspirations with you.'

'Aspirations built on the suffering of others are no aspirations at all, Ulrich. I had written to you expressing my distress over the pain Gessler's rule inflicts upon your own people, yet your reply seemed to gloss over that.'

Ulrich's gaze dropped to the forest floor, avoiding her piercing stare. 'I thought...I thought it was the best way to secure a future for us, to enable us to be together.'

Bertha's voice softened but lost none of its intensity. She could see the cloud of confusion in Ulrich's eyes. She did not want to hurt this man whom she was falling in love with. But she did want him to see Gessler's courting of him for what it was. She wanted the old Ulrich back. 'You speak as if you've forgotten who you are. Ulrich of Rudenz, nephew of Baron von Attinghausen, who is a pillar of the Swiss and who speaks his mind to the Austrians, a bastion of hope for the Swiss people's heritage.'

'But what has that heritage brought us but poverty and isolation? The world is changing, Bertha. Surely we must change with it. Perhaps you haven't considered the good that can come from power and progress.'

'Then help me understand,' she challenged, her eyes never leaving his face, as he raised his eyes to meet hers. 'Explain to me how the man I knew, the man I...' she hesitated, then forged ahead, '...love, could turn his back on everything he once held dear. You used to tell me about the wondrous Swiss stories of courage you heard when you were growing up.'

She noticed the uncertainty in his expression. She wanted to reach the man she believed still existed beneath the gilded exterior.

'I thought I could make a difference from within, with you by my side,' he said, his voice low.' By gaining not just Gessler's favour, but the favour of all the governors. That by becoming part of the system, I could soften their approach, bring in protections for my countrymen.'

'You will be a puppet in a system that's brought terrible suffering to your people. To *our* people. Have you seen the prison fortress being built in Altdorf?'

'Only from a distance.'

'Think of the cries of children whose fathers will rot in those dungeons. What of the widows whose bodies are violated and whose lands are seized by Austrian nobles? How can you turn away from them?'

She saw his shoulders sag, realization dawning in his eyes. 'What have I done?'

The distant blare of hunting horns pierced the air, startling both of them. The sound echoed through the glade.

'They're returning this way, they'll be looking for me.' Bertha's gaze darted towards the forest. 'We have little time left.' She grasped his hands, her touch both gentle and insistent. 'Promise me you'll consider what I've said. Our people need you, Ulrich – I need you – to stand against this tyranny.'

'Bertha, I—' he began, his voice catching.

'No,' she interrupted. 'Don't answer now. Later today we're both required to attend Gessler. But on the morrow, visit the construction of the prison, see for yourself the cruelty, speak to farmers about the taxes, look around you at the court to the nobles' indifference. I know the path of honour is a dangerous one, but it's the only one that leads to true freedom.'

The hunting horns sounded again, closer now. Bertha glanced over her shoulder, then turned back to Ulrich. In a swift, unexpected motion, she reached up and cupped his cheek, her touch sending shivers through him. 'Remember this moment. Think about what I've said, what's at stake.'

He leaned into her touch, tears welling in his eyes. And then she pulled away, and he watched as she made her way back across the glade and into the forest.

***

As Bertha's footsteps faded, Ulrich remained rooted in place, his mind reeling. This had not been the romantic rendezvous he'd imagined. He'd known of Bertha's discomfort at aspects of the Austrian rule but it was far greater than he'd been aware. He had not taken it seriously, he'd been distracted, swept up by the promise of greatness he'd seen in the offers and accolades he'd received from Gessler's court. Bertha's words had been blunt. He'd hated the disappointment in him that he'd seen in her eyes.

He felt that his heart would explode with the love he felt for her. Her courage, her determination, her sense of right and wrong – all as captivating as her stunning beauty.

He wandered, following the sound of a nearby stream. When he reached it, he stood and gazed at its clear waters rushing over smooth stones. He lifted his face to the breeze and allowed the serenity of this place to wash over him.

Had he allowed himself to be blinded by the twin devils of ambition and false promises?

I've been a fool.

After a while of reflection, he began to head back the way he had come, Bertha's words resonant in his mind.

Our people need you...I need you.

Even in memory, her voice carried a strength that seemed to cut through his confusion.

After a while the forest began to thin, and Ulrich found himself at the edge of a cliff overlooking a vast valley. The waterfall he'd been hearing streamed down the opposite side, its mist catching the sun and creating a shimmering rainbow. He felt something in his breast that he hadn't felt for a long time, a swell of pride in this land, and he realized, as his tears fell freely, how much he'd missed that simple sense of belonging.

Further along, he came to a fork in the path. One way led to Altdorf and Gessler's court. The other to his uncle's castle. He needed to think deeply about everything Bertha had said but, in the meantime, he had to return to the court, his attendance was required for several events, as was Bertha's.

But even as he reached the point where he had left his horse tied to a tree, and then rode on to Altdorf, he felt the overwhelming need to visit his uncle, the baron, as soon as possible, his mood sullen now by how he'd left things on his last visit.

Chapter Twelve

The afternoon sun cast strips of shadow across the northern end of the town square in Altdorf, along the opposite side of where two of Gessler's guards stood watch over their bizarre charge. Friesshardt shifted his weight from one foot to the other, his armour creaking in protest. His gaze went to the cap perched atop the pole – a symbol of authority that seemed to mock him with its very presence.

'Another day of guarding this blasted hat,' he muttered to Leuthold, who stood beside him with an equally dour expression. 'And hardly a single bow this morning from these ungrateful peasants.'

Leuthold grunted in agreement. 'What did you expect? They resent us as much as we resent this duty. Only the lowest rabble wander by.' There was a pole with another of Gessler's caps at the prison as well as here in the town square, and Gessler intended to have others mounted throughout the cantons.

'Most are taking the long way round rather than bow to this,' Friesshardt said. The futility of their task gnawed at him. He scanned the square, noting the sidelong glances and whispered conversations of stragglers in the distance. A silent rebellion that set his teeth on edge.

As they stewed in their frustration, Frieshhardt's gaze fixed on a man, a crossbow slung across his back, walking with a young boy, deep in conversation, heading in their direction.

***

Tell and Walter entered the sprawling town square. As they'd approached, it had seemed to Tell that it was less crowded than usual.

'Papa,' Walter said, his young voice filled with curiosity, 'is it true that the trees on the mountains, if they are wounded by a hatchet, will bleed? That they weep for our land?'

'And who told you this?'

'The master herdsman who passes by our land each week. Sometimes he tells stories to the local children. He says that the trees have a charm upon them, and if injured by men, the hand of that man who struck them will rise out of the man's grave.'

'That's quite a story.'

'Is it true, Papa?'

Tell smiled down at his son. 'Ah, Walter, the legends of our forests run as deep as their roots. Some say the trees bleed when our freedom is threatened, their sap turning red as a warning.' He looked across the distant Alps and motioned for Walter to follow his gaze. 'I think that the trees do have a charm that protects us. You see the white horns of those glaciers atop the mountains?'

'Yes, Papa, the ones that thunder when they send down the avalanches.'

Tell threw his glance back, at the buildings and stalls along the square's perimeter. 'Parts of all the cantons might have been buried under those avalanches but for those charmed trees that stand like a bulwark, arresting the fall of the snow.' He was mindful of his next words. 'But remember, my son, it's not just the trees that protect us. It's the strength of our people, our love for this land, that truly safeguards our liberty.'

The boy nodded solemnly and Tell could see in the boy's expression how his young mind grappled with his father's words. How he wished he could shield his son from the harsh realities of their world, but he knew that knowledge and preparedness were the greatest gifts he could offer.

As they walked on, the boy's eyes wandered about the square and he saw the cap. 'Look papa, what's that cap on the pole?'

Tell glanced in the direction Walter pointed. 'We'll speak of it later. Come on.'

But before he'd taken a few more steps, Friesshardt, flanked by Leuthold, stepped into their path in a swift motion, his hand resting on the hilt of his sword. 'Halt!' he barked. 'You there, archer! You've broken the law by not bowing to the hat.'

'I meant no disrespect,' Tell said. 'We were talking and—'

Friesshardt glared at him. 'Your excuses mean nothing. The word has been spread throughout the canton for many weeks about the fate for those not bowing before the governor's cap.'

Walter's eyes widened with fear. 'We did not see the cap,' he cried out, his shrill voice carrying across the square. He raised his arm and pointed. 'The pole is over there.'

'Only a few paces, well within the required space for paying respect to the empire.'

Tell placed a protective hand on Walter's shoulder. He scanned the growing crowd that had heard Walter's cry as they edged toward the scene, noting the outrage on their faces. 'There's no need for this,' he said, keeping his voice calm. 'Surely we can resolve this misunderstanding without—'

But Friesshardt was already signalling to Leuthold. 'Seize him.'

'Help! Someone help my father!' Walter shrieked.

As the guards advanced, Tell's mind raced. He could easily overpower them, but what then? The outcome for his family, for the entire town, would be harsh. And yet submitting to such petty injustice was not in his nature.

The crowd began to grow and press closer, their murmurs becoming louder. Tell caught sight of Father Rosselmann pushing his way to the front.

'Please, gentlemen,' the priest called out, his hands raised in a gesture of peace. 'Let us not act hastily. Surely there's no need for violence on this day.'

Tell felt a glimmer of hope at the priest's intervention, but it was quickly snuffed out by Friesshardt's sneering response.

'Stay out of this, Father. The law is clear, and it will be enforced.'

As the tension in the square mounted, Tell's gaze met Walter's. The boy's eyes were filled with a mixture of dread and unwavering trust that made Tell's heart ache. Whatever happened next, he knew he had to protect his son at all costs.

Many of the men and women in the crowd had recognized Tell and they called out for the soldiers to leave him alone.

From the corner of his eye, he saw Hedy's father, Furst, and Stauffacher, hurrying from another corner of the square. They'd been waiting, for their meeting with Tell, at a prearranged spot near the market just beyond the square. They'd heard the boy's shriek.

A sudden hush fell over the square, rippling outward like a stone dropped in still water. Tell felt the change before he saw its cause, a prickling sensation at the nape of his neck. He turned, his heart sinking as he caught sight of the approaching entourage.

The clatter of hooves on cobblestones seemed unnaturally loud in the eerie silence that had descended. Governor Gessler rode at the head, his imposing figure cutting a stark silhouette against the afternoon sky, a falcon perched on his shoulder, a symbol to those around him of his power. Tell had heard about the governor's penchant for having the falcon with him when he rode in a procession, although this was the first time he had seen it.

Flanking Gessler, Tell recognized the head of Gessler's entourage, Rudolph de Harras, followed by Baron Attinghausen's nephew, Ulrich of Rudenz, and Bertha, the heiress Tell had encountered at the prison. Riding alongside them was a young man in glittering regal attire, and Tell recalled hearing that the Austrian Emperor's nephew, Duke John of Swabia, would be touring the canton.

A horn blast from De Harras announced Gessler's arrival as the entourage's armed attendants formed a ring of lances around the square.

'Make way for the governor!' De Harras's voice echoed around the square.

Tell's eyes were drawn to Ulrich, the young nobleman's face a mask of conflicted emotions. Tell knew of the baron's concerns about his nephew's attraction to the pageantry of Gessler's court. For a fleeting moment, their gazes met, and Tell saw a flicker of something – regret? shame? – before Ulrich looked away.

Gessler dismounted, his cold eyes sweeping the scene before settling on Tell. 'What have we here?' he asked, his voice deceptively soft.

Friesshardt stepped forward, bowing low. 'My lord, this man refused to pay homage to your symbol of authority.'

Tell's mind raced. He knew his next words could mean life or death, not just for him, but for Walter and perhaps the entire town. He inhaled deeply, steadying himself.

'Governor,' Tell said, his voice calm despite the turmoil within, 'I assure you, this is merely an oversight on my part. I was lost in conversation with my son and failed to notice the hat. No disrespect was intended.'

Gessler's lips curled into a smile that never reached his eyes. 'An oversight, you say?' He took a step closer.

'You are the archer who showed insolence at the prison site.'

'I have paid the fine, Governor.'

'The renowned archery champion, William Tell, whose keen eyes are said to rival those of an eagle?'

Tell's throat was dry. He could feel Walter trembling beside him, could sense the collective breath of the crowd being held. 'Even the sharpest eyes can sometimes miss what's right before them,' he said.

Gessler's gaze bore into him, as did those of the falcon on his shoulder. 'Indeed,' he murmured, the cold smile still playing on his lips, as his eyes searched Tell's face for any hint of defiance. 'And yet, I find myself wondering. A man of your... reputation. Could it truly be mere chance that led you to ignore our symbol of authority?'

The gears clicked over in Tell's mind. How could he convince this man of his sincerity without grovelling? The very thought of bowing and scraping before Gessler made his skin crawl, but the alternative... He glanced at Walter, anxiety gripping his heart.

'My lord,' Tell said, choosing each word with painstaking care, 'I am but a simple huntsman. My reputation, such as it is, comes from necessity, not pride. I assure you, my oversight was genuine.'

As Gessler considered his words, Tell caught sight of Bertha von Bruneck again. The noblewoman's face was a mask, but her eyes betrayed a hint of sympathy. For a moment, Tell dared to hope that this might yet end without further consequence.

But then Gessler's smile widened like a predator who had just spotted weakness in its prey. 'A simple huntsman,' he repeated softly. 'We shall see about that, Tell. We shall see.' He stared at Walter. 'Is this your son?'

'Yes, my lord.'

'Do you have others?'

'Two boys, my lord.'

'And which do you love more?'

'Both are equally dear to me.'

Gessler's eyes glinted with cruel amusement as he raised his voice, addressing the crowd. 'Let us put this marksman's skill to the test, shall we?' He turned back to Tell, his words dripping with malice. 'I am myself a falconer, so I understand what it takes to develop skills. You hunt chamois and the story goes that shooting from a distance, you never miss. Is this true?'

'Every huntsman has their misses,' Tell said.

'And in a contest, your arrow, shot from eighty paces, has been known to split an apple perched on a tree branch more times than not. Is that also true? Speak up.'

'Yes, my lord.'

'You claim oversight, Tell. Very well. Prove your loyalty to me and your prowess in one stroke. From eighty paces, you will shoot an apple that sits upon your son's head.'

The crowd gasped collectively. Tell staggered back as if physically struck, his face draining of colour. 'My lord,' he said, his voice raspy with breath, 'surely you jest.'

'I do not jest, Tell, not when it comes to the law, and not with the likes of you.'

'I beg you, Governor, please reconsider this command.'

'You will shoot,' Gessler's voice rose, 'or both you and the boy will be put to death.'

'Please,' Tell pleaded, his pride forgotten in the face of this unthinkable task. 'I'll do anything else you ask. Punish me if you must but spare my boy.'

Bertha cantered her horse a few steps closer, her elegant features stamped with concern. 'Governor,' she said, 'surely there are other ways to test a man's loyalty. This... this is unnecessarily cruel.'

Ulrich hesitantly added his voice. 'My lord, perhaps the lady has a point. We could—'

Gessler silenced them both with the sweep of his hand. 'Enough! I have made my decision.' To Ulrich, he added, 'So the dandy speaks out, despite my generosity to him for a brighter future than he would otherwise have known. You need to grow a backbone, sir. I will speak with you later about your attitude.' He flashed a look of disappointment at Bertha.

Ulrich shrank back.

Duke John of Swabia was watching quietly, with interest.

Gessler then turned again to face Tell. 'I have no more time to waste on this. You will prove your loyalty or you and the child will face the gallows.'

Murmurs of horror rippled through the crowd.

Tell's anger flared. 'You would hang a child?'

'The boy will be put in shackles until he is a young man. And then he will swing.'

Tell saw his father-in-law, Furst, begin to push forward past the crowd but Stauffacher grabbed his arm and stilled him, whispering in his ear. There was nothing more that could be gained by those two attracting attention to their presence.

Tell's panic threatened to overwhelm him. How could he possibly take such a risk with Walter's life? And yet, to refuse would mean certain death for them both. He looked at the row of soldiers with their lances. His hands trembled as he reached for his son, desperate to shield him from this madness. Hedy's face flashed before him and her words replayed in his mind.

I have a bad feeling about today, William... Please, I beg you, stay home...

But he hadn't listened, hadn't given her intuition, her sense of foreboding, any credibility.

His heart sank as he realized the futility of further argument against Gessler. He closed his eyes, offering a silent prayer for strength and guidance.

When he opened his eyes again, his gaze was steady, his voice low but firm. 'Very well, Governor. If this is what you demand, I have no choice but to comply.'

I can do this. I can save my son.

Walter's voice cut through the tense silence. 'Papa, you can do it. I know you can.'

Tell turned to his son, marvelling at the child's courage. Walter's small frame seemed to grow taller as he stood straighter, chin lifted in defiance of the fear that gripped the crowd. 'I trust you, Papa. More than anyone in the world.'

Gessler commanded his soldiers. 'Prepare the boy.'

Tell embraced his son before the soldiers removed him.

The crowd watched in horrified silence as the soldiers led Walter to the ancient linden tree at the centre of the square. They were handed ropes and they bound him to the tree, not roughly, but with a lightness of touch that showed their own discomfort with the task.

Tell was focused on the action, and even across the distance he caught the voice of one of the soldiers, 'Stand still now, young master,' the man said, almost apologetically, as he placed the apple atop Walter's head.

Tell watched, his throat constricting, as his son stood straight and proud against the tree.

A collective gasp rippled through the onlookers. Tell could feel their fear, their outrage, their helplessness. It mirrored his own, set to overwhelm him.

To be just a mere fraction off target would kill his son, spearing his forehead, or one of his eyes.

'Now, Tell.' Gessler's voice sounded to Tell as the voice of the devil might sound, devoid of heart or soul, exhilarated at the idea of great suffering. 'Your chance to prove this remarkable skill, save yourself and your son, and prove your undying loyalty to me.'

As he stepped forward to take his position, Tell's eyes locked with his son's. In that moment, despite the distance between them, father and son shared a silent understanding.

Hedy's plea that very same morning invaded his thoughts.

Bring yourself, and our son, safely home to me.

He swallowed hard, sweat on his brow, and he pushed Hedy's voice and face, and everything else, from his mind.

His hands trembled as he reached for his quiver, his fingers brushing against the familiar feathered fletching. With movements that belied his inner turmoil, he selected two arrows. The first, he slipped discreetly into his belt; the second, he notched to his bow.

'Steady now,' he said to himself, willing his hands to stop shaking. A bead of sweat trickled down his brow, and he blinked hard, fighting to keep his vision clear. The weight of the impossible task before him pressed down on his shoulders.

A movement at the front of the crowd, who were being held back by the guards, momentarily distracted him. He saw a small girl's head pop between the legs of the adults, her eyes wide with distress. Tell recognised the child from church. Elsi. A friend of Walter's. He did not want her to witness this. He could only hope her face would disappear from the front as the adults inched forward in front of her.

He refocused on his task.

As he raised his bow, an eerie hush fell over the square, leaving only the thundering of his own heartbeat in his ears. He took a deep breath, trying to centre himself.

How many times, in practice, and in contest, had his arrow missed the apple and thudded instead into the bark of a tree?

How long since he'd even attempted such a feat?

'Lord,' he prayed silently, his eyes fixed on the distant apple atop his son's head, 'guide my hand. Protect my boy.'

Walter's voice carried across the square. 'Papa, I'm not afraid. I trust you.' But there was a waver in the boy's voice that hadn't been there before.

Tell felt a surge of pride at his son's bravery. He forced himself to nod, not trusting his voice to remain steady if he spoke. As he drew back the bowstring, a strange calm settled over him. The tremble in his hands stilled, his vision sharpened, and the world narrowed to a single point – the apple that held his son's life in balance.

Time seemed to freeze in that terrible moment – Tell's bowstring drawn taut, Walter standing impossibly still, the crowd barely breathing.

With one final, steadying breath, Tell gathered his resolve.

His fingers tightened, feeling the tension, and time slowed as he pulled the crossbow's trigger, launching the arrow with a twang. For a split second the sun glinted off the silver tip, making it seem almost ethereal as it soared towards its target with lightning speed, Tell watching its trajectory with eagle-like focus. But something did not seem right. He gasped, his breath catching in his throat, and he feared he'd made the slightest of miscalculations, the arrow a fraction too low, slicing through the air now at his son's unmoving, trusting face.

Chapter Thirteen

The arrow whistled through the air, a blur of motion cutting across the square.

The crowd gasped, a sound that swelled and then abruptly died as the arrow found its mark. The apple exploded into fragments, pieces scattering to the ground around Walter's feet.

For a heartbeat, silence reigned. And then the square erupted with the people's relief. All were amazed. There were gasps and murmurs of amazement, the anxiety breaking like a dam giving way to a flood.

Walter's voice rang out, clear and triumphant. 'Papa! You did it!'

Relief flooded through Tell, nearly buckling his knees. His aim had been true. He staggered, his bow dropping from his fingers. 'Merciful God,' he said, his voice barely audible. 'Walter,' he called, fighting to keep his composure. 'Are you unharmed?'

'Yes, Papa.'

As the soldiers moved to unbind Walter from the tree, Tell's gaze snapped to Gessler. The governor's face was a mask of shock and barely concealed fury.

De Harras commented that this was an extraordinary feat that would be told by the people throughout the land, no doubt adding to Tell's stature. Gesler did no more than shoot De Harras a look of indignation.

The tension in the square shifted, anticipation building as the crowd waited to see how Gessler would respond.

Walter stood unharmed, his eyes wide with relief and awe.

Tell's hand moved unconsciously to the second arrow tucked into his belt. Its presence was both a comfort and a reminder of the choice he had made. If the first arrow had strayed... He shuddered, pushing the thought away.

'Walter,' he called out, his voice rough with emotion. 'Come to me, son.'

As the crowd swelled forward, Walter began to move through it, and Tell's gaze swept over the assembled faces. He saw fear, yes, but also hope and a growing determination. The little girl, Elsi, was leaping and clapping, and Tell knew that whatever came next, he had done more than save his son's life. He had given his people a reason to believe that tyranny could be challenged, that the indomitable spirit of the Swiss would not be broken by Austrian cruelty.

As Walter reached him, Tell pulled his son into a fierce embrace, whispering words of pride and love and, once again, the crowd erupted, this time with cheers and applause. Tell's heart thundered in his chest, the adrenaline of the moment giving way to a rush of overwhelming emotion. His vision blurred with the promise of tears as he held his son, the gravity of what could have been crashing over him in waves. The crowd's jubilation seemed distant, muffled by the blood rushing in his ears.

Gessler's cold, imperious voice cut through the celebrations and silenced the crowd in an instant. 'A master shot, I grant you.'

'Thank you, my lord.'

'But enlighten me, Tell, why did you take the second arrow from your quiver?'

The atmosphere in the square changed abruptly. Tell straightened, keeping Walter close to his side. He met Gessler's cruel gaze, acutely aware of the arrow still tucked in his belt.

'It is the custom of all archers, my lord.'

'I've heard of no such custom.'

'It is not well known, Your Excellency.'

'The purpose of such a custom?'

'A skilled archer always carries a spare. It is... a precaution.'

Gessler's eyes narrowed, clearly unsatisfied with the response. 'A precaution against what?'

'For when an archer is on the hunt, and the first shot fails to fell a chamois.'

'But you are not on a hunt.' Gessler took a step forward, gesturing. 'You had some other purpose. Tell me another lie and I will have you shot before a firing line of my own archers. But speak truth, and you have my promise your life will be spared.'

Tell felt every eye upon him. He looked at the son whose life he'd been forced to gamble with, and his eyes then swept across the faces of his countrymen.

'Since you guarantee my life in front of everyone here, I'll tell you plainly.' He drew the second arrow from his belt and held it up, meeting Gessler's gaze with sudden, terrifying directness. 'If my first arrow had struck my child, this second one was for you, my lord. And believe me – I would not have missed.'

For a long moment, silence reigned. Then, Gessler's harsh laughter shattered the stillness, sounding almost as though it echoed off the stone buildings that ringed the square. It was a sound devoid of mirth.

'How admirably honest of you, Tell.' Gessler's lips twisted into a crooked sneer. 'And how foolish. Did you think your skill with a bow would protect you from the issues of such treasonous thoughts?'

Tell remained silent.

Gessler's eyes glittered with malice. 'I am a man of my word, Tell. I promised to spare your life if you spoke the truth, and so I shall.' He paused, savouring the moment. 'But your freedom? That, I'm afraid, is forfeit. You shall live out your days in the dungeons of the Austrian empire, where your rebellious spirit can rot along with your bones.'

A murmur of protest rose from the crowd, quickly silenced by Gessler's glare. Tell felt a cold dread settle in his stomach, but he refused to show fear.

Gessler gestured to his guards. 'Bind him. Take him to my boat. I'll see him safely locked in the Kussnacht castle's prison wing myself.'

The guards moved swiftly, rough hands grasping Tell's arms. He offered no resistance as they bound his wrists tightly with coarse rope.

His face remained impassive, a mask of stoic acceptance, but inwardly, his heart ached. What had he done? Words of defiance to inspire the crowd but at what cost when you are speaking to a madman?

'Papa! No!' Walter lunged forward, small hands clutching at Tell's shirt. 'Please, don't take him!'

Ignoring the bindings on his wrists, Tell resisted the guards' handling and knelt beside his son. 'Listen to me, Walter, you've shown more courage today than many men do in a lifetime. I need you to be brave once more. Can you do that for me?'

Walter's eyes were red-rimmed but determined. 'Yes.'

Tell managed a smile. 'That's my boy. Now, I need you to return home, your grandpapa will take you, and I need you to take care of your mother and your little brother. Can you do that for me?'

Walter nodded solemnly. 'I will protect them.'

'Be strong for your mother. I will find a way back to you, I promise.'

The crowd's voices grew louder, a mixture of anger and fear. One voice rang out above the others.

'This is an outrage!' Stauffacher pushed his way to the front, Walter's grandfather, Furst, trailing him. 'This is a violation of rights. Tell has committed no crime worthy of imprisonment!'

Gessler's other guards moved to restrain Stauffacher but Gessler motioned for them to hold back. He confronted Stauffacher, man to man, a display of strength to the watching crowd. 'Rights, Stauffacher?' Gessler spat. 'You have only the rights I choose to grant you. Tell's defiance is a threat to order, to the very authority of the Emperor himself.' He gaze swept across the assembled villagers. 'Let this be a lesson to all who would dare challenge my rule.'

As the guards began to lead him away, Tell felt another shift in the crowd. Faces that had moments ago beamed with pride were now distorted in disbelief.

'They can't do this!' a woman cried out.

'Tell is one of us!' said another villager.

Tell did not want his action to cause grief to any one of those men and women. He called out to them. 'Do not throw your lives away today in futile resistance. Our day will come, but not like this.'

The crowd's fervour dimmed, replaced by a feeling of helplessness.

As he was marched towards Gessler's waiting boat, moored at the Lake Uri dock not far from the town, Tell's attention was drawn to storm clouds in the distance, moving out from the mountain, and the sudden gusts of wind, sweeping across the lake, whipped his hair about his face. He said a silent prayer of thanks that those winds had not reached the shore just minutes earlier, when they would have buffeted the arrow.

He cast one last look over his shoulder at the town, his eyes searching for Walter.

The wind picked up, whistling through the streets and whipping cloaks into a frenzy. Leaves and debris skittered across the cobblestones.

His gaze locked with that of his father-in-law and a world of understanding passed between them. Furst gave an almost imperceptible nod, his face grim.

Furst's arms were around Walter's shoulders, and they stood, with Stauffacher alongside them, catching their last glimpse of Tell before he was beyond their vision.

Tell had kept his promise to Hedy that her son would return safely. But his foolishness meant it was only half of his promise that he'd been able to keep, and he feared for what lay ahead for his family.

'Keep moving,' one of the guards barked. Tell was shoved forward, across the dock's plank, and onto the waiting boat.

Chapter Fourteen

The rough hemp ropes bit into Tell's wrists as the guards thrust him into a corner at the stern. From there, the captain, directing his oarsmen, would be able to keep the prisoner in view, as would Gessler and the guards.

Tell's eyes surveyed the vessel – a sturdy oak longship with high sides, built from oak trunks and fastened with large iron nails, boasting benches for a dozen oarsmen, a mast on which a sail was raised, the boat's dragon-headed prow a remnant of Norse influence. Perhaps, Tell thought, this arrogant governor fancied himself as a Viking conqueror.

Before boarding, Gessler had instructed his entourage to escort Duke John back along the roads to the Altdorf castle, while announcing his intention to oversee the transport of his prized prisoner to the small prison across the lake. 'But when the new Altdorf dungeons are complete,' he said to Tell, 'you'll be sent there, where your punishment will be far more unpleasant than mere incarceration.'

Tell flinched, recalling the Master Mason's words that the dungeons held an array of torture devices.

As Tell was forced to his knees, he caught the anxious glances exchanged between the guards. Their hands fidgeted on weapon hilts as they eyed the gathering storm. They'd heard the murmurs of the crew that perhaps the launch should be delayed until the storm had passed.

'My lord,' one guard ventured, 'perhaps we should delay—'

'We leave now,' Gessler snapped. 'Or would you face my displeasure rather than a bit of rain?' He glanced at his boat's captain. 'We have sailed in storms far worse than this one looks, have we not?'

'We have, my lord.'

Turning back to the guards, he said, 'That should settle the nerves, then, of my cowardly guardsmen.' He didn't wait for a response. 'Launch!' he commanded.

The crew's oars dipped into the slate-gray waters, and the boat lurched away from the shore.

But they were not far into the journey when the winds surged in strength, turbulent gusts whipping across the lake. The craft pitched, and several oarsmen cursed under their breath.

'Steady, men!' barked the captain, his knuckles white on the tiller.

Tell noted the change in the air, the intense, metallic taste that preceded a tempest. But not just any tempest. The rapid advance of dark clouds and the savagery of the wind reminded him of the storm that erupted when he'd ferried Baumgarten across another part of the lake. He recalled that the father of Werni, a fellow hunter, had predicted a series of sudden, unnatural tempests over many weeks, his superstitious belief that the Dark Talkers were venting their fury at the injustices inflicted on the Swiss.

Tell allowed himself a grim smile at the memory.

'Something amuses you, bowman?' Gessler said as he regarded his captive.

Tell didn't flinch as he met the governor's gaze, despite the spray that stung his eyes. 'Only that you may soon learn the folly of challenging these waters, my lord. They bow to neither man nor cap.'

A peal of thunder punctuated his words, the black clouds lit momentarily by a flash of lightning, and two of the guards jumped. Gessler sneered at Tell's words but before he could respond a massive wave crashed over the bow, drenching everyone and wiping the sneer from the governor's lips. The boat lurched violently, and Tell braced himself against the bulwark.

The Uri basin waters flowed into the greater Lake Lucerne. It was vast and deep, and its waters churned into frothy peaks, lifting the boat and then dropping it into a trough, hindering the efforts of the rowers as they pushed and pulled their oars through the water. Tell scanned the distance, the wind-driven rain a whirlpool in the air, spreading, darkening, the thunder roaring across the sky, and he thought again of Werni's father's Dark Talkers.

They are sending a hurricane.

'Secure the mainsail!' the captain bellowed.

Tell's muscles tensed as he tried to avoid being thrown across the deck. He could sense the fear radiating from the crew as they scrambled across a deck that was awash with water, their desperation unmistakable as they struggled to carry out the order.

'We're taking on water,' one of the sailors cried out.

'Start bailing,' the captain told them. He shot a look at Gessler. 'This storm is far worse, my lord, than it first appeared.'

Or you simply told Gessler what he wanted to hear against your better judgement, Tell thought.

Gessler was clutching the side of the bulwark, straining to keep his footing, water running in rivulets down his coat. 'I expected better of you,' he roared back at the captain. 'Now show your mettle and get us through this.'

Tell closed his eyes for a brief respite against the salt-laden sprays, steadying himself as best he could as the boat rocked violently. His father's words echoed in his mind, a lesson from long ago: 'The lake demands respect, William. It gives life, but it can take it just as swiftly.'

He opened his eyes as another deafening crack of thunder split the air, and he saw several of the oarsmen cross themselves. Surveying the mayhem, he caught sight of his bow and quiver. They'd been placed portside, alongside the guards, but had slid back and forth across the deck, ignored by everyone, tantalizingly close yet frustratingly out of reach.

Another enormous wind thumped the boat, and it tipped on its side before righting itself, but there was a loud crack and the mast split, and then its two splintered columns of wood were ripped away into the lake. It happened in just seconds and now the exhausted oarsmen were at the mercy of the storm without the backup of a sail.

'Put your backs into it, men,' the captain bellowed again, shouting to be heard above the wind which howled now like a wounded animal.

The rain came down in a torrent then and together with another enormous wave, the boat began to take on water faster than the crew could bail it out.

'We need a shelter where we can anchor from this,' the lead oarsman shouted to the captain.

Tell watched as the captain ran his eyes over the distant shoreline, which was barely visible through the torrent. The man looked stricken and Tell realized that for all his gusto the captain had never faced a squall anywhere near as feral as this.

'We don't know these waters well enough,' another crewman's voice raised above the roar of the waves.

'The prisoner does,' yelled the oarsman in front of him.

The first man's eyes darted to Tell, recognition flickering in their depths. Tell locked eyes with him and gave a nod.

The oarsman turned his head, catching the attention of the captain. 'Master, our prisoner is both an archer and a skilled sailor. I've heard even the fishermen say he knows the lake better than any of them.'

Tell saw an opportunity but he kept his face impassive, not daring to betray his emotions as the captain exchanged an uncertain glance with Gessler.

There was another sickening crack, followed by a chorus of panicked cries.

'The steering oar has snapped,' the lead oarsman called to the captain.

The boat tipped steeply to its side again, several of the oarsman thrown from their benches.

As the boat rocked back and forth, at the mercy of the savage swells and the relentless deluge, Tell saw his chance. 'Governor, Captain, I can lead us to safety.'

Cries of agreement erupted from the crew as they grappled to maintain their places.

'Help us, Tell.'

'Untie him!'

'Madness,' one of the guards was heard to shout back.

For a split second, the captain's eyes squinted as he appraised the prisoner, and then his head whipped about to face the governor.

Gessler, his arrogance gone in the face of the disaster facing him, was struggling now to grip the side of the boat. He saw the questioning look in his captain's glance.

With his face contorted with rage and indecision, Gessler turned his gaze to his prisoner. 'You expect me to trust you, Tell? A traitor to the crown.'

'You think I would leap over the side and drown? I can be trusted to save all our lives.'

'Tell knows the shores of Lucerne,' an oarsman shouted.

Another massive wave engulfed the boat. This time, one of the crew was swept overboard. Lost.

'God, have mercy!' The cries of the crew were swallowed by the roar of the wind.

'There's a rock shelf that juts into the lake,' Tell called out. 'I can guide us to shelter in the bay beside it.'

Gessler, his face pale, hesitated only a moment before shooting a look at his guards. 'Untie him!' he barked. 'But if he tries anything, use your swords!'

As the ropes fell away from Tell's wrists, he flexed his fingers, relishing the return of circulation. 'The steering oar,' he said firmly, taking command. 'Where is the spare?'

Two crewmen stumbled forward, struggling under the weight of the replacement oar that they picked up from the port side. Once it was in place, thrust through the oarlock on the side of the stern, Tell grasped it, the feel of it in his hand grounding him as the boat creaked and groaned and rocked. 'Hold fast' he called.

Planting his feet wide on the deck and grunting with exertion, he fought to take control of the boat's direction. 'Row hard, men,' he directed the oarsmen.

The boat lurched, fighting against his command.

Tell tried to recognize, through the veil of rain, the shapes on the far shore. He knew which direction they needed to take, and he watched the pattern of the waves closely. And saw what he was looking for. 'Hard to port!' he ordered. 'We need to catch those swells!'

It would take every ounce of strength from every oarsman on board, riding the swells, fighting the wind, for him to guide the boat to the shore. Every nerve end screamed. He wrestled with the steering oar, the wood slick with rain, every violent pitch of the boat threatening to tear the oar from his grasp or snap the wood as it had the last one.

'Pull harder!' The wind was louder than ever and his voice so hoarse, Tell wasn't certain if he was being heard. He hoped Gessler had been swept overboard, but the rest of these men he was determined to save.

Time lost all meaning, and he wasn't certain if they'd been rowing and steering for minutes or hours, lashed by rain, his body pounded by wind, when he caught sight of a familiar silhouette in the distance. A rocky ledge, barely visible through the swirls of water. It was the place he was looking for. And it meant they were within reach of the bay where they could anchor.

He shouted words of encouragement, telling the crew he'd sighted the cliffs of the Axen.

The rock shelf appeared ahead of them. Bringing the boat into shallower waters along its edge would enable the crew to see out the storm in relative safety with its ring-stone anchor dropped. Tell's eyes measured the distance, factoring in the wind and the boat's momentum. His navigation needed to be as precise as possible given the conditions so that they rounded the tip of the craggy outcrop safely and then followed its line to the shallows.

But that was not all Tell had in mind.

'Now! Hard to port' he roared, and the crew threw themselves into a frenzy of motion, oars slicing through the churning waters as the boat pulled toward the side of the rocky shelf. One of the crew cried out that this was madness, that the boat would be hurled against the jagged undersides of the outcrop but Tell knew it was a chance they had to take. The crew's only chance of salvation. And Tell's only chance at something else entirely.

The cliff face rushed past, close enough to reach out and touch. Tell worked the steering oar to direct the boat away from the outcrop and toward the less choppy waters of the bay.

He had just seconds to act.

He spied his crossbow and quiver against the bulwark.

The boat, dangerously close to the rock's edge one moment, veering away the next.

One prayer to God, one deep breath.

Tell's muscles coiled like a tightly wound spring, then released as he freed his grip from the oar, reached out, grabbed his bow and quiver, rose from the bench, and then launched himself from the boat's deck. All in one fluid motion. Taking just seconds.

For a breathless moment he was airborne, suspended between the boat and the rock shelf, the wind and the waves a dull roar in his ears. And then he landed on the flat, narrow top of the shelf, shuffling to find balance on the slick stone.

Behind him, chaos erupted on the boat. 'Stop him!' Gessler shrieked. But no one would have the courage to try the same feat. Even if they wanted to attempt it, the boat was careening away from the outcrop toward the bay's calmer waters. The gap too wide. The moment gone.

Tell didn't hesitate. Slinging his bow and quiver over his shoulders, he scrambled up the rocks, propelling himself with every crevice and ledge that his fingers found. Rain lashed his face, vicious gusts of wind threatening to tear him from the cliff. He hugged the rock face, climbing higher, fuelled by sheer adrenaline.

As he neared the summit, lightning split the sky, and he caught sight of the churning lake below, the boat now a mere speck tossed about by the waves.

Finally, after what seemed an eternity, his hand grasped the top of the cliff. With a final surge of strength, Tell pulled himself over the edge and onto solid ground, casting his bow aside and rolling onto his back as he caught his breath. The rain pelted his face, but he welcomed it, feeling more alive than he had in days.

After a moment, he rose to his feet, surveying the wilderness before him. Dense forest stretched as far as he could see, offering both shelter and possibility and he felt a strange calm settle over him.

There was a fisherman's cottage not far from here and if he could find the trail and reach the cottage, he would be able to dry his clothes and take shelter until the storm was gone.

After that, he needed to return to his home, but only briefly, to ensure Hedy and his sons were not at risk from the governor's retribution.

Tell was an outlaw now, and he knew he couldn't simply return to the simple life of a hunter and family man. The time had been thrust upon him to become an active part of the planned rebellion. Any other option had been ripped away.

There could be no doubt now that the tyranny of men like Gessler had to be confronted. Otherwise, no Swiss man, woman, or child was safe.

He thought of Ruodi, of Baumgarten, of Melchthal's father.

The image of his son's trusting face flashed before him, followed by Hedy's worried eyes. His heart ached, but he knew what he had to do.

Chapter Fifteen

Shadows crept across the stone walls of Attinghausen Castle's bedchamber. Baron von Attinghausen lay still beneath warm furs, his silver hair spread across the pillow like a crown.

Daniel Furst perched on a carved wooden chair beside the bed, his hands clasped tight. Werner Stauffacher stood at the window, his broad shoulders tense beneath his cloak. Melchthal paced the flagstones, each footfall muffled by rush matting.

'It was dangerous for you to come here,' Stauffacher said to Melchthal.

'I'll be here only briefly,' Melchthal said. 'But I had to pay my last respects to a man who's been a champion of the people.'

The baron's chest rose and fell in shallow movements. His skin had taken on the pallor of old parchment, stretched thin across noble features that had commanded respect throughout Uri for decades.

'He's gone.' Furst's voice cracked, barely above a whisper.

Stauffacher turned from the window, crossing to the bedside in two long strides. He bent close, eyes fixed on the baron's face. A white feather lay across Attinghausen's lips, stirring with the faintest breath.

'No.' Stauffacher straightened, relief softening the lines around his eyes. 'Look there.'

Furst leaned forward, squinting in the dim light. The feather trembled again, a gossamer dance that spoke of life's tenuous hold.

In the company of Stauffacher, Furst had been returning Walter home to his mother, when they'd received word that the Baron was on his deathbed. They'd diverted to the castle, and Furst had sent a messenger to his daughter so that she would know her son was with him.

The boy was crouched quietly beside the bed of the old man, still distraught over the arrest of his father.

Melchthal ceased his pacing, his expression tipping between hope and resignation. The three men exchanged glances, each knowing that while death had not claimed the baron yet, it was close.

Outside, a raven's harsh call split the evening air. A strong wind gusted, rattling the shutters.

The door opened. Hedy Tell stumbled into the chamber, her cloak askew, hair wild from her desperate ride through the gathering dusk.

'Walter!' Her eyes darted across Furst's and Stauffacher's faces until they found her son. She crossed the room in three strides and swept him into her arms, pressing his face against her shoulder. Her fingers trembled as they smoothed his hair.

'Mother, I'm fine.' Walter's voice came muffled against her cloak.

Hedy held him at arm's length, scanning his face. The colour drained from her cheeks as her relief gave way to fury. 'How could he? My own husband – to shoot at our son's head! Has he gone mad?' Her voice rose. 'I heard what happened in the square. An apple! As if our child were nothing more than a target for sport!'

'Daughter.' Furst rose from his chair, joints creaking. He laid a steadying hand on her shoulder. 'William had no choice. Gessler's men surrounded them both. The tyrant gave him two options – shoot the apple in an attempt to save his son's life or they would both be executed.'

'But to risk—' Hedy's voice broke.

'Father's the best marksman in all the cantons,' Walter pulled back from her embrace, chin lifted with pride. 'I knew he wouldn't miss.'

'William chose the only path that he could,' Furst said. 'Had he refused, both he and Walter would face the gallows. At least this way, he gave them a chance.'

Hedy's fingers hooked into Walter's tunic. Fresh tears spilled down her cheeks as the horror of what might have been crashed over her.

'But Walter would have been held in a cell until he was much older, so there would have at least been hope!' Her voice echoed off the chamber walls. 'What father places his child before a crossbow? The same weapon he's used to fell countless beasts?' Her fingers dug into Walter's shoulders, pulling him closer. 'He should have refused. The people could have begged for William to be spared rather than risk—' She choked on the words.

And then she reared on the others. 'And where were you all?' Her gaze swept across the room, settling on each man in turn. 'You stood in the square and watched this madness unfold. Watched as my husband was arrested and carted off. After everything William has done...' Her eyes bore into Stauffacher's. 'When Baumgarten was desperate for help, pursued by Gessler's wolves, my husband didn't hesitate. He rowed out into that storm without a thought for his own safety.'

Stauffacher's shoulders slumped. 'The square was ringed with soldiers. Any move would have meant—'

'Meant what? Death? Better that than to watch a father forced to shoot at his own child's head!'

Her knees gave way. She sank onto the chair her father had vacated, drawing Walter against her side. 'They've taken him to the dungeon at Küssnacht. You know what that place is like – stone walls pressing in, darkness thick as tar.' Her voice dropped to a whisper. 'William needs the mountains. Needs clean air and open sky. He'll wither and die in there.'

Tears tracked down her cheeks. 'He's not made for chains and iron bars. Every breath in that cell will be torture for him. And for what? Because he didn't bow to Gessler's hat? Because he is revered by the people for his archery?'

The baron's eyelids fluttered. His papery hand lifted from beneath the furs, reaching toward some unseen presence, diverting everyone's attention.

'Ulrich.' The name escaped his lips in a rasp. 'Where is my nephew?'

Stauffacher stepped closer to the bed. 'He's not here, my lord. He rides with Gessler's entourage to the court.'

'Gessler's court.' Bitterness tinged the baron's voice. 'While his homeland stands on the brink.' His fingers curled into the blanket. 'Tell me of Rütli. What news from the meadow?'

The men exchanged glances. The Baron had been informed of the meeting's outcome weeks before, but he was clearly not of right mind. Melchthal moved to the bedside, dropping to one knee. 'Representatives from Uri, Schwyz, and Unterwalden met in the middle of the night. Thirty-three men swore oaths beneath the stars.'

Colour bloomed in the baron's wan cheeks. His eyes, which had been clouded with pain, sparked with renewed life. 'Without nobles to lead them?'

'The people and some of the young nobles stood together to choose their own path,' Stauffacher said. 'They've found their strength.'

'The beginnings of a confederacy.' A smile transformed the baron's face. He pushed himself up against the pillows, struggling with the effort. 'Then the Swiss need not rely solely on us nobles. Look here.' He pointed toward Walter, who stood pressed against his mother's side. 'Your grandson, Furst, represents the future.'

His voice grew stronger. 'The peasants have discovered their own worth, their own power.' He sank back, chest heaving. 'This is what I've prayed to see – the common folk and the imperial class rising together, claiming their birthright against the Austrians as free men.'

'The league stands ready,' Melchthal said.

The baron nodded, satisfaction settling over his features. 'Then our future is secure.' He pushed himself higher against the pillows. His voice seemed to gain strength with each word, his gaze fixing on each person in turn. 'Austria's princes think themselves mighty, yet they build their power on shifting sand. They cannot crush what grows wild and free in these mountains.'

He gripped the blankets with surprising strength. 'The Swiss spirit runs deeper than noble blood. It flows through every peasant's veins, every shepherd's heart.' He was rambling now and yet, Furst thought, he was making perfect sense. 'Let the Habsburg princes send their armies. They'll find our people as unmovable as the Alps.'

116

The baron reached out, catching Furst's hand in his right and Stauffacher's palm in his left. His grip was iron-strong, belying his frail appearance.

'Stand together,' he said, pulling them closer. 'Unity is your shield, your sword, your salvation.' His fingers tightened around theirs. 'Promise me. Promise you'll hold fast to each other, no matter what comes. The people need leaders who remember their roots.'

'You have our promise,' Furst said.

The Baron's eyes clouded over, his breath fading, and then he glanced with a sudden start at a fixed point beyond his bed, as though the past, present, and future were laid out before him in his final moments. 'The territories will join as one and have the name that's been spoken of by the cantons' leaders, inspired by our founding fathers in Schwyz. Switzerland, a land united.'

There were no more words. The Baron's eyes stared straight ahead, no longer seeing. His body without breath.

'Dear Lord,' said Furst, as he and Stauffacher, recoiling in shock, and then, composing themselves, extricated their fingers from those of the baron.

The baron's seneschal, who had been observing from just inside the door, crossed himself and, with a silent prayer, left to inform the staff of their master's passing.

And then the chamber door burst open once more. Ulrich von Rudenz stumbled across the threshold, his court attire splattered with mud from his desperate ride. His eyes locked onto the still form beneath the furs, and the colour drained from his face.

'Uncle?' His voice cracked. He crossed the room in three strides, dropping to his knees beside the bed. 'No, please – I came as fast as I could, as soon as I was given word.'

The baron lay motionless, his features peaceful in death.

Ulrich's shoulders shook as he gripped his uncle's lifeless hand. 'Forgive me. I was blind, chasing empty glory at Gessler's court while you...' He pressed the cold fingers to his forehead. 'You were right about everything.'

He straightened, turning to face the gathered witnesses. Tears rolled down his cheeks. 'After witnessing the actions in the square today, after hearing what the heiress von Bruneck has had to say, I renounce my allegiance to Austria. My sword belongs to the Swiss – to the people and their freedom.'

Rising to his feet, his hand fell to his sword hilt. 'I'll tear down Gessler's castles stone by stone if I must.'

'Stay calm,' Furst said. 'We honour the baron best by ensuring that the plans for rebellion are followed to the letter.'

Tears ran from Hedy's and Walter's eyes, mother and son holding each other tightly.

The toll of the castle bell shattered the night's silence, announcing the baron's passing to the valley below, and its mournful note echoed off the chamber walls.

Chapter Sixteen

Tell pressed his back against the cold granite. The Austrian soldiers' shouts bounced off the valley walls, their accents ringing out in the pristine mountain air.

'There are tracks here!' A voice called from below. 'He's heading towards the ridge.'

They'd worked out his path faster than Tell had hoped. His thoughts drifted to the fisherman's family who'd sheltered him – the father's tense face, the children's wide eyes as he'd slipped away before dawn. He'd been careful, swept away his footprints, scattered pine needles across the yard to cover his tracks.

The fisherman had been amazed by his story the afternoon before and only too pleased to help. Night fell, and Tell slept, secure that no one was coming for him in the dark while the storm raged.

But he could only assume now that when he'd left the hut early that morning, the storm having passed during the night, Gessler had set sail at the same time, reaching Brunnen shortly after and ordering the troops stationed there to hunt down the escapee.

A rock clattered down the slope. Tell remained motionless, casting his eyes over the landscape. The afternoon sun cast shadows across the gorge, creating patches of darkness between the trees. To his right, a wall of granite rose towards the clouds, its surface scarred by winter storms and dotted with hardy mountain flowers. On his left, dense thickets of mountain pine offered cover, their branches low and tangled.

The sound of boots on loose scree grew closer. Tell's fingers brushed the familiar grip of his crossbow as he mapped his route. The main path curved around the mountain's shoulder, but he knew better. There was a shepherd's track, barely visible unless you knew where to look, that cut through a narrow ravine. It would take him higher, where the soldiers' armour would slow them down.

He traced the line with his eyes – past the lightning-struck pine, through the gap between two boulders, then up the natural stone steps hidden by years of fallen leaves. The route was treacherous. He remembered it from a hunting journey years before.

'Spread out!' The commander's voice echoed.

Tell's lips curved into a grim smile. These lowland soldiers didn't understand the mountains. They saw only obstacles where he saw passages, only danger where he saw sanctuary.

He heard them trudge through the undergrowth, and their commander's voice cracked like a whip across the gathering. 'Check every hollow, every crevice. Tell might be a huntsman who knows these mountains but he's also just a man who can be tracked and cornered like an animal. The Governor has assigned another thirty of his best men to join us from Kussnacht, an unprecedented number for a single outlaw.'

A breathless soldier's voice. 'Sir, we found fresh prints by the stream, heading higher in the direction of the ridge.'

'Finally.' The commander was quick to issue instructions. 'You three, follow the streambed. The rest of you, take up covered positions here, forming a perimeter, in case he doubles back. He's clever, but he's also tired. We'll flush him out.'

Tell imagined that Gessler had offered the commander a glorious future if he delivered the prisoner back.

His boots found purchase on the moss-covered rocks, each step calculated to avoid loose stones that might betray his position. Birdsong and rustling leaves provided cover for his movement through the undergrowth.

He pressed his back against a weathered pine trunk, its rough bark catching at his leather jerkin. The distant sound of metal on metal, sword scabbards striking against armour as the soldiers moved through the undergrowth, reached his ears. Tell held his breath, counting the seconds between each clank.

A flash of red and white through the trees – Austrian colours. Tell dropped to his haunches, sliding sideways behind a lichen-covered boulder. The sound of boots crunching on dried pine needles grew closer.

'There's fresh tracks here.' The soldier's voice carried clearly through the still air.

'Could be anyone's. These paths see hunters daily.'

Tell's fingers pressed into the damp earth as he made himself smaller behind the rock. The conversation above him continued.

'Wait.' Footsteps approached Tell's hiding spot. 'Something's not right here.'

Tell held his breath. A loose pebble rolled under the soldier's boot, tumbling down the slope mere inches from Tell's position. The guard's shadow fell across the ground beside him.

Silence stretched out, broken only by the distant cry of an eagle. Tell remained motionless, aware that the slightest movement might give him away.

'What is it?' The second soldier's impatience flared.

'Thought I saw... no matter. Must've been a deer. They're clever around here, always hiding behind rocks.'

The shadow withdrew. Tell listened as the footsteps receded, waiting until they faded completely before allowing himself to breathe normally again.

His thoughts drifted to Hedy's face, the way her eyes had crinkled with worry the last time he'd seen her. The memory of her fingers brushing against his sleeve, her whispered plea for caution, twisted like a knife in his chest. Their home in Bürglen felt a lifetime away now.

The Austrians might have already visited their cottage. His jaw set hard at the thought of soldiers bursting through their door, frightening Hedy, demanding to know if she'd seen him since his escape. They'd suspect her of lying when she told them he hadn't returned there. But Hedy was clever, she'd know what to say, how to protect herself and their sons. Her father, and Stauffacher, would be lending their support.

121

A branch cracked in the distance. Tell pushed away from his hiding spot, keeping low as he navigated between the trees. The terrain sloped downward, and the rushing sound of water grew louder with each step. He followed it, away from the steep path which had led the soldiers to higher ground.

The stream cut through the valley like a silver blade, its waters swollen from the storm. It was as wide and as deep as a river in that spot and rushing toward a cliff edge where it transformed into a spectacular waterfall. White foam crashed against dark rocks, creating a thunderous roar that would mask his crossing – if he survived it. The current looked strong enough to sweep a man off his feet.

Tell studied the water's path, searching for the safest route. A fallen tree stretched partway across the stream, its trunk worn smooth by the elements. Beyond it, a series of partially submerged rocks created a treacherous path to the far bank.

He pressed his palm against the log's surface, testing its stability. The bark was slick with moss, but the wood beneath felt solid. Tell eased himself onto it, moving with the grace of a mountain cat. The stream churned beneath him, sending up a fine mist that beaded on his clothing.

The log ended abruptly, leaving a gap between its tip and the first of the stepping stones. Tell gauged the distance, his muscles tensing for the leap. The soldiers' voices echoed from somewhere on the higher shelf, spurring him to action.

He looked at the ravine's jagged walls ahead of him, his experienced eyes measuring the width between them. Barely the span of his outstretched arms. The path twisted like a snake through the mountain's belly, disappearing around a bend. Water trickled down the moss-covered stone, making the footing treacherous.

He recognised this shortcut, he had used it once, years ago, whilst tracking a wounded stag. But that was when the ground was dry and sure. Now, with the storm-swollen water seeping through every crack, it was a different challenge entirely.

The sound of voices drifted down from above. Tell recognised one of the voices as that of old Franz from the valley, one of Gessler's conscripted guides. Tell pursed his lips. Of course, Gessler would force local hunters to aid in the search. The tyrant knew these mountains harboured too many secrets for his Austrian soldiers alone to uncover. It was an explanation of how the soldiers had advanced in his direction so quickly.

Tell slipped into the ravine's mouth, his shoulders brushing both walls. The air grew colder, damper. Each step required careful consideration – loose shale here, a deceptively sturdy-looking handhold there. The sides of his boots found grip on tiny ledges, some barely wider than his thumb.

He squeezed through a particularly tight section. The walls pressed in, scraping against his quiver. Above, a sliver of sky peeked through the ravine's lips. The voices grew closer, echoing off the stone walls.

'The ravine, check the ravine!' Franz's voice carried clearly down the channel.

Tell's heartbeat was rapid and he took long, slow, quiet breaths to calm it. The path ahead vanished into shadow. One wrong step in the darkness would mean a broken ankle, or worse. But turning back wasn't an option. Not with Gessler's men traversing every known mountain and valley trail to Bürglen.

Tell heard the soldiers' boots scraping against stone above. From the edge of the ridge up there, they would be able to look down on the slope and the hills beneath. The commander's voice dripped with barely contained frustration. 'Split up. Two men, go back and down the slope to that stream, check the crossing. The rest of you, spread out along these ridges. I want eyes on every possible escape route.'

Metal clinked against stone as the soldiers shifted position. Tell pressed deeper into the ravine's shadows, his back against the cold rock. Above, loose pebbles skittered down the cliff face as boots disturbed them.

The sound of scrambling boots and muttered acknowledgments followed. Tell counted at least eight distinct sets of footsteps moving away from the area above, their rhythm betraying their exhaustion. The commander resumed barking orders, his voice growing fainter as they moved further away.

Tell edged forward from the ravine's shelter, each movement calculated against the loose stones beneath his feet. The soldiers' voices had faded to almost nothing but distant echoes carried on the wind. He scanned the ridgeline. It was clear of movement.

The hidden cave lay just ahead, its entrance obscured by a curtain of moss and trailing vines. Tell slipped inside, the familiar musty scent of earth and stone welcoming him into its depths. He'd used this shelter before, on the hunting expedition. Several days in the wilderness with fellow hunter, Werni.

His chest heaved as he settled against the cool wall, legs aching from hours of moving stealthily through rough terrain. Water dripped somewhere in the darkness, marking time like the gears of a clock.

The scope of Gessler's search struck him then. The number of men being used, spoke of the governor's rage. More soldiers than Tell had ever seen committed to a single pursuit. Assisted by local guides, they could cover every path, every crossing between here and Bürglen.

Hedy's face flashed in his mind again. The thought of her waiting, watching from their home's windows for any sign of him, sent a fresh wave of anxiety through his tired body. But attempting to reach her now would only lead Gessler's men straight to their door.

He pressed his palms against his eyes. Gessler's resources weren't endless. Even the governor's influence had limits – he couldn't keep this many men away from their regular duties in the towns and villages forever. The search would have to be scaled back soon.

Until then, Tell would have to trust in Hedy's strength, in her ability to protect their home and family. He'd seen that strength before, countless times. She would understand his absence, know that staying away now meant keeping them all safer in the end.

Chapter Seventeen

Gessler paced his chamber, his fists clenching and then unclenching. The afternoon sun filtered through the small window. He wanted to smash his fist against the stone wall but he suppressed the urge.

The door creaked open. Rudolf De Harras entered, his armour still dusty from the search. He removed his helmet and stood rigid, waiting.

'Three days.' Gessler's voice cut through the air. 'Three days since that peasant made fools of my finest men and *me*.' He stopped at the window, staring out at the mountains that sheltered his prey. 'Do you know what I heard in the marketplace today? They whisper his name like a prayer. William Tell, the man who defied Gessler.'

'My lord—'

Gessler raised his palm to silence him. 'Every hour he remains free, my authority bleeds.' He turned, his face a mask of controlled rage. 'The common folk grow bolder. I see it in their eyes, that spark of defiance. Tell me how a single bowman avoids a troop of Austria's best.'

'He knows these mountains better than any man alive, my lord. It's been reported to me our men tracked him to the eastern ravines, but—'

'Excuses.' Gessler's hand slashed through the air. 'I don't want excuses. I want Tell's head on a pike outside these walls. Let his precious Swiss compatriots see what becomes of rebellion.'

'We've doubled the patrols around Bürglen. His family—'

'His family?' A cold smile spread across Gessler's face. 'Yes, his wife. His boy. The same child who stood so bravely while his father shot the apple.' He stopped before De Harras, close enough that the captain could smell the wine on his breath. 'Perhaps it's time we reminded Tell of what he has to lose.'

De Harras had brought a worn map with him and he spread it across the table, his finger pointing out the ridges and valleys. 'The locals speak of hidden paths through these peaks. Ancient routes known only to shepherds and hunters. Tell's used them all his life. Every cave, every stream, every cliff face.'

Gessler's fingers drummed against the oak surface of the table. The map before him blurred into meaningless lines and shadows.

'Even our guides stumble in these passes. Tell moves like a ghost through the rocks. Three hunting parties lost his trail near the western ridge. But he must be tiring while I've ensured our men are rested and replenished each day.'

'William Tell.' Gessler spat the name like poison. 'Such an English name for a Swiss peasant who thinks himself above the law. Did his mother fancy herself some noble lady, giving him such pretensions?'

De Harras straightened. 'I'm told his grandfather crossed from England two generations past. Settled in Uri, married local. Tell's parents christened him Wilhelm but Tell's mother often referred to him as William, in memory of her father, and it's the name he became known by at archery contests.'

'William.' Gessler rolled the word on his tongue, his lip curling. 'The common folk love that, don't they? Their hero with the fancy name.'

Gessler's hand slammed against the map. 'His name matters nothing. What matters is that he bleeds like any other man and bleed he will.' His rings scraped against the oak as he dragged his fingers across the surface. 'I want every cave searched, every shepherd questioned. Break their bones if you must but find him.'

De Harras bowed his head. 'Yes, my lord.'

'And there's something else.' Gessler's voice dropped as he moved closer to De Harras. 'That foolish girl, Bertha. I've seen how she watches the peasants in the square. Such... sympathy in those pretty eyes.' He exhaled a breath of frustration. 'And young Ulrich, following her like a lost pup, and becoming brazen enough to question me at the town square. The two of them whisper together in corners, thinking no one notices.'

De Harras stiffened. 'You suspect—'

'I suspect everyone,' Gessler said. 'Watch them both. Every conversation, every glance, every step they take outside these walls. If they breathe a word to Tell's sympathizers...' He left the threat unspoken.

'They are nobles, my lord. To spy on them—'

'Noble blood means nothing if it's tainted with treachery.' Gessler picked up his goblet, his knuckles whitening around it. 'Bertha especially. Such a delicate flower, yet I see steel beneath those silk skirts. Report everything to me. Everything.'

***

De Harras pressed against the cold stone wall, his breath a whisper in the night air. The torches along the castle corridors had burned low as midnight approached, casting elongated shadows that danced across the weathered stones. He gazed at Bertha von Bruneck's window above. It glowed with candlelight.

After leaving Gessler that afternoon, De Harras had arranged for his men to keep watch on both the heiress and the Swiss noble Ulrich von Rudenz, whom he'd never liked. Rudenz was an upstart in the Austrian court. As for Bertha, De Harras himself took the first shift, with another man arranged to relieve him as the clock struck twelve but before that man arrived, a shadow crossed the light. De Harras sank deeper into the alcove as a figure appeared in the window. Bertha's slender form emerged onto the balcony. She paused, scanning the courtyard below.

The hem of her dark cloak brushed against the stone as she withdrew back into her chamber. Moments later, the door to her quarters opened with the faintest creak of iron hinges. She stepped into the corridor, hood drawn low over her fair hair.

De Harras counted her footsteps as she passed his hiding place. Her boots made little sound on the worn flagstones – she was treading as softly as possible, he realized. This wasn't her first midnight excursion.

He gave her a dozen paces before following. The castle's shadows became his allies as he tracked her progress through the winding passages. Each time she paused to check her surroundings, he melted into doorways or behind pillars, his own dark clothing rendering him nearly invisible.

Bertha navigated the castle's maze, avoiding the regular patrol routes. She chose paths De Harras hadn't expected – servant's corridors and forgotten passages that came from her knowledge of the castle's architecture.

De Harras matched her pace, maintaining enough distance to remain undetected while keeping her in sight. He made certain to tread lightly as well.

He watched as Bertha slipped through the castle gates, her dark cloak blending with the night. The moon hung low, lighting her way. She wove through alleyways, past shuttered shops and silent homes.

A cat darted across her path. She froze, pressing against a weathered wall and then she continued on her way, the streets stretching empty before her.

Each turn she made was calculated. Past the baker's shop, through a gap between buildings barely wide enough for passage.

The route led to the old tannery district. Workshops that had fallen into disrepair due to Austrian taxes that had driven the craftsmen away. Bertha ducked into a low doorway, vanishing into the darkness of a derelict building.

De Harras crept closer. Through a crack in the wall, lamplight flickered. Voices murmured, too low to distinguish words. He moved around, finding a better vantage point behind a stack of rotting barrels.

'The Swiss cannot endure much longer under Gessler's boot,' a man's voice emerged clearer now. De Harras thought he recognised the voice but couldn't immediately place it.

'My position in the castle gives me access to his plans,' Bertha's voice, edged with determination, carried across the space. 'He means to break the people's spirit through force. New troops arrive within the week.'

'We must warn the valley settlements,' another voice said, 'they're most vulnerable.'

'I'll arrange for supplies to reach Tell's family,' Bertha said. 'The area is being patrolled too frequently for Hedwig Tell or her boys to travel far but I can ensure food reaches them.'

De Harras pressed closer, memorizing each voice.

He had heard enough. He couldn't confront this group alone, so he'd return to the castle, and organise soldiers to go to the workhouse, though he feared the rebels would have dispersed before his men got there.

He scurried back through the night, relishing the favour he'd gain with Gessler once he'd reported his discovery.

***

The moon had slipped behind clouds by the time Bertha retraced her steps through the castle gates. Her cloak trailed against stone as she walked the familiar corridors, mind still echoing with the resistance meeting's plans.

A torch guttered in its bracket, casting wild shadows across the walls. The usual night sounds of the castle – creaking timber, distant guard calls, the flutter of roosting birds – had fallen silent.

Bertha's steps faltered. The air felt thick, charged with an unseen presence.

I'm imagining things.

But as she rounded the corner to her chamber, dark figures peeled away from alcoves and doorways. Steel rasped against leather as swords cleared sheaths.

'Lady von Bruneck.' De Harras stepped into the torchlight. 'You're charged with conspiracy against the crown.'

The blood drained from Bertha's face as De Harras pushed back the hood from her head, but her chin lifted. 'What conspiracy? I merely took a walk to clear my head.'

'Through the tannery district?' De Harras's lips curved. 'Meeting with rebels?'

Two soldiers seized her arms. Bertha didn't struggle as they bound her wrists with rope, though her eyes blazed with fury. 'You overstep, De Harras. I answer to the emperor, not Gessler's lackeys.'

'You'll answer to Governor Gessler himself.' De Harras gestured to his men. 'Take her to the prison wing.'

The soldiers marched her forward. Bertha held her head high, her steps dignified despite her bonds.

Her blonde hair caught the flickering torchlight as she walked. Though her wrists burned from the coarse rope, she refused to give De Harras and his men the satisfaction of seeing her discomfort. She kept her gaze fixed straight ahead, her delicate features composed into a mask of aristocratic disdain, but it only masked the shock of discovery. Her heart raced and the fear rose within her.

The castle's prison wing consisted of three cells, for the temporary detaining of prisoners before they were transported to one of the canton's jails. Bertha was pushed into the cell at the end of a short corridor, and her breath caught in her throat as the key turned in the door's lock and the bolt slid home with a final, echoing clang.

There was no window, and the cell was a compact square, with no light. Bertha stared into the darkness that surrounded her, and although she knew the area was small, it seemed to her that the darkness was an abyss that went on forever.

What have I done?

***

De Harras strode into Gessler's chamber, where the governor stood at the window overlooking the courtyard, which was bathed in morning light.

'My lord, Lady von Bruneck is secured in the prison wing.'

Gessler turned. He'd been incensed ever since hearing the news earlier. 'Give me the full details.'

'She met with unknown rebels in the tannery district. They spoke of supply routes, safe houses. Unfortunately, those men had dispersed by the time guards could get there.' De Harras stepped closer. 'When confronted on her return to the castle, the lady maintained the pretence of an evening walk.'

'Of course she did.' Gessler's laugh held no warmth. 'Our noble lady, slumming with peasant rabble.' He crossed to his desk. 'The new cells at Altdorf are ready for their first occupants. They should provide adequate accommodation for one of her... standing.'

'The guards report she hasn't spoken a word since her confinement last night.'

'She'll speak.' Gessler's rings glinted as he poured wine into a goblet. 'They all do, eventually.'

Chapter Eighteen

Tell adjusted the rough woollen hooded cloak around his shoulders, matching his pace to that of the shepherd family. He carried a crude staff, a poor substitute for his crossbow, but necessary for the disguise.

A cart rattled past, the driver paying them no mind. Tell kept his head bowed, noting how the youngest shepherd child skipped alongside her mother, lending authenticity to their group. He'd been fortunate to encounter them, kind folk who understood the value of silence and shared glances rather than words, and who would quietly lend their support to the rebellion being planned.

The slate-roofed manor of Werner Stauffacher rose before them, gleaming in the afternoon sun. The shepherd family paused at the fork in the road, the father giving a subtle nod before leading his flock toward the market square.

Tell's boots crunched on the gravel path leading to Stauffacher's door. He scanned the tree line and the road, searching for any sign of Austrian colours. Nothing stirred but the leaves.

His knuckles rapped against the oak door. The sound echoed his heartbeat, too loud, too conspicuous. But before he could retreat into the shadows, the door creaked open.

Stauffacher's eyes pierced through Tell's shepherd's garb, recognition flooding his weathered face. 'William?'

'Werner.' Tell's voice was barely above a whisper.

Stauffacher grabbed Tell's arm, pulling him inside with surprising strength. 'By all that's holy, man.' His embrace was fierce but brief.

'We'd heard of your escape, but...' He stepped back. 'You're taking a devil's risk coming here.'

Tell's eyes adjusted to the warm interior of Stauffacher's home. Tapestries adorned the stone walls, their rich colours defying the Austrian attempts to break Swiss spirits. Carved wooden beams stretched overhead.

'Gertrude's at market.' Stauffacher gestured toward a chair. 'Sit, William. You look half-dead on your feet.'

Tell sank into the offered seat, his muscles aching from days of evading pursuit. 'What news?'

'Baron Attinghausen...' Stauffacher's voice faltered. 'He passed four days ago. With his dying breath he spoke of our cantons united under one name. Switzerland.'

Tell had known the old baron was failing, but the loss still cut deep. 'A good man. One of the last true nobles.'

'There's more.' Stauffacher leaned forward. 'Ulrich von Rudenz was there at the end. He's renounced his Austrian allegiance, sworn himself to our cause.'

'Ulrich?' Tell straightened. 'That's unexpected.'

'As you know, he witnessed the events at the town square that day. That, and the baron's death, has changed something in him. He's already gathering support among the younger nobles while playing a double game, still pretending to be part of the Austrian court.'

'And my family?' The question burned in Tell's throat.

'Your house is watched. Hedy and the boys are safe, but there are Austrian eyes on every approach.' Stauffacher cleared his throat. 'They're counting on you trying to return home.'

Tell pressed his lips into a thin line. The thought of Hedy and their sons under watch made his blood boil, but he forced the anger down. Attinghausen's legacy, the people's unrest, Ulrich's conversion – the pieces were falling into place. Their resistance was growing stronger, even as the Austrians tightened their grip.

'There was a clash near Altdorf two days past.' Stauffacher poured dark wine into wooden cups. 'Austrian troops tried to confiscate grain from the miller's stores. The townspeople fought back.'

Tell's fingers closed around his cup. 'Casualties?'

'Three dead. One Austrian, two of ours.' Stauffacher's face hardened. 'But it sparked something. The next morning, a group of peasants refused to pay their taxes. In Schwyz, they're burning the Austrian tax records.'

'Gessler's response?'

'More troops in the villages. Doubled patrols on the roads.' Stauffacher leaned forward. 'But his men are spread thin. The mountain passes need guarding, the towns need watching, and he's got too many of his men searching for you.'

Tell absorbed this. 'The nobles?'

'Split. Some, like Ulrich, have thrown in with us. Others...' Stauffacher shrugged. 'They're waiting to see which way the wind blows.'

'We can't wait much longer.' Tell drank from the mug. 'Winter's coming. Once the passes freeze...'

'The Austrians will have any rebellion trapped.' Stauffacher nodded. 'But move too soon, without proper coordination—'

'And the rebellion will be crushed piecemeal.' Tell put his mug down. 'What about arms?'

'We've been stockpiling. Hunting bows, farming tools, old swords. The blacksmiths work through the night.' Stauffacher took a deep breath. 'But we need more time to distribute them, to train the men, as per the original plan agreed at the Rutli meadow, to infiltrate the castles at Christmas.'

'Time we no longer have.' Tell frowned. 'Each day Gessler's grip tightens.'

'Agreed.' Stauffacher spread his hands on the table. 'But one false move...'

Tell nodded.

Through Stauffacher's window, he caught glimpses of children playing on the road. Their laughter carried memories of Walter's voice, of Hedy's smile as she watched their son grow. The Austrian guards who watched their home would see those same scenes, those precious moments that should belong only to his family.

He flexed his fingers. Every instinct screamed at him to return home, to protect them directly. But that path led only to capture – or worse.

'The rebellion needs you, William,' Stauffacher's words echoed his thoughts. 'The people were inspired by your feat at the town square, they chant your name. But no one would fault you for —'

'I will fight for them, and for my family,' Tell cut him off, his voice low but firm. 'Every Austrian fortress we tear down, every tyrant we drive from our lands, it's all to give Walter and Tristan a future where they can walk free. Where Hedy needn't fear soldiers at her door.'

The truth of it settled in his bones. This wasn't a choice between family and cause. They were one and the same. His bow would serve both his country and his loved ones.

'I am with you,' Tell said, meeting Stauffacher's gaze. 'But first, I need to ensure Hedy, Walter, and Tristan's safety. They must be moved somewhere beyond Gessler's reach.'

Tell traced a route in his mind – the hidden paths between cottages, the shadowed alcoves where Austrian patrols wouldn't think to look. His fingers adjusted the shepherd's staff, testing its balance. Not his crossbow – that waited for him in a shed at the shepherd's home, Tell would retrieve it later – but the staff would serve well enough as a walking aid for the old man he'd pretend to be.

'The western approach.' Tell's voice was barely above a whisper. 'There's a gap in the tree line where the brook bends. The guards won't expect anyone to ford it there, not with the main bridge so close. A way to approach my house, and a way to lead Hedy and the boys into hiding.'

Stauffacher nodded, his face grave. 'Take care, William. These aren't common soldiers. Gessler's picked his best hunters for this task.'

'And they'll be looking for a hunter.' Tell's lips curved in a grim smile. 'Not a decrepit old shepherd with a limp.'

Through the window, he caught sight of a familiar figure on the road – Gertrude Stauffacher, her market basket balanced on her hip. Werner followed his gaze and his expression changed, concern pinching his features.

'Best you go now.' he clasped Tell's shoulder. 'Gertrude believes in the rebellion, but the less she knows at this point, the less she will worry. God speed, my friend.'

'Keep the fires burning, Werner. We'll need their light soon enough.' Tell slipped through the side passage, its walls still holding the day's warmth. The stones beneath his feet were worn smooth by generations of comings and goings. As he emerged into the gathering dusk, he pulled his cloak tighter, hunching his shoulders in the manner of age.

Behind him, he heard the main door open, Gertrude's voice carrying clearly: 'Werner? You'll never believe the price of wool in the market today...'

Tell melted into the shadows, leaving the warmth and safety of Stauffacher's home for the uncertainty of the encroaching night.

Chapter Nineteen

Ulrich pulled his cloak tighter as he slipped through the alleyways of Altdorf. The cobblestones gleamed with recent rain, reflecting the pale moonlight. His boots made soft splashing sounds despite his careful steps, each one reminding him of the gravity of his choice.

His uncle's final moments weighed heavily upon him. Baron Attinghausen's withered features, peaceful in death, had stirred something within Ulrich's soul. The family signet ring on his finger felt heavier with each passing hour.

The distant howl of a wolf echoed off the mountainside, causing him to pause beneath an overhanging roof. The sound carried with it memories of hunting trips with his uncle, lessons about leadership and duty that he'd been too proud to truly hear. Now those words rang clear as crystal in his mind.

A patrol of Habsburg soldiers marched past the end of the alley. Ulrich pressed himself against the wall, holding his breath until their torchlight faded into the darkness. The near encounter only strengthened his resolve.

Before long, he reached the old weaver's workshop. Its worn wooden door bore the secret mark – three vertical scratches that looked natural to any casual observer. Ulrich paused, his heart skipping a beat. The moon cast shadows from the surrounding buildings, creating strange patterns on the ground before him.

Taking a slow breath to steady his nerves, he pushed open the door. The hinges creaked softly as he stepped into the dim interior. Dozens of faces turned toward him, lit by lanterns. The assembled rebels watched him with a mixture of hope and wariness.

Jakob Muller emerged from the crowd, his lined face breaking into a warm smile. He clasped Ulrich's hand firmly.

'Welcome, Ulrich of Rudenz,' Muller said, the use of Ulrich's inherited title carrying both respect and expectation.

Muller spoke to the gathering, motioning to Ulrich as he did, telling the group that their visitor was here to address them.

Ulrich stepped forward, his shoulders squared beneath his cloak. 'My friends, tonight I stand before you not as a noble, but first and foremost as just another Swiss man. I see what we all see, that for too long have we watched Gessler's cruelty poison our lands. For too long we have bowed our heads whilst our brothers and sisters suffer beneath his boot. And it is the same with the other cantons and their Austrian governors.'

The assembled rebels' eyes fixed upon him. A few elder members crossed their arms, their faces showing doubt.

'I bring more than just words.' Ulrich gestured to a side wall where three young noblemen stood together. They'd arrived separately and earlier than Ulrich. 'These men have pledged their swords to our cause, and some of you here tonight will have already spoken with them. Heinrich von Halwil, whose family have hunted in the mountains for generations. Conrad von Meggen, whose estates produce many of the crops that feed us. And Friedrich von Sarnern, builder, whose cottages have sheltered our people for many years.'

Murmurs rippled through the crowd as the nobles stepped forward, each removing their signet rings and placing them upon the rough wooden table in a sign of solidarity.

'When the time comes, I suggest that we unite the various groups throughout the cantons by lighting signal fires. First from Mount Pilatus, then answering flames from the Rigi and Säntis. Every valley, every village will know when the hour has arrived.' Ulrich spread a crude map across the table, pointing to marked locations. 'Our forces must strike as one, or not at all.'

Muller nodded slowly, his initial scepticism melting into fierce determination. Others pressed forward, and they studied the map. Even the most hesitant among them straightened their backs, catching the fire in Ulrich's eyes.

'The nobles' support gives us access to weapons, horses, and men trained in warfare,' Ulrich said. 'But make no mistake, this fight belongs to every Swiss soul. From the highest peak to the lowest valley, we stand together or fall divided.'

The rebels gathered around the wooden table under flickering lantern light as Muller spread out detailed lists of available weapons and supplies.

'The blacksmiths in Schwyz have been stockpiling arrowheads for months,' he ran his finger along the parchment. 'We've hidden them beneath loads of farming tools.'

'And what of the crossbows?' A gruff voice said from the back.

'One hundred in Altdorf alone,' one of the nobles, Heinrich, replied. 'Another three hundred spread across the smaller villages, all to be added to the existing supply of regular bows.'

Ulrich nodded as each rebel leader reported their resources. The pieces were aligning – weapons cached in barns and cellars, horses ready in remote stables, messengers arranged to carry notes between the valleys.

'Each district needs a commander,' Muller pointed to various locations on the map. 'Someone who knows the terrain and the people.'

The discussion continued, roles assigned and plans refined, until a voice cut through the murmurs.

'Where's Lady Bertha? She usually attends these meetings with news from the castle.'

The question sent a ripple of unease through the gathering. Heads turned, searching the shadows as if expecting to find her hidden among them.

'Lady von Bruneck remains our steadfast ally,' Ulrich's voice carried across the room, steadier than he felt. 'Her absence tonight does not change that. Her position at the court is precarious, she must be careful. It's possible she did not feel she could sneak away on this occasion.'

But his words did little to quell his own rising concern. He knew that Bertha, since involving herself with this Altdorf chapter, had never missed a meeting without sending word. Her insights into Gessler's movements proved invaluable as the network of those planning the rebellion grew. As these confederates returned to developing those plans, Ulrich's thoughts drifted to his last conversation with Bertha – her determined expression as she'd promised to bring crucial information about the garrison's rotations.

He pushed down the knot of worry in his stomach. He'd been staying at the Attinghausen castle but on the morrow, he would seek her out. He had the uneasy sense that something wasn't right.

Muller suggested that leadership from Ulrich would be a further boon to the groups throughout Uri and the assembled men voiced their agreement. Old Hans, his beard streaked with grey, stepped forward and pressed a weathered hand to his chest. 'We stand with you, Ulrich Von Rudenz. Your uncle would be proud to see this day.'

Others joined in, pledging their support with quiet intensity. Muller clasped Ulrich's shoulder. 'You've given us hope, my lord, in the genuine support now of many from the noble class. Something uncertain for too long.'

Ulrich looked at their faces – farmers, craftsmen, merchants – all willing to risk everything for their homeland. The uneasy mantle of leadership pressed down on him.

As the rebels melted away into the shadows, departing in twos and threes to avoid detection, Ulrich remained in the workshop. His mind raced with all that needed to be done. The task before them still seemed, in moments of reflection like this, insurmountable.

***

The early morning found Ulrich approaching Altdorf castle, his formal attire ensuring no guards questioned his presence. He strode through the familiar stone corridors. Servants scurried past with downcast eyes as he made his way toward Bertha's quarters.

As he reached her chambers, he was stunned by the sight of a guardsman, standing with his pike in front of her door, blocking his path.

'The Lady von Bruneck is no longer receiving visitors.' The guard's words carried a note of finality.

'Why? What has happened?'

'By order of Governor Gessler, she's been arrested for treason and conspiracy against the crown. She's held in the castle's cells awaiting transport to the new prison.'

The words struck Ulrich like a mace to the chest. His vision blurred for a moment as the implications crashed over him. The corridor seemed to tilt beneath his feet.

'On what evidence?' His voice came out hoarse.

'That's not for us to say, my lord. Best you take it up with the governor himself.'

Blood pounded in Ulrich's ears as he turned away from the guards. His feet carried him mechanically down the winding stone stairs, past tapestries and suits of armour that had once seemed so impressive but now felt like hollow symbols of oppression.

Bertha. In the dungeons. The thought twisted in his gut like a knife. He'd seen those cells. Dark, damp holes carved into the bedrock beneath the castle. No place for anyone, least of all her.

His hands formed into fists as he strode through the castle's main hall. Servants scattered from his path, perhaps sensing the storm of emotions radiating from him. The morning sun struck his face as he emerged into the courtyard, but he felt only cold.

This changed everything. And nothing. The rebellion would proceed, but now it carried an even greater urgency for him. The woman he loved in chains. Every moment Bertha spent in those cells was a moment too long.

Ulrich descended the castle steps. The looming conflict with Gessler and the Habsburg oppressors had never felt more personal.

Chapter Twenty

Hedy's fingers curled into fists as Austrian boots trampled across her threshold, marking muddy prints on the wooden planks she'd scrubbed the previous afternoon. The soldiers' weapons clinked against their armour as they spread through the cottage, their presence poisoning the sanctuary of her home.

'Stand aside,' barked the lead soldier.

Hedy planted herself in front of Walter and Tristan, both boys pressing against her skirts. 'This is the third day in a row you've searched. You've found nothing before, and you'll find nothing now. And with two of your guards stationed permanently outside, they would know if my husband had snuck in here.'

'We're following orders.' The soldier's eyes scanned the room. 'No chances are being taken, especially now that conflict has escalated between the villagers and our troops. I will ask you again this morning, do you know where your husband has gone?'

'I have no idea what's happened to him.' Hedy lifted her chin and then, raising her voice, she said, 'My children cannot sleep for fear of these raids.'

The other soldier roughly searched through the kitchen for any signs Tell had eaten there, plates crashing to the floor, fragments of pottery scattering across the boards. Walter flinched at the sound and young Tristan trembled.

'The violence in the cantons grows worse by the day,' the leader said, stepping closer. 'As for your children's fears, tell us where your husband has gone and these searches end.'

'I know nothing of violence except what you bring into my home.' Hedy's voice cut through the air. 'You break our belongings, frighten my children, and dare to speak of trouble?'

The soldier's face reddened. 'As I said, we have our orders. The governor himself—'

'The governor can come himself if he wishes to terrorise women and children.' Hedy's heart thumped and her mouth was dry, but her voice remained defiant. 'Or perhaps he's too much of a coward for that?'

Her skin crawled as the soldier's fingers dug into her arm, yanking her forward. The stench of foul breath filled her nostrils as his face loomed closer. She twisted away, but his grip locked on, crushing her flesh against bone.

His mouth crashed against hers, rough and demanding. Bile rose in her throat. She wrenched her head back and spat in his face. The back of his hand caught her cheek, snapping her head sideways. The force sent her stumbling, knees striking the wooden floor.

'Mother!' Walter launched himself at the soldier, small fists hammering against leather and steel. His face contorted with rage as he struck again and again.

The soldier backhanded Walter, sending him sprawling across the floor. 'Insolent brat.'

Hedy's vision blurred, but she forced herself upright, touching her split lip. Blood stained her fingertips. In the corner, Tristan's shoulders shook with silent sobs, tears streaming down his face as he pressed himself against the wall.

'You're brave when facing children,' Hedy said, her voice raw but unwavering. She pushed herself to her knees, meeting the soldier's gaze with burning defiance.

Walter scrambled back to his feet, chest heaving. Though his cheek reddened where he'd been struck, his eyes blazed with the same fire as his father's. He positioned himself between Hedy and the soldier, small hands balled into fists.

143

Hedy's heart lurched as rough hands seized her arms, dragging her toward the basement door. The soldier's rancid breath was on her neck as he sneered.

'Time for some private entertainment.' His fingers dug into her flesh.

'Let her go.' The second soldier's voice cracked like a whip. 'There's no time for that. The governor wants Tell found. Now. We need to keep moving.'

Hedy's captor hesitated, his grip loosening. 'A few minutes won't—'

'Our orders are clear.' Steel rang in the second soldier's tone. 'Put them all in the basement, out of our way. We need to check the other rooms.'

The first soldier shoved Hedy toward the basement steps. Walter rushed to steady her before she stumbled, his small hand finding hers in the gloom. They descended into darkness, Tristan's footsteps pattering behind them.

The basement air, heavy with the scent of earth and stored vegetables, pressed against Hedy's skin. Light filtered weakly through the ground-level window and across the dirt floor. She guided the boys to a corner furthest from the steps, pulling them close as the door above slammed shut.

She listened as boots scraped across wooden planks overhead and strained to hear the muffled voices drifting through the window.

'...waste of time...'

'...governor wants daily searches...'

'...there have been a rash of false sightings of Tell...'

Hedy leaned closer to the window, desperate to catch more fragments of conversation of the two guards stationed at the front of the cottage.

She pressed her ear against the horn sheet that covered part of the window, heart quickening as the guards' voices drifted through.

'That mountain pass north of the old chapel will catch the mountain rebels unaware.' The first guard's voice carried clearly in the morning air. 'Captain says we'll have three hundred men through there in a few days.'

'Aye, the mountaineers won't expect us to know about that hidden route.' The second guard chuckled. 'The Swiss vermin think they're the only ones who know these alps.'

Hedy's breath caught. The chapel pass. She and William had spent countless summer days there in their youth, gathering berries and hunting for mushrooms. Few were aware of its precise location through the treacherous mountain terrain.

The guards went on with their conversation. 'The rebels won't stand a chance once our men come through behind them.'

Hedy's mind raced. The Swiss rebel forces would be massacred if caught between two Austrian armies. She had to warn them somehow. But with guards posted outside day and night...

Her gaze fell on Walter, huddled in the corner with his younger brother.

Boots thundered overhead as the search party descended the stairs. The basement door creaked open, flooding the space with harsh light.

'Nothing found,' the lead soldier growled. 'You can come out.'

Hedy shepherded her boys up the stairs, keeping her expression neutral despite her racing thoughts. She watched as the soldiers filed out, their armour clanking with each step.

The door slammed shut behind them, leaving only the two permanent guards posted outside. Hedy's fingers curled around the windowsill as she stared at the mountains looming in the distance. She knew what she had to do.

She led the boys quietly back down into the basement. She picked up Tell's hunting horn from a shelf, and then she gathered her sons close in the dim basement. Her lips brushed Walter's ear, voice barely a whisper. 'Remember how Father showed you how to slip through this window?'

Walter nodded, his eyes bright with understanding.

'Good lad. Now help your brother through first.' She calmed her breathing as she watched Walter guide Tristan to the narrow opening. The younger boy's shoulders caught for a moment before he wriggled through.

Hedy passed the horn through to Walter, and then she squeezed through the opening, sucking in her stomach so as not to get stuck.

Autumn leaves crunched beneath their feet as they crept along the house's foundation. Hedy pressed herself flat against the rough stone, peering around the corner. The guards stood rigid at their post, faces turned in the direction of the village square.

They darted between patches of shadow, Hedy's skirts gathered close to avoid rustling. The path to the Meier farm stretched before them, a gauntlet of open ground that set her nerves aflame.

At the edge of the tree line, Hedy pulled her sons close.

'You'll stay with the Meiers until I return.' Her voice cracked. 'Whatever you hear, whatever happens, stay hidden.'

Walter's fingers clamped around the horn. 'But Mother—'

'Promise me.' Hedy cupped his face in her hands. 'Your father and I need you and your brother safe.'

Tears spilled down Tristan's cheeks as he clung to her. Hedy gathered him close, pressing kisses to both their foreheads. Her chest ached as though her heart might shatter.

'Go now.' She gave them a gentle push toward the farm. 'Quick and quiet, like your papa taught you.' She knew the Meiers would understand when Walter explained the situation. She knew how fiercely they wanted to defy the Habsburg masters.

Hedy watched until her boys disappeared into the confines of the property. Only then did she allow herself a single, shuddering breath before turning in the opposite direction, toward one of her other neighbours.

Hedy crouched behind the woodpile at the edge of the Odermatt property, her fingers tracing the simple patterns carved into Tell's hunting horn. William had spent countless evenings working on those designs, each groove and swirl telling their story. The day they'd met in the mountain meadow. Their wedding feast. Walter's and Tristan's births. The horn carried their memories and their love.

She pulled her shawl tighter, the touch of the horn against her chest both familiar and strange. William had taught her its calls – three short blasts for danger, two long ones for safety, and another pattern of blasts that meant 'I love you. How often had those sounds echoed across the valleys, guiding him home?

146

The morning mist clung to the ground as Hedy slipped between the shadows of trees and outbuildings. Austrian patrols had grown more frequent as they combed through the village each day. But she knew every hidden corner, every secret route between the cottages. William wasn't the only one who'd learned to move unseen.

Iris Odermatt's cottage lay ahead, smoke curling from the chimney. It was a year now since Iris's husband died. The Austrian soldiers claimed he'd resisted arrest, but everyone knew better. These past few weeks, since Iris's resolve had hardened, and in memory of her husband, her home had become a quiet centre of resistance, passing messages between those who fought for freedom.

Hedy touched the horn once more, drawing strength from its presence. The knowledge she carried could save thousands of lives, but she feared it would be too difficult and take too long to get word to the right people. Her children were safe with the Meiers. Now she had to do her part.

She moved forward, keeping low, her steps silent on the dew-dampened grass. The shadows welcomed her, wrapped around her like old friends as she made her way to Iris's back door.

Chapter Twenty-One

Hedy burst through Iris's door, her chest heaving as she pressed it shut. The widow jumped from her chair by the hearth, dropping her mending.

'The Austrians.' Hedy gripped the back of a chair to steady herself. 'They're using the old mountain pass, the one that cuts through beneath the snow line. I overheard the soldiers talking.'

Iris's face paled. 'That pass would let them surround our people in the mountains.'

'Yes, but I know that ridge.' Hedy leaned forward, her voice raspy. 'William and I hiked there often before we married. The forest ends right where the snow begins. This time of year, the snowpack is building but can be unstable.'

Understanding dawned in Iris's eyes. 'You mean to trigger an avalanche?'

'Your husband's tools – the axes and flints. I need them.' Hedy's fingers dug into the worn wood of the chair. 'If I can start fires along the trees on the slope, the heat will melt the snow. The water will seep into the ground beneath.'

'Creating unstable soil conditions.' Iris pressed her hand to her mouth. 'But Hedy, the risk.'

'I know, but it's the only way,' Hedy said. 'Once enough water infiltrates the soil, the pressure builds. The ground loses its strength. One good shift and the whole slope will come down, blocking their passage completely.'

Iris crossed to the storage chest where her husband's tools lay. 'The forest fire itself could draw attention.'

'By then it won't matter. The avalanche will already be underway – or it won't.' Hedy watched as Iris lifted the lid. 'But if it does work, then the pass will be blocked.'

Hedy raked her fingers anxiously across her neck. 'The fires need to be small but numerous, spread across the lower tree line where it meets the snow. The heat has to be constant enough to melt through.'

'But how many fires?' Iris's brow furrowed. 'It sounds impossible.'

'Hundreds. Each one carefully placed to create the right conditions.'

Iris sank into her chair. 'Days of work, then? Just to set them?'

'At least. But what choice do I have? That pass will give the Austrians the advantage they need. I've walked those slopes with William. I've seen the scars where past avalanches tore through. The conditions are perfect. I just need to exploit them.'

'Perfect?' Iris shook her head. 'I'll go with you, I can't let you try this alone. But two women alone in those woods, trying to start hundreds of fires before the Austrians arrive? Hedy, surely that's madness.'

'Not alone.' Hedy straightened. 'Karl Leuzinger knows those woods better than anyone. He's cut timber there for twenty years.'

'The woodsman?' Iris said. 'Yes, and he'd know exactly where to place the fires for the greatest effect.'

'He is a good man, a friend of William's, and he hates the Austrians as much as we do.' Hedy pushed away from the chair. 'And he's your neighbour, on the north side. Will you help me convince him?'

Iris stood. 'Of course. His cabin's just past the mill. But he'll see the madness of this idea, Hedy, and maybe he'll convince you of its folly.'

***

Hedy and Iris crept across the meadow that separated Iris's home from Karl's cottage.

It emerged in the distance, smoke curling from the chimney, carrying the scent of pine. It meant that Karl was at home, as Hedy had hoped.

They reached the cottage and Hedy's knuckles rapped against the wooden door.

When the door creaked open, it revealed a face marked by years of exposure to the harsh Alpine elements. Karl Leuzinger's eyes widened at the sight of them, dark brows lifting beneath his greying hairline in recognition and surprise.

'Hedy Tell? Iris Odermatt? What brings you here this frosty morning?' He ushered them into the warmth of the cottage.

'The Austrians plan to use the old mountain pass,' Hedy said. 'The one below the snow line.'

Karl drew his brows together. 'That passage would give them the advantage.'

'Unless we cause an avalanche.' Hedy drew the path on an imaginary map in the air. 'Small fires along the tree line, where the forest meets the snow. Enough heat to weaken the ground beneath.'

Karl stroked his beard, eyes distant. 'I've not heard of anything like that ever being done.'

'But it could work, could it not?'

Karl nodded. 'Yes. It could work. The conditions are right, especially after the rash of storms this past month – wet snow, unstable soil.' He shook his head. 'But the timing and the placement would need to be perfect.'

'Will you help us?'

Karl thought for a moment longer and then nodded slowly. He crossed to his workshop corner. 'We'll need my longest ropes, shovels for digging fire pits.' He pulled out a rolled canvas. 'And my tent – we'll have to camp up there while we work.' He turned back to them, his face grave. 'I won't lie. This could easily fail. But by God, it's worth trying.'

***

Hedy's fingers worked methodically through Karl's old hunting pack, sorting essential supplies. The steel striker, wrapped in oiled cloth. Dried meat and hard cheese. Extra wool socks. Her movements slowed as she

150

touched the hunting horn at her belt, its presence a constant reminder of what was at stake.

Karl laid his climbing ropes in coils, checking each length for wear. He told Hedy they might not be needed but he intended to be prepared, and they could be used to pull logs and heavy branches from one spot to another. His experience showed in every decision he made. The tent canvas rustled as he folded it.

Iris divided dried herbs and bandages between the packs, her healer's instincts preparing for any possibility. Her quiet strength complemented Karl's knowledge and Hedy's determination. The three worked in comfortable silence, broken only by occasional suggestions or requests.

'We make a fine trio,' Karl said at one point, a mischievous grin stretching from ear to ear. 'A madman and two madwomen.'

Hedy smiled, allowing herself a moment of levity. 'Perhaps madness is the best defence we have.'

The climb began as afternoon shadows lengthened across the valley and later, they reached the slopes where early snow crunched beneath their boots. Hedy's breath frosted in front of her face as she followed Karl's lead through the treacherous terrain. Above them, jagged peaks pierced a steel-grey sky, their snow-covered flanks gleaming like polished armour.

Wind whipped around them, cutting through layers of wool and fur. Hedy pulled her scarf tighter, grateful for the warmth of exertion. Iris's cheeks had reddened from cold and effort, but her steps were steady. Karl hiked the slope with the sure-footed grace of one born to the mountains, finding paths with seemingly little effort.

At the level where the forest met the snowline, they unpacked their tools. Karl drove stakes into the frozen ground, securing guide ropes for the work ahead. Hedy positioned the kindling and larger pieces of wood. Iris arranged their supplies in groups, each pile representing a potential fire point along their planned route.

No words were needed as they worked.

As night fell, Hedy huddled near the small campfire, her mind drifting to Walter and Tristan. The Meier family would keep them safe, but her heart ached at the distance between them. Her gaze wandered to the hunting horn. The firelight caught the worn brass, reminding her of evenings spent watching William clean and polish it after his hunts.

Karl's snores rumbled from inside the tent. As the sun had gone down, he'd declared their setups were ready for them to begin the fires first thing in the morning. Iris sat at the tent's opening, looking up at the stars while Hedy pulled her cloak tighter against the biting wind. A wind like that on the morrow would help their cause. It was a mission that could change everything – or fail on a grand scale. Either way, there would be no second chance.

She slipped into the tent and slept and the next thing she knew dawn had broken crisp and clear across the mountaintop.

It wasn't long before the three of them were hard at work, Karl's axe biting into branches while Hedy and Iris gathered kindling. The first flames caught easily in the dry wood that they'd stored in the tent or under canvas sheets, and an hour later columns of smoke curled up through bare trees.

Hour after hour they moved along the tree line, setting fire after fire. Hedy's arms burned from the effort of chopping and carrying wood. The fires spread steadily, melting the snow in expanding circles.

By midday, a dozen fires dotted the slope. The heat had turned patches of snow to slush, water seeping into the soil beneath. Hedy paused to catch her breath, watching rivulets of snowmelt carve dark paths down the mountainside.

The first rumble came mid-afternoon as they lit the final fires for the day. A deep, resonant sound that Hedy felt in her bones. The ground trembled beneath her feet as the rumble grew into a thunderous roar. Snow began to slide, slowly at first, then faster, gathering speed and mass. She could hardly believe it. The first avalanche had begun, sooner than she could have hoped.

'Let's move to higher ground!' Karl's voice cut through the din. 'Quickly.' He waved frantically to them and Hedy and Iris sprinted for the shelter of the trees that weren't burning, higher up the slope. Hedy was stunned by how much faster, all of a sudden, the fires had taken hold and how much more unstable the ground was than any of them had anticipated.

Glancing over her shoulder as she ran, Hedy watched in awe as the initial avalanche thundered down the mountainside, a massive wall of white that devoured everything below, obliterating trees and rocks in its path with terrifying force. Hedy could feel the vibrations through her boots as the thunderous mass of snow and debris swept downward, consuming the burning forest like a demented beast. The roar was deafening, drowning out even the crackling of the flames. Each tremor sent jolts through her body.

Pride and relief flooded through her – they'd succeeded beyond her wildest hopes. The pass would be completely blocked, the Austrian forces thwarted. But her moment of triumph shattered as a loud crack split the air above them.

This past couple of hours the fires had burned hotter and spread faster than any of them could have hoped for. Hedy's eyes snapped upward to see the ridge above them shifting, impacted by the heat and vibrations. The snowpack groaned, a sound that made her blood run cold.

No.

'Run!' she screamed, but her voice was lost in the thunderous roar that followed. The world turned white as a second avalanche, this one above them, crashed down. Hedy stumbled backward, her boots slipping on the slope as her heart thumped louder than she could believe possible. The ground beneath her feet simply vanished, leaving her suspended in a terrifying moment of weightlessness before the inevitable fall. Snow enveloped her from all sides like a freezing shroud, crushing the air from her lungs with merciless force as she tumbled helplessly in its grip. The world became a dizzying blur of white and shadow, each slam driving what little breath remained from her body.

Through the chaos, she caught a glimpse of Iris and Karl being swept away, their bodies tossed like leaves in a storm, dark forms tumbling end over end against the stark white backdrop. She watched in horror as their flailing limbs disappeared, Karl's arm reaching out, grasping for something, anything, before vanishing. Iris's scream cut off abruptly as the snow swallowed her whole. The sight burned itself into Hedy's memory even as the avalanche carried her along, spinning her until she lost all sense of direction. Snow filled her mouth, her nose, pressing in from all sides. The world shrank to a suffocating whiteness as the slide dragged her into its abyss.

The avalanche's momentum slowed, its crushing grip loosening as Hedy felt herself being tossed one final time. The snow dumped her like discarded debris, her body rolling to a stop against something hard and unyielding. The sudden stillness felt wrong after the violent chaos.

She lay motionless, lungs burning as she tried to draw breath through the packed snow around her face. Her right arm was pinned awkwardly beneath her body, but her left hand found a pocket of air near her face. She clawed at the snow, desperate to create space to breathe.

The snow pressed in from all sides, a freezing coffin that threatened to become exactly that if she couldn't free herself. Her fingers scraped against ice crystals until they broke through to open air. Hedy gasped as fresh oxygen rushed into her starved lungs, the cold air painful but welcome.

Working her trapped arm free sent daggers of pain through her shoulder, but she forced herself to keep moving. The snow shifted around her as she wiggled upward, following the path her hand had carved. Her head broke the surface and she blinked against the harsh sunlight reflecting off the pristine white expanse.

The landscape before her was unrecognizable. Where there had been forest now lay a barren field of snow and broken trees. Massive chunks of ice and rock dotted the slope like scattered building blocks. The silence pressed against her ears, broken only by the occasional settling of snow and the distant crack of stressed timber.

She pushed herself to her knees, every muscle screaming in protest. Blood trickled down her face from a cut above her eye, staining the snow crimson. Tell's hunting horn still hung at her belt, somehow having survived the tumble.

'Iris!' Her voice sounded weak and foreign in the stillness. 'Karl!'

Only the wind answered.

A further low rumble echoed across the mountainside, and Hedy's blood turned to ice. Her gaze swept upward, tracking the sound to its source – another wave of snow breaking loose from the ridge above. A movement caught her eye – Karl's tent canvas, torn and fluttering from a broken tree branch protruding from the snow field.

Grief crashed over her. Karl and Iris, gone. Their bodies lost somewhere beneath the endless white. But survival instinct kicked in as the rumbling grew louder. She stumbled toward a cluster of massive boulders, dragging herself through the snow. Her fingers, numb with cold, clawed at the caught tent canvas until it came free.

The rock formation created a natural alcove, and in desperation Hedy scooped snow away from the base of the largest boulder. The skills William had taught her about winter survival surfaced through her panic – how to pack snow, where to position supports, how to maintain airflow.

She wedged the canvas across the opening between two rocks, creating a crude roof. More snow packed against the sides formed walls. The rumbling grew to a roar as Hedy squeezed into the cramped space, pulling the last section of canvas across the entrance.

The avalanche hit with the force of a battering ram. She curled into herself as her shelter shifted, snow and debris thundering overhead. The space tilted, sliding deeper into the mountain's grip. Soil and smatterings of rocks crashed against the canvas as the shelter wedged tighter into what felt like a small crevasse.

When the movement finally stopped, Hedy found herself trapped in complete darkness save for a slit between the boulders through which she could see the sky. The walls of her refuge had held, but they were now pressed so close she could barely move. She pushed against the canvas, but it wouldn't budge. The shelter was pinned tight by who knew how much snow and earth. She was alive but completely trapped.

Her fingers trembled as she grasped Tell's hunting horn. The cold had seeped into her bones, but she refused to let despair take hold. The space between the rocks felt like a tomb, yet she drew strength from memories of summer days spent practicing signals with William in these same mountains.

She pressed the horn to her lips and blew. The distinctive three-note pattern – short, long, short – echoed across the mountainside. Her heart soared at the sound, so familiar and full of hope. Again and again, she sent the call into the gathering dusk, pausing only to catch her breath.

The horn's brass grew slick with moisture from her breathing, but she maintained her grip. Each blast took more effort than the last as exhaustion crept through her body. Still, she persisted. William had to be out there somewhere in the mountains and the sound of the horn echoed across the mountain and the nearby valley. It wouldn't mean anything to anyone else but it would to William. She prayed he would hear the call.

Between calls, Karl and Iris flooded her mind. Karl's quiet confidence as he'd planned the fire positions. Iris's gentle strength as she prepared their supplies. They'd lost their lives and Hedy couldn't shake the dreadful feeling that she was responsible. This mad attempt to block the pass had been her idea.

Hours passed. Hedy's lips grew numb, her breaths coming in ragged gasps. Darkness crept through the small gap in the rocks, bringing with it a bone-deep cold that made her shiver uncontrollably. Still no answering call came.

Fear clawed at her chest as night settled over the mountain. What if William was too far away? What if no one could hear her desperate signals? The horn slipped from her fingers as tears froze on her cheeks. She was alone, trapped in this icy prison, with only the memory of her friends' courage to keep her spirit from breaking.

Chapter Twenty-Two

Tell crouched behind the trunks of ancient pines. The morning sun bathed his cottage, illuminating two Austrian guards who lounged near his front door. Their helmets gleamed as they passed a flask between them, their laughter carrying across the distance.

At quarter-hourly intervals one of the guards circled the perimeter. Tell watched the man pause near Hedy's herb garden, plucking a sprig of rosemary and crushing it between his fingers.

The familiar sight of his home stirred an ache in his chest. He focused on the worn path to the basement window, barely visible from his position. That small opening had saved him countless times when returning late from hunts, allowing him to slip inside without waking the household.

Tell studied the guards' positions, noting their casual demeanour. They seemed more interested in their flask than their duty.

Darkness would be his ally. The new moon would cloak his approach, and the basement window remained hidden from the guards' line of sight. Tell settled in for the wait as the sun crept toward the horizon. His fingers absently followed the grain of his bow, which he'd retrieved from the shepherd's hut the day before, as he counted the guard's rounds, memorizing the rhythm of their patrol.

The basement window would be tight – he'd need to remove his quiver to squeeze through. But he knew every creaky floorboard, every shadowed corner of his home. Once inside, he could move undetected.

He backed away from his vantage point, melting into the forest shadows. The Meier farmstead lay a quarter mile west through dense woodland, close enough to his home that Hedy would likely have sought help there if needed. While he waited for nightfall, Tell would see if they could confirm whether his family was safe, and seek out any other information on what had occurred since Tell had left Stauffacher's home in Steinem the day before.

Pine needles cushioned his footfalls as he wound between the massive trunks. A jay's mocking call made him freeze, pressing against a fallen log while scanning for movement. But only branches swayed in the chill breeze.

The familiar path felt different now, each rustle and snap of twigs setting his nerves on edge. He chose his route, avoiding the well-worn track that Austrian patrols would watch. Instead, he picked his way through a ravine choked with brambles, the thorns catching at his sleeves.

The stream crossing posed the greatest risk. Tell crouched in the undergrowth, watching and listening. The burble of water would mask approaching footsteps. After several long minutes of silence, he darted across the exposed rocks, staying low.

The Meier's barn came into view through the trees. Tell circled wide around the pasture, noting the cattle still grazing peacefully. No signs of soldiers or disturbance. Smoke rose steadily from the chimney – another good sign.

Rather than approach directly, Tell worked his way to the back of the property where thick hedgerows provided cover. Through gaps in the foliage, he could see Alban Meier splitting wood in the yard. The steady rhythm of the axe and Alban's relaxed posture suggested all was well.

Tell weighed his options. Alban was a trusted friend, but approaching openly carried risk, both for himself and the Meiers if soldiers were watching the farm. He would need to wait until Alban was inside, away from any prying eyes that might spot their meeting.

Tell slipped through the back door of the Meier farmhouse after he'd seen Alban go in for a break. Alban's wife Maria dropped her mixing bowl with a clatter, flour dusting the floor. Her hand flew to her mouth to stifle a cry of surprise.

'William! Thank the heavens.' She rushed to embrace him, flour-covered hands leaving white prints on his jerkin.

Alban burst through another doorway at the sound. His face broke into a broad smile. 'You old fox! We've been sick with worry.'

'Papa!'

Tell's heart leaped at Walter's voice. His son barrelled into him, small arms wrapping tight around his waist. Tell dropped to one knee, pulling Walter close, drinking in the familiar scent of his boy's hair. Tristan toddled over more slowly, thumb in mouth, but his eyes lit up as Tell gathered him in with his other arm.

'My boys.' Tell's voice was rough with emotion as he held them both. Walter's shoulders shook with silent sobs. Tell stroked his back, murmuring soft words of comfort.

'They arrived the morning before yesterday,' Maria explained quietly. 'Hedy brought them but didn't come in herself, we didn't see her...'

Tell's head snapped up at the mention of Hedy, but Maria's words were interrupted by approaching footsteps outside. Alban quickly ushered them away from the windows, into the back room where fresh hay had been laid out as beds for the boys.

'The patrols have passed once or twice a day for the past few days,' Alban said. 'But you'll be safe here for now.'

Tell nodded gratefully, still clutching his sons close. Walter's fingers were tangled in Tell's shirt as if afraid his father might disappear again. Tristan had already fallen asleep against his chest, tiny breaths warm against Tell's neck.

'The soldiers came again, Papa.' Walter's voice trembled as he pulled back from Tell's embrace. 'They struck Mother. One tried to take her to our basement...' He swallowed hard. 'But another soldier stopped him.'

Rage burned in Tell's chest. 'What happened then?'

'Mother overheard them talking about secret troops coming through the mountain pass. She sent us here with the Meiers, then left for the mountain.' Walter's eyes shone with fierce pride. 'She took your hunting horn and said she would stop the Austrians from using that pass.'

Tell's blood ran cold. He had seen the massive avalanche from miles away while travelling the back roads the day before – a wall of white thundering down the mountainside, the sound reaching him even at that distance. At the time, he'd also seen the columns of smoke, a forest fire that would have dislodged the unstable snow, and he'd wondered at its cause.

The guards he'd seen outside his cottage would have known by now that neither Hedy nor the boys were inside but were clearly remaining on guard in case of his return.

'Mother said she knew how to make the snow fall,' Walter said. 'That she remembered where you showed her the weak spots in the ridge.'

Tell's chest constricted. He knew the pass Walter spoke of, knew its dangers intimately. The thought of Hedy there, deliberately starting an avalanche of such magnitude...

'Mother is the bravest person I know,' Walter declared. 'Besides you, Papa.'

Tell managed a tight smile, though his heart raced. The avalanche he'd witnessed had been catastrophic, far larger than any natural slide he'd seen in recent times. That Hedy had achieved such a feat spoke to her determination and courage. But the risks... Dear God, the risks she'd taken.

'She hasn't snuck back here this morning?' Tell already knew the answer but asked it anyway.

Walter shook his head. 'No, Papa.'

Tell closed his eyes briefly, fighting to maintain his composure. Pride in Hedy's boldness collided with terror for her safety. She had acted to protect their people, just as he would have done. But the magnitude of that avalanche...

He paced the small back room, his mind spinning through the implications of Hedy's mission. His wife knew those slopes as well as he did, she'd hiked them countless times at his side. But causing an avalanche of that magnitude would have required her to be dangerously close to the unstable snowpack.

He knelt before his sons, placing a hand on each of their shoulders. 'I need to find your mother. You understand that, don't you?'

Walter's chin lifted, his eyes bright with unshed tears. 'Yes, Papa. We'll stay here and help the Meiers.'

'That's my boy.' Tell squeezed Walter's shoulder. 'You're the eldest. I'm counting on you to look after Tristan and help Maria with the chores.'

Tristan's lower lip trembled. 'But when will you come back?'

'As soon as I can, little one. The Meiers will keep you safe until then.' Tell pulled them both into a loving embrace. 'Your mother and I have taught you well. You know to stay hidden if soldiers come, and to help each other no matter what happens.'

Walter straightened, clearly taking the responsibility to heart. 'We won't let you down, Papa.'

Tell gathered his bow and quiver, checking his knife was secure at his belt. The mountain pass lay several hours' journey north. He would need to move fast to reach it before nightfall and he hoped to meet Hedy, safe and on her way back to the Meiers. The alternative, that Hedy might be trapped somewhere in that vast expanse of snow and rock made his chest tighten with dread.

He touched the hunting horn at his belt – its twin to the one she carried. Their signal had provided a form of communication over the years when he was the one out on the mountain. He said his goodbyes to Alban and Maria, who wished him Godspeed, and he headed off.

He would search every ridge and valley until he found his wife.

***

Tell moved through the forest. The familiar paths felt different now. Where he once tracked deer and chamois, he now searched for signs of Hedy. His keen hunter's eyes caught details others might miss; broken twigs, disturbed moss, any hint of recent passage.

The looming peaks grew larger with each mile, their snow-capped summits piercing grey clouds. He picked up his pace as he recognized landmarks from countless hunting trips – the lightning-split oak, the distinctive boulder shaped like a sleeping bear. These markers guided him toward the pass where Hedy would have attempted her desperate plan.

Evidence of the avalanche's devastation became clear as he ascended. Splintered trees lay scattered like broken matches. Massive snow drifts filled valleys that had been clear just days ago. The scale of destruction surpassed anything Tell had witnessed in his years in these mountains. The snowpack had been more unstable than Hedy would have anticipated, and the avalanche was likely to have occurred naturally within months, maybe weeks. Hedy's efforts had brought it about sooner.

He paused at a ridge overlooking the pass, studying the changed landscape. The main slide had carved a new path down the mountainside, leaving bare rock exposed where thick forest had stood. Debris and fallen trees created a maze of obstacles. Somewhere in this chaos, Hedy might be trapped or injured.

Tell spotted blackened areas where fires had burned. He had no doubt Hedy started the fires but to achieve what she had in such a tight window of time, she must have had help.

The wind carried the crisp scent of snow and wet earth, along with something else. Wood smoke. Tell froze, analysing the faint trace. Fresh campfire smoke. Someone else was up here. He would need to be alert for both signs of Hedy and any Austrian patrols that might be searching the area.

Tell's boots crunched through patches of snow as he picked his way around fallen trees. His father's voice echoed in his memory, teaching him to read the mountain's moods, to understand its rhythms, and respect its power. Those lessons, passed down through generations of Swiss mountain folk, had shaped him into the man he was. His mother had died while he was still young and his memories of her were like wisps in the wind. What he recalled most about her was the same kind and serene nature that he also found in Hedy. His fondest memories of his mother were the winter nights when he'd snuggled with her in bed and she'd sung him to sleep with an old Swiss folk song. *'Hear the herdsmen call from the valley below/Echoes of home where wild rivers flow/Safe in the arms of the night so sweet/Dream of the freedom beneath your feet.'*

162

'The mountain gives and takes as she pleases,' his father would say, 'but she always provides for those who know her ways.'

The fresh scent of woodsmoke made him pause behind a massive boulder. He reached for the horn at his belt but stopped himself. The smoke meant others nearby, likely Austrian soldiers searching the avalanche zone. Using the horn would only draw their attention.

His father's other lessons rang clear. Patience, caution, choosing the right moment to act. Tell had learned those skills tracking prey through these same forests. Now they might mean the difference between finding Hedy and being captured.

He traced the ridge line with his eyes, calculating routes that would keep him hidden while covering the most ground.

The feel of his bow across his back reminded Tell of another lesson, one he hoped he was instilling in his sons. True strength lay not in weapons or force, but in unwavering devotion to what was right. Hedy embodied that principle in her bold action to protect their people.

He moved forward as the dusk began to gather. The mountain's challenges – treacherous footing, bitter cold, the threat of discovery – seemed small compared to his burning love for Hedy and his need to find her.

Chapter Twenty-Three

The distant echo of a horn pierced the mountain air. Tell froze mid-step, his heart leaping in his chest. Three short blasts, two long. Hedy's distress signal. His legs nearly buckled with relief at this proof she was alive, even as dread knotted his stomach at what danger she faced.

He oriented himself toward the sound, calculating the horn's location based on how the mountains bounced the echo. The call came again, weaker this time, from high on the eastern slope where the avalanche had carved its path.

His muscles ached as he charged upward through the deep snow. Sweat dampened his skin despite the biting wind that whipped across the exposed ridge. Tell's breaths came in ragged gasps, the thin mountain air offering little sustenance, but he pressed on.

The horn sounded once more, barely noticeable now. He recognized the failing strength behind each blast. Hedy's energy was fading. He scrambled over fallen trees and around massive snow drifts, his hands bloody from gripping ice-crusted branches to steady himself on the slope.

Years of hunting these peaks had honed Tell's endurance, yet this desperate climb tested every limit. His thighs trembled with each step through ankle-deep snow. His lungs felt scraped raw by the frigid air. None of it mattered. Hedy needed him, and he would not fail her.

The horn fell silent. He pushed harder, fighting the mountain's resistance. Somewhere ahead, Hedy waited. He would find her. He had to find her.

The acrid scent of woodsmoke drifted across the slope. Tell's nostrils flared, the scent was stronger than it had been before. Were Austrian soldiers making camp nearby? What were they doing up here? He suspected they'd seen the fires earlier, and then the avalanche, and were checking the landscape for any signs that rebel groups had caused this, either intentionally or unintentionally. He dropped low, pressing against an outcrop as voices carried on the wind. The crunch of boots in snow echoed from somewhere below.

Another blast from Hedy's horn rang out, closer now. Tell edged forward, using the boulders and fallen trees for cover, taking care to avoid loosening rocks that might betray his position. Had the soldiers been drawn by the sound of the horn?

Tell crested a ridge and his breath caught. Twenty feet below, a mass of snow and debris created a natural bowl between massive boulders. At its centre, a narrow crevice descended into darkness. A flash of movement caught his eye – fingers gripping the edge of a torn canvas.

'Hedy?' he called.

'William!' Her voice was weak.

He trudged toward the crevasse.

'I'm trapped. Not enough space to climb out.'

He belly-crawled to the edge, peering down. Hedy was wedged in a tight space between the rocks, snow, and soil that were packed around her makeshift shelter. Only a small opening remained, barely wide enough for him to see her face in the shadows.

'I'll get you out.' He assessed the situation. The boulders were immovable, but the packed snow... 'Can you move at all?'

'Just my arms. Everything else is pinned.'

Tell nodded, already forming a plan. 'I saw a fallen pine back there. The branches will work as picks to break up this snow. Once it's loose enough, we can dig you free.'

He scrambled back through the snow, his heart pounding as he located the fallen pine. He snapped off the sturdiest branches, testing each one's strength against his palm. The sharpened ends would serve as crude ice picks, not ideal, but they would have to do.

Back at the crevice, Tell wedged the first branch into the packed snow above Hedy's shelter. He loosened small sections at a time to avoid starting another collapse.

'The snow's starting to give,' he called down, driving another branch into the compressed mass. 'Just hold on.'

Hedy's fingers appeared through the widening gap, brushing against his boot. He redoubled his efforts, methodically breaking apart the frozen barrier between them.

The opening gradually expanded as Tell cleared away chunks of snow and soil. Hedy's face came into fuller view, her eyes bright with relief. Tell reached down, gripping her outstretched hands.

'Ready?' he asked, bracing his legs against the boulder.

Hedy nodded. Tell pulled, feeling her body shift upward through the space. She gasped as she broke free, tumbling into his arms. Their lips met in a desperate kiss. Tell held her close, his fingers tangling in her hair.

'So cold in there last night I swear I thought I'd died.'

'I thought I'd lost you,' he said against her temple.

Hedy cupped his chin in her hands. 'Never.'

Tell helped her to her feet, supporting her as she found her balance on the unstable snow. His heart swelled with pride as he gazed at her face, marked with exhaustion but undefeated.

'The avalanche has completely blocked the pass. The Austrians can't bring their reinforcements through.' Tell brushed a strand of hair from her cheek. 'You've done what an army couldn't.'

Hedy leaned into his touch. 'There was no way to spread word throughout the cantons in so short a time, so I had to act. The rebel groups wouldn't have stood a chance against a surprise attack.'

'You've given us time to organize, to strengthen our defences.'

Hedy's expression crumpled, her fingers digging into Tell's arms. 'But Iris and Karl... they helped me set the fires. When the snow came down...' Her voice broke. 'They were swept away. I couldn't reach them, couldn't save them.'

Tell hugged her tight, feeling her shoulders shake with suppressed sobs as a flood of tears streamed down her cheeks. 'They chose to stand with you, knowing the risks,' he said. 'Their sacrifice protected countless lives. Their neighbours, their families, their homeland.'

'But their deaths are on my hands. If I hadn't asked for their help—'

'Then the Austrians would have crushed the rebellion before it began Their sacrifice hasn't been in vain.'

Tell tensed at the sound of boots crunching through snow. His hand found Hedy's, squeezing in warning as voices carried across the slope.

'There! By the rocks!' The harsh accent of an Austrian soldier shattered the silence.

Tell's muscles coiled, ready to move. He scanned their surroundings, marking the dense stand of pines thirty yards to their left. The trees would provide cover, but the open ground between offered no protection.

'Halt! In the name of Governor Gessler!'

Tell put his lips to Hedy's ear. 'When I say run, *move*. Don't look back.'

The first arrow whistled past his ear sooner than he expected. 'Run!'

They burst into motion, feet churning through the snow. Tell angled their path, using the uneven terrain to throw off the archers' aim. More arrows hissed through the air, thudding into the snow around them.

Hedy stumbled. Tell caught her arm, keeping her upright as they pushed forward. Blood stained her sleeve where an arrow had torn through the fabric. Her face was pale but determined as she matched his pace stride for stride.

'Almost there,' Tell shouted.

They reached the tree line as another volley of arrows split the air. Tell yanked Hedy behind a massive pine trunk, pressing her against the rough bark as arrows splintered into the wood. Her breath came in ragged gasps.

'Let me see your wound,' Tell said, gently pulling back the torn fabric. The arrow had carved a shallow groove across her bicep, but the bleeding was already slowing.

Tell drew his bow in one fluid motion, nocking an arrow as naturally as breathing. The familiar yew wood settled against his palm, an extension of his arm after decades of daily use. He guided Hedy deeper

167

into the pine grove, positioning her behind him as he sought the perfect vantage point.

Years of hunting had taught him to read terrain instantly. The slight rise to his left offered both cover and a clear line of sight. Tell moved like a shadow through the trees. The first soldier appeared at the edge of the clearing, crossbow raised.

Tell's mind cleared, his focus narrowing to the space between heartbeats. The same stillness that had steadied his hand when aiming at the apple atop Walter's head settled over him now. His breath slowed, muscles relaxing into the familiar draw.

The soldier's neck presented a clean target from the side angle. Tell released, the arrow in flight before the man could spot his position. The Austrian dropped without a sound, his weapon falling into the snow.

In one continuous motion, Tell shifted right, drawing another arrow. The second soldier charged forward, alerted by his companion's fall. Tell tracked the man's movement, compensating for the uneven ground and the soldier's speed. The distance was greater now - perhaps sixty yards but Tell had made harder shots while hunting chamois in these same mountains.

His arrow caught the soldier in the gap between chest plate and shoulder guard. The man stumbled, his sword arm dropping as he crashed face-first into the snow.

Tell scanned the darkening sky. The twilight was spreading. The soldiers' bodies would be discovered soon – their absence would alert others at their post.

'We have to go,' Tell said, touching Hedy's shoulder. 'More patrols will come searching before long.'

Hedy nodded, her face tight with pain. Tell led them down the slope, choosing a path that balanced speed with stealth. His boots found traction on hidden rocks beneath the snow, marking safe steps for Hedy to follow.

His muscles tensed at every snapping twig, every rustle of wind through the pines. He kept Hedy close, supporting her when the steep terrain threatened her balance.

The familiar shapes of the valley emerged as they descended – landmarks Tell had known since childhood. He guided them through a ravine, using the natural formation to mask their tracks. The wind picked up, erasing their footprints in fresh powders of snow and grass.

Light glowed from the Meier farmhouse windows as they approached through the twilight. Tell paused at the tree line, studying the surrounding area for signs of Austrian patrols. Satisfied they weren't being watched, he led Hedy across the open ground to the barn's side entrance.

Inside, warmth and the scent of hay enveloped them. Tell helped Hedy sink onto a wooden bench, exhaustion overcoming her. Their boys would be in the house, safe with the Meiers, but Tell knew he couldn't risk staying long. The Austrians would search every farm and homestead within miles once they discovered the dead soldiers.

Hedy and the boys could stay hidden in the basement area that Tell knew the Meiers had under their barn.

'Rest,' Tell said, crouching beside Hedy. 'I'll check on the boys, and let Alban and Maria know the situation. But I will need to move on.'

'William, you should hide here with us.'

'I can't hide, not with our whole country on the verge of an uprising unlike anything we've ever seen.'

'You're being hunted high and low,' Hedy said. 'What will you do?'

'I have to put an end to this madness.'

Chapter Twenty-Four

Bertha's wrists chafed against the rough rope as she sat on the cold stone floor of her cell. The iron-studded door creaked open, and two guards entered.

'Look at her now. Not so high and mighty without her silk dresses,' the taller guard sneered, his face twisted in a cruel smile.

The shorter one circled her like a vulture. 'Those delicate hands weren't made for prison rope, were they, my lady?' He yanked her bonds, making her wince.

Bertha met their mocking gazes with steel in her eyes. 'How brave you both are, tormenting a bound woman. Is this what passes for valour in Gessler's ranks?'

The taller guard's hand twitched toward his sword. 'Watch your tongue, traitor.'

'Speaking of watching, where is your master?' Bertha's voice cut through the musty air. 'Does Governor Gessler lack the courage to face me himself? Or does he prefer to hide behind his lackeys while they do his dirty work?'

The shorter guard grabbed her arm. 'The governor doesn't waste his time with—'

'With what? With those who dare speak truth to his tyranny. Tell him I await his presence. Unless, of course, he fears what a mere noblewoman might say to shake his carefully constructed facade of power.'

The taller guard's smirk widened as he leaned against the cell wall. 'The governor has special plans for you. A public spectacle to remind these peasants what happens to noble traitors.'

Bertha studied their faces, noting the uncertainty beneath their bravado. 'Like the spectacle with Wiliam Tell? We both know how well that worked out.' She shifted on the cold stones, her chains rattling. 'Each time Gessler tries to crush the people's spirit, he only fans the flames. The Swiss are showing they aren't cattle to be beaten into submission.'

'Silence!' The shorter guard's hand trembled as he yanked her to her feet.

'Your own fear betrays you,' Bertha said. 'You've seen it in the villages, haven't you? The way people gather in whispers, the defiance in their eyes. The outbreaks have already led to deaths on both sides. Gessler's cruelty has united them like never before.'

They grabbed her arms and marched her from the cell. The castle corridors stretched before them, torch flames casting dancing shadows on the stone walls. Their footsteps echoed off the vaulted ceiling, a hollow rhythm that reminded Bertha of funeral drums.

Other guards they passed straightened at attention, their eyes following her progress. Bertha held her head high, refusing to show weakness despite the ropes that bit into her wrists and the prison rags in which she'd been forced to dress. She wondered how many acts of cruelty to which this castle's ancient stones had borne witness.

Her legs trembled as the guards marched her across Altdorf Square, but she refused to let her steps falter. The morning sun cast shadows from the infamous pole where Tell had defied Gessler's cruel game. Now his cap still perched atop it, a reminder of both submission and rebellion.

Faces turned toward her, a sea of conflicting emotions. Some villagers dropped their eyes, shoulders hunched in fearful deference. Others lifted their chins, their gazes meeting hers with quiet strength. A woman clutched her child closer, whispering something that made the girl's eyes go wide.

'Look upon your noble traitor,' the herald bellowed. The ropes dug deeper as the guards forced Bertha to her knees before the pole.

The rough hemp fibres cut into her flesh, but Bertha barely felt the pain. Her heart beat faster as she surveyed the gathered crowd. These were her people now. Once she might have thought of them as subjects to rule over. But now they were souls bound together in their yearning for freedom. An old man raised a fist. A youth's eyes blazed with barely contained fury.

A murmur rippled through the assembly. 'Shame,' someone said. 'Shame on Gessler.'

The guards yanked her bonds tighter, but Bertha refused to cry out. Let them see her strength of character. Let them witness how nobility truly behaved. She thought of Tell's unwavering stance in this very spot, of his son's brave trust.

More voices joined the whispers now. 'The lady stood with Tell,' they said. 'She's one of us.'

Bertha's heart swelled. These weren't just peasants watching a noblewoman's fall from grace. They were Swiss men and women recognizing a shared spirit of resistance. Each murmur of support, each defiant gaze, strengthened their sense of unity.

The wheels of a Royal carriage kicked up stones that pelted Bertha's legs as she was forced to trudge behind it, each step a battle to maintain her footing on the rutted road. The guards flanking her traded crude jokes about noble ladies and their delicate sensibilities.

'Not so proud now, are you?' One guard yanked her chain, causing her to stumble. 'Walking in the dirt like a common criminal.'

Bertha kept her eyes fixed ahead, refusing to acknowledge their taunts. She'd seen how they fed on reactions, how their cruelty grew with each sign of weakness. The late autumn wind cut through her thin, ragged tunic, but she wouldn't give them the satisfaction of seeing her shiver.

'Maybe we should make her crawl the rest of the way,' another guard suggested, drawing raucous laughter from his companions.

The unfinished walls of Altdorf prison rose before them, scaffolding clinging to the grey stone like skeletal fingers. Workers swarmed over the structure, hammering and hauling stone blocks into place.

Dust filled the air, coating Bertha's throat and making her eyes water. The prison seemed to grow more menacing with each step, its half-built towers already casting long shadows across the courtyard. Iron bars glinted in the windows that had been completed, while others gaped like empty eye sockets, waiting for bars to be embedded. When the towers reached their full height, they would loom over the nearby town square as a constant reminder of the Austrian Emperor's rule.

Gessler's carriage halted at the prison gates. Through the settling dust, Bertha could see the temporary wooden door that would eventually be replaced with iron-bound oak.

Her shoulders screamed in protest as the guards yanked her forward, their iron grips bruising her arms. Her feet caught on the uneven stones, but she refused to cry out when they dragged her across the rough ground. The newly laid mortar still leaked between the blocks, leaving damp trails down the prison walls.

'In you go, my lady,' one guard sneered, shoving her hard enough to make her stumble. 'Your new chambers await.'

The stale air hit her like a physical force as they hauled her further into the prison wing. Torches cast wavering shadows. Water dripped somewhere in the darkness.

The guards pushed her down the corridor. Their boots scraped against the floor, the sound mixing with the rattle of keys and the creak of both metal and leather armour. Bertha forced herself to memorize every turn, every doorway, though her head spun from their rough handling.

A cell door groaned open on uneven hinges. Without ceremony, they shoved her inside. Bertha caught herself against the back wall, the damp stone cold beneath her palms. The door slammed shut with a boom that echoed through her bones.

'Sweet dreams,' a guard called through the small window in the door. Laughter followed, fading as the guards' footsteps retreated down the corridor.

173

She pressed her forehead against the cool stone, letting its solid presence ground her. The cell reeked of mildew and worse things, in spite of its being newly built, but she refused to let the conditions break her spirit. Her discomfort meant nothing compared to the suffering of the Swiss people under Gessler's rule.

She traced her fingers along the rough stone wall as her eyes adjusted to the darkness. There was a faint sliver of light coming from somewhere, filtering under the door from the corridor. In the corner there was a pallet of straw for bedding. Her mind wandered to Ulrich, her heart aching at the uncertainty of his fate. Had he discovered her imprisonment? Was he safe, or had Gessler's men seized him as well?

The guards' earlier conversation echoed in her thoughts. 'The governor has rushed to the mountain pass,' one had said. 'Some avalanche caused havoc with his plans.' The news had piqued her interest. It was as though the mountain itself had joined the Swiss resistance.

A rat scurried across the floor, its claws scratching against stone. Bertha wouldn't put it past the guards to have planted the creature in there deliberately. She pulled her knees closer to her chest, trying to preserve what little warmth remained in her body. The damp chill had settled into her bones, making each breath a reminder of her confinement.

She closed her eyes, picturing the faces of the villagers in the square. Every act of cruelty only served to unite them further, binding noble and peasant in common cause.

But doubt gnawed at her resolve. The walls seemed to close in, the silence broken only by distant echoes and the steady drip of water. How long could she endure this solitude? The thought of years spent in darkness, cut off from the world above, sent a chill through her flesh.

Bertha pressed her fingers against her temples, fighting back the rising panic. The Swiss cause would triumph – she clung to this belief like a lifeline. Yet she couldn't shake the fear that her mind might fracture before she saw that day arrive. The darkness felt alive, watching, waiting to consume her sanity piece by piece.

Chapter Twenty-Five

Tell crouched behind a fallen oak, watching a figure approach along the forest path. The stranger's gait seemed familiar, the slight limp marking him as old Falstaff, the travelling merchant who'd traded with Tell's family for years. Still, Tell waited until Falstaff passed close enough to confirm his identity before stepping out.

'Falstaff,' Tell kept his voice low.

The merchant startled, then broke into a relieved smile. 'William Tell! The saints be praised.' He clasped Tell's arm. 'We feared the worst when word spread of your escape.'

'What news from the cantons?' Tell's eyes scanned the surrounding trees as they spoke.

'Gessler rages like a wounded bear. The avalanche that blocked his secret pass...' Falstaff shook his head in admiration. 'But there's worse coming. A sympathetic soldier warned that the Austrian reinforcements found another route. They march to join Gessler at Kussnacht.'

Tell bit down on his lip. 'How many men?'

'Many hundreds. Maybe more. And Gessler's called in his forces from across Uri to gather there with those reinforcements. Word is they plan to crush the uprisings in one swift strike.' Falstaff's voice dropped further. 'But Ulrich von Rudenz and Melchthal have assembled a rebel stronghold near Kussnacht. They prepare to meet Gessler's attack.'

Tell absorbed this, calculating distances and timing in his mind. The rebels would need every advantage against such numbers. His knowledge of the area here would be vital.

'When do the Austrian forces arrive?' Tell asked.

'Two days, perhaps three. The mountain passes slow their progress.'

Tell thanked Falstaff and the two men embraced before going on their separate ways.

Later, Tell approached the rebel outpost as dusk settled over the valley. Torchlight flickered between the trees, revealing clusters of men sharpening weapons and checking bowstrings. The familiar scent of pine smoke mixed with the metallic tang of fresh-forged arrowheads.

'William Tell!' Ulrich strode forward, clasping Tell's forearm. His noble bearing remained, but his fine clothes had been replaced by practical leather and wool. 'We'd hoped you'd find your way here.'

Melchthal appeared at Ulrich's shoulder, his face breaking into a broad grin. 'The legend himself joins our cause.'

Tell took in the scene. At least two hundred men moved with purpose through the camp. Farmers and craftsmen worked alongside merchants and minor nobles, their usual social barriers dissolved by common purpose. Near a large fire, a blacksmith hammered crude spearheads while others fitted them to wooden shafts.

'You've built quite the force,' Tell said.

'And more arrive each day.' Ulrich gestured to a group of young men practicing with crossbows. 'These are sons of nobles who've pledged themselves to our cause. They bring not just their strength, but their family resources.'

'Every one of Gessler's cruelties only swells our ranks further,' Melchthal added.

A cheer went up from one end of the camp where men successfully raised a defensive barrier of sharpened logs. Strategically placed, it was a barrier against any unexpected approaches along the nearby path.

'We've prepared as best we can,' Ulrich said, leading Tell toward the command tent. 'But your experience of the land would be invaluable in positioning our forces.'

Around them, men called out greetings, their faces lighting with recognition and hope at Tell's presence.

'I bring news of the Austrian reinforcements,' Tell said as they ducked into the tent. 'We'll need every advantage we can get.'

Tell studied the crude map sketched in the dirt floor of the command tent, noting the possible approaches to Kussnacht. Ulrich paced behind him, stress radiating from his every movement.

'Our scouts confirm Gessler left Altdorf for his Kussnacht estate,' Ulrich said. 'But we've lost track of his exact route.'

'He's a serpent, slithering through the shadows,' Melchthal spat.

Tell traced the mountain paths with a stick. 'These roads all funnel to Kussnacht. His reinforcements must use one of them.'

'And that's where we'll strike.' Ulrich said. 'He's taken Bertha, imprisoned her in Altdorf for supporting our cause. I'll not rest until—'

'Bertha?' Tell's head snapped up. 'When?'

'Three days past. And she's since been thrown into that new prison wing like a common criminal while the work goes on around her to complete the other cells and towers.' Ulrich's voice cracked with emotion. 'She risked everything to help us, and now...'

Melchthal placed a steadying hand on Ulrich's shoulder. 'The network that Furst and Stauffacher established has already spread word. Rebels gather from every canton, moving toward Kussnacht. In time, we will reach Bertha at Altdorf. The villagers rise with us.'

'How many?' Tell asked.

'Hundreds,' Melchthal replied. 'Perhaps thousands. They come with farming tools turned to weapons, with hunting bows, with generations of stored rage.'

'Then we must coordinate their arrival,' Tell said. 'Time it precisely with our attack.'

'Yes.' Ulrich's eyes blazed.

Tell traced the shoreline on the crude map, his hunter's instincts piecing together Gessler's most likely movements. The governor was nothing if not calculating. He would avoid the well-travelled roads where rebels might lie in wait.

'If his entourage has not been seen on the roads then I predict he's taken to the water,' Tell said, tapping the lake's edge. 'Heading to the shore near Kussnacht where he keeps horses. From there, the ravine provides cover all the way to his estate. The same route he took when he attempted to transport me to the Kussnacht prison.'

Ulrich leaned closer, studying the passage. 'The hollow way? It's treacherous ground.'

'Exactly. Few travel it, and the high rocks on either side make it defensible with a small force.' Tell's fingers sketched the ravine's twisting path. 'But those same walls will trap him once he's committed to the route. My best guess is that's his route.'

Melchthal nodded slowly. 'We could position men along the ridge.'

'I'll lead them,' Ulrich declared, his jaw set with determination. 'If that's his route we'll catch him in the hollow way before he reaches Kussnacht.'

Tell rose from his crouch, already formulating his own plan. 'Head off before the dawn. Take forty men, enough to block both ends of the ravine, but not so many they'll slow your approach.' He adjusted the quiver at his hip. 'I'll move ahead alone through the forest. I know paths that will get me there first.'

'Alone?' Ulrich pursed his lips. '...That's too dangerous.'

'One man moves faster than forty,' Tell replied. 'And I can traverse ground your men couldn't manage. I'll scout his approach and signal when he enters the trap. And if I get the chance to bring Gessler down before your arrival, I'll take it.'

'What signal?'

Tell raised his hunting horn. 'The sound of this horn carries far and wide. If you hear it—'

Ulrich clasped Tell's arm, understanding in his eyes. 'Then may God speed your path, my friend.'

Tell nodded grimly. It was time to get as much sleep as he could through the night. He was used to rising before the sun, and in the morning, as the others roused, he slipped out of the tent, leaving Ulrich to gather his forces. The forest beckoned, its familiar shadows offering both challenge and sanctuary. Here, at least, Tell knew he held the advantage.

He moved through the forest like a shadow. He thought of that day in Altdorf square – the apple, Walter's brave face, Gessler's twisted smile. His hand gripped a low branch as he pulled himself up a steep incline.

The forest whispered around him, branches creaking in the wind. He'd walked these paths countless times hunting, but today his quarry was different. The thought of Hedy trapped in that avalanche, of Walter forced to stand before the crowd – each memory stoked the fire in his chest.

Patches of morning sunlight filtered through the canopy as Tell picked his way across a streambed. The stones slid beneath his feet, but his balance never wavered. Like these waters cutting through rock, his purpose had been shaped by time and pressure. He was no longer just a hunter, no longer simply a father protecting his family. The tyranny that threatened his homeland had transformed him into something more.

He reached the ridge above the hollow way as the sun climbed higher. Below, the narrow ravine carved a twisted path between steep rock walls. He found a natural alcove in the cliff face, partially hidden by a gnarled pine. The position offered clear sight lines in both directions while keeping him concealed from anyone passing below.

Settling into place, Tell drew his crossbow and checked the mechanism. The familiar routine centred him, pushing aside doubts and distractions. He positioned himself behind the pine's trunk, his body still and alert as he surveyed the empty path below. Here, wedged between earth and sky, Tell waited with the patience of a hunter who was certain his prey would come.

His fingers skimmed the surface of his crossbow. His father had carved this weapon, teaching him not just marksmanship but the responsibility that came with such skill. 'A bow serves justice or tyranny,' his father had said, 'depending on the heart of the man who wields it.'

The memory brought a half-smile to Tell's face. His father would have understood this moment.

A merchant's cart rattled through the ravine below, the wooden wheels echoing off the stone walls. Tell tracked the movement. But it was just a trader and his son, their voices carrying up as they talked about the day's market prices.

Dappled light played across Tell's position. A group of pilgrims passed next, their religious songs bouncing off the rocky walls. Each time, Tell's body coiled like a spring, only to relax slightly as innocent travellers moved on.

He thought of the lessons he'd taught Walter about patience during their hunting trips. 'The deer comes when it comes,' he'd explained, 'but your mind must stay ready.' Now those same teachings served a darker purpose. This was no longer about feeding his family, it was about freeing his homeland.

Two monks deep in discussion passed. There were more travellers than Tell had expected. He remained motionless, his awareness extending to every shadow and sound in the ravine.

His ears caught the first hints of an approaching melody – strings and drums, the sound growing clearer, an upbeat tune that was the last thing he expected to hear.

A group of travelling musicians rounded the bend below, their brightly coloured clothes stark against the grey stone walls. Three men played lutes while another kept rhythm on a small drum. They sang with cheerful voices about spring love and pastoral scenes.

In all his years of hunting these paths, Tell had never encountered wandering minstrels in this treacherous ravine. Most travellers hurried through, anxious to reach open ground. Yet these musicians strolled casually, as if performing for an audience that wasn't there.

The lead singer gestured dramatically as he performed, his eyes scanning the ravine walls in a way that seemed too deliberate for a simple traveller. Tell pressed closer to the pine trunk, ensuring his position remained hidden. Something about their carefree manner felt forced, rehearsed.

The musicians passed directly beneath his position, their music nearly drowning out all other sounds from the ravine. Tell forced himself to breathe slowly, maintaining his focus despite his confusion. His hunter's instincts screamed that this display was more than it appeared – perhaps a distraction or a signal of some kind.

Chapter Twenty-Six

Tell watched as a group of villagers emerged behind the musicians, wearing festive clothing. He recognized Stuffi among them, the old ranger's familiar gait unmistakable even from this distance.

After a moment's hesitation, Tell shouldered his crossbow and made his way down the slope. Stuffi's presence meant these people could be trusted.

'Wilhelm!' Stuffi's thin, lined face broke into a broad smile as Tell approached. The old ranger had always referred to his friend by his birth name. The two men clasped hands warmly. 'I hardly expected to find you here, old friend.'

'Nor I you,' Tell replied. 'What brings you through the hollow way?'

Stuffi gestured to the procession. 'We escort young Valentin to his wedding feast in Kussnacht. The musicians lead us to the banquet hall where his bride awaits.'

Tell watched the celebration unfold around him. Women carried baskets of bread and flowers, while men passed around wine skins and laughed at old jokes. Their joy seemed to belong to another world entirely, one where children still played in village squares and couples still dreamed of building lives together.

'Life goes on,' Stuffi said softly, noting Tell's expression. 'Even in these dark times, people find reasons to celebrate.'

Tell nodded, unable to speak for a moment. He thought of his own wedding day, of Hedy's smile as they'd danced under summer stars. Now he stood alone in this ravine, waiting to end a man's life.

'You should join us,' Stuffi offered, though his eyes showed he already knew the answer.

'I cannot,' Tell said. The gap between their paths had never felt wider than in this moment - Stuffi leading people toward celebration while Tell remained behind, committed to his solitary vigil.

His hand rested on his crossbow. 'The governor – have you seen him on the road?'

'Yes,' Stuffi nodded, lowering his voice. 'Not an hour past. Gessler, that snake De Harras, and a dozen armed men. They'd just pulled their boat to shore when we passed. Making ready to take this very path to Kussnacht.'

Tell's nerves pulled taut. This was the confirmation he needed.

'Come with us, Wilhelm.' Stuffi gestured to the celebrating crowd. 'What better disguise than a wedding party? No one would think to look for you among the revellers.'

Tell shook his head, his eyes hard as flint. 'I have business here that cannot wait.'

'Wilhelm —'

'Get your people to the banquet hall quickly,' Tell cut across him. 'Take no delays, no stops for music or dance. There will be trouble on this road today.'

Stuffi studied his friend's face, understanding dawning in his wizened features. He nodded once, sharply, and squeezed Tell's shoulder before turning back to the wedding party.

Tell watched as Stuffi hurried the musicians and guests along, his cheerful voice masking the urgency of their departure.

But Stuffi turned back when he saw that one of the peasant women had broken from the group and approached Tell. His heart sank as he realised the woman had been watching him closely and had overheard snippets of his conversation with Stuffi. The woman's seven children clustered around her skirts like chicks around a hen. Her eyes fixed on him with desperate intensity.

'I joined the procession after they passed the shore. Is it true what I just heard? Gessler travels this road today?'

Stuffi cleared his throat. 'Wilhelm, this is Armgart Mechthild. Her husband—'

'Gessler threw him in chains,' Armgart's voice was raw. 'For nothing more than speaking against his cruel taxes. My children haven't seen their father in months.'

Tell was acutely aware that the children stared up at him with hollow eyes that spoke of too many hungry nights.

'The wedding feast was to be our first joy since then,' Armgart said. 'My friend's celebration... a moment to forget our troubles.'

'You must join the others,' Tell urged. 'This path will not be safe once Gessler passes.'

Stuffi nodded in agreement, gently taking Armgart's arm. 'Come, the procession moves ahead without us.'

Tell watched as Stuffi guided Armgart and her children toward the celebrating crowd. But while the rest of the party disappeared around a bend in the ravine, Armgart's pace slowed. Her children tugged at her dress, trying to hurry her along, but she kept falling behind.

She turned back once, meeting Tell's gaze. Tell saw his own rage at Gessler's tyranny reflected in her face.

He lifted the hunting horn to his lips. The clear note echoed through the ravine, bouncing off stone cliffs before fading into silence. He hoped Ulrich and Melchthal would recognize the signal and quicken their pace.

His position above the hollow way offered a perfect vantage point. The crossbow felt alive in his hands, an extension of his will. Years of hunting had honed his skills for this moment – though never before had his quarry been human. The thought should have troubled him more, but memories of Gessler's cruelty, of the apple on Walter's head, of Hedy's bruised face, of Bertha von Bruneck's imprisonment, of Iris and Karl's deaths, hardened his resolve.

Emperor Albert would need to understand that his appointed governors couldn't terrorize the Swiss cantons without consequence. An end to Gessler would send that message clearly.

The clip of hooves on stone drew Tell's attention. He tensed as he peered down the ravine. First came two guards. Behind them rode Gessler, his falcon perched on his shoulder like a projection of his ego, as it had been the day Tell had seen Gessler at Altdorf prison. De Harras followed close beside him, their heads bent in conversation. More guardsmen took up the rear.

Tell drew back the crossbow string, his breathing steady.

He listened for any sound of Ulrich's approaching forces but heard only the steady approach of hooves and the soft murmur of voices below. Tell wondered if his signal had reached them in time, if they were close enough to capitalize on the chaos that would follow his shot.

The horses drew closer. Tell sighted down his arrow, tracking Gessler's movement through the ravine.

His concentration broke as movement caught his eye. His heart lurched. Armgart Mechthild emerged from behind a cluster of trees further down the pass, her seven children trailing behind her like ducklings. She hadn't continued with the wedding party after all.

She marched directly into the path of Gessler's approaching horses, her thin frame somehow commanding the narrow space. The guards drew their mounts up short, hands moving to their weapons.

'My lord governor!' Armgart's voice rang off the ravine walls. 'Mercy! Justice! I beg you!'

Tell watched helplessly as she dropped to her knees, her children clustered around her. His finger eased off the trigger.

'My husband rots in your dungeons while our children starve!' Armgart's words came fast and desperate. 'He spoke only truth about the crushing taxes. Show mercy, I implore you! Without him, we have nothing. No bread, no hope!'

The oldest boy, no more than ten, stepped forward. 'Please, sir. Our father is a good man.'

The children's gaunt faces and threadbare clothes told their own story of suffering. Armgart remained on her knees, but her head was held high, a mother's fierce courage driving her to this desperate act.

'We will work harder, pay what we can,' she pleaded. 'Only give him back to us. Look at these children. They need their father!'

Tell watched as Gessler's face twisted into a sneer, his hand raised to silence Armgart's pleas. The governor's eyes held no trace of compassion as he gazed down at the kneeling woman and her children.

'Clear the road,' he barked. 'Your husband's punishment is just. He dared question my authority, and now you compound his crime by wasting my time with these pathetic displays.'

De Harras moved his horse forward, the animal's hooves inches from Armgart's skirts. 'You heard the governor. Move aside.'

Members of the wedding party emerged from around the bend, they'd turned back, looking for Armgart, their festive mood evaporating at the scene before them. Stuffi stood at their head, his weathered face lined with concern.

'Your husband will serve as an example,' Gessler said, his voice carrying clearly. 'Let his fate teach others the price of defiance. Now remove yourself and these brats from my path before I decide they belong in chains as well.'

Tell's finger was on the trigger, his blood boiling at Gessler's threats against the children. The governor's words only confirmed what Tell already knew – there could be no reasoning with such a man, no appeal to mercy or justice. Only action would end his reign of terror.

His muscles tensed as he watched Gessler's horse paw the ground, its iron-shod hooves striking sparks from the stones. The governor's face had transformed into a mask of pure malice, his previous sneer deepening into something far more dangerous.

'Last warning,' Gessler said. 'Remove yourself and these worthless offspring, or we ride through.'

Instead of retreating, Armgart threw herself flat on the road, pulling her children down beside her. Their small bodies formed a living barrier across the path. 'Very well, then, trample us!' Her voice cracked with desperation. 'Better to die here than watch my children starve!'

Tell's breath caught in his throat. Surely even Gessler would not murder this innocent family. His hands steadied on the crossbow as he watched Gessler's movements. The wedding guests gasped in horror.

'You see?' Gessler's voice rang out through the ravine. 'This is what comes of showing too much mercy. I have been far too mild a ruler for these ungrateful peasants.' He straightened in his saddle, his voice rising to address the gathered crowd. 'Let it be known throughout the land that new laws will remedy this defiance. The time for gentle governance is over.'

Gessler raised his hand, signalling his men to form up beside him. The horses were restless, their riders tightening their grips on the reins.

'Forward!' Gessler commanded, spurring his mount toward the prone figures of Armgart and her children.

Tell's fingers tensed on the crossbow's trigger as Gessler's horse pranced forward. A death sentence for Armgart and her children. He had seconds to act.

Time seemed to slow. Tell drew a steady breath, his focus narrowing to Gessler's chest. The distance, the wind, the angle, all these calculations passed through Tell's mind in an instant.

The lives of Armgart Mechthild and her children were now dependent on him.

His arrow flew, cutting through the air with falcon-like precision. Before Gessler could complete his charge, the shaft struck home. The governor's words died in a choked gasp as the arrow found its mark.

Gessler toppled from his saddle and hit the ground, his falcon shrieking and flying off. His horse reared, adding to the sudden chaos as guards shouted and weapons were drawn.

De Harras leaped from his mount, kneeling beside his fallen master. Blood spread across Gessler's chest where Tell's arrow protruded.

'This... Tell's work,' Gessler wheezed, barely able to form words, his face contorted in pain. His fingers clutched weakly at the shaft. 'God, have mercy on me...'

Tell watched as the life drained from Gessler's eyes, feeling neither triumph nor remorse, only the quiet certainty that justice had finally been served and more lives saved.

Turmoil erupted in the ravine below. De Harras barked orders, his composure shattered. The guards' horses wheeled in confusion, their riders torn between protecting their fallen leader and searching the ridge for more attackers.

Armgart sprang to her feet, scooping up her youngest child. She thrust him skyward, her voice ringing with fierce joy. 'Look! The tyrant lies dead! The forces of justice strike down those who torment us!'

The wedding guests pressed forward, their earlier fear transformed into a surging wave of triumph. Tell caught glimpses of familiar faces among the crowd, faces that had too long borne the sting of Gessler's venom.

Movement along the ridgeline caught his attention. Ulrich's men emerged from the forest on both sides of the ravine, their bows drawn and arrows trained on the Austrian guards. Their sudden appearance transformed the pass into a trap.

'Surrender your weapons!' Ulrich's voice boomed across the ravine. 'Your master is dead, and you are surrounded. Lay down your arms and live!'

De Harras's hand hovered over his sword hilt as he assessed their situation. His men exchanged uncertain glances, their earlier confidence evaporating.

'The monks at Küssnacht have been sent for,' a peasant's voice carried up from the crowd. 'They'll tend to the body proper-like.'

'Austrians do not surrender!' De Harras's voice boomed. 'There must be blood paid for the governor's death!' He wheeled his horse around, pointing at Ulrich's positions. 'Archers, nock arrows! Take aim at these rebel dogs!'

The Austrian guards raised their bows, but Ulrich's voice cut through their movements.

'Fire!'

A deadly rain of arrows descended from both sides of the ravine. Tell tracked two guards as they jerked in their saddles, arrows finding gaps in their armour. They toppled from their mounts, hitting the ground with dull thuds that made the remaining soldiers flinch.

Tell stepped out from his cover, keeping his crossbow trained on De Harras.

'De Harras!' he shouted. 'Look up. My arrow killed Gessler, and my next shot will find you if you don't order your men to surrender.'

De Harras's eyes widened as he recognized Tell. The commander's gaze darted between Tell's unwavering crossbow and his own depleted forces.

'Stand down,' De Harras said. 'Lower your weapons.' His shoulders slumped as his remaining men dropped their bows.

Tell watched from his position as Ulrich's men descended into the ravine. The Austrian guards dismounted under the rebels' watchful eyes, their proud bearing diminished by defeat. Melchthal collected their weapons while others bound their hands with rope.

De Harras stood rigid as Ulrich himself secured his bonds, the commander's face a mask of contained fury. 'This death will not go unanswered,' he said.

The sound of Latin chants drifted through the pass, growing stronger as the Brothers of Mercy approached. Their brown robes brushed the ground as they walked, heads bowed beneath their cowls. The wedding guests parted to let them through, many crossing themselves at the sight.

Tell lowered his crossbow as he watched the monks gather around Gessler's body. He recalled that their monastery was not far from here. Their ancient prayers echoed off the stone walls, transforming the narrow space into an impromptu cathedral. The solemn words seemed to mark more than just a man's passing – it was as though they sensed the end of an era was coming.

Armgart Mechthild stood with her children, tears of relief streaming down her face as she watched the monks prepare Gessler's body for transport. Her children gripped her skirts. Around them, the wedding guests who had witnessed Gessler's final moments of inhumanity now watched his ignoble end with quiet satisfaction.

The Brothers lifted Gessler onto their cart, their chants never faltering. As they began their slow procession toward Küssnacht, Tell wondered if the tyrant's death would be the beginning of great change. Where there had been fear in people's eyes as they'd returned looking for Armgart, he now saw hope. Where there had been submission in so many Swiss people, he saw the straightening of backs and lifting of chins of the people in the ravine.

The sound of the monks' chanting faded gradually, carried away by the mountain winds. In its wake, Tell could feel a different kind of silence settle over the ravine, not the fearful quiet of oppression, but the peaceful stillness of liberation.

He stood tall on the ridge, his crossbow lowered but still ready. The wind whipped his cloak as he gazed down at the gathered crowd below.

'People of Uri!' His voice carried across the ravine. 'I am William Tell! Let it be known that by my hand, the tyrant Gessler has fallen. No longer will he force fathers to shoot apples from their sons' heads. No longer will he imprison honest men for speaking truth. No longer will he threaten to trample children in the road!'

The crowd turned toward him. Tell saw the glow of hope in Armgart's eyes as she clutched her children closer.

'Our cottages and our mountains can be our own again!' Tell said.

A cheer erupted from the wedding guests. The bound Austrian guards seemed to shrink at the sound.

Tell raised his arm above his head and both the rebels and the villagers did the same. The first true blow for Swiss freedom, struck in a narrow mountain pass. There could be no turning back now.

Chapter Twenty-Seven

Daniel Furst and his wife Elsbeth woke in the middle of the night to a loud rapping on the front door.

Elsbeth gasped. 'Daniel...''

'Stay here,' Furst said. He pulled a coat around his shoulders and strode to the front door, his nerves on end, fearing a raid by Gessler's men. He swallowed hard, braced himself, and opened the door – not to a troop of soldiers but to a lone peasant, a farm worker who was part of his messenger network, who had gone to join Ulrich's rebel stronghold in the mountains.

'I bring news of Gessler's demise,' the messenger blurted out.

Furst stepped back as though struck. 'What?'

'Ulrich, Tell, and a band of men are headed here to Uri to stage a dawn raid on the soldiers stationed in the Altdorf town square and at the prison...'

Furst motioned for the messenger to enter. 'Come in, man. You need sustenance after your long ride. And then, you must go to the homes of our supporters through the valley, and to Werner Stauffacher in Schwyz, and I will do the same here in the town...'

'Yes, sir.'

'We must have them group together with their weapons at the Uri tanner's workshop, then march to join Ulrich's men when they arrive.'

The messenger nodded.

'And what of Arnold of Melchthal?' Furst asked.

190

'He and Baumgarten led another group of our rebels for a dawn raid on Governor Landenberg's castle in Sarnen. And then they march to confront the Austrian guard throughout Unterwalden.'

Furst's brow raised in understanding. With Gessler vanquished, a simultaneous raid on the commanders of those other cantons would further fan the flames of the rebellion.

Furst took a moment to calm himself. He was thankful that his daughter, Hedy, and his grandsons were safe in hiding on the Meier farm. The revolt was happening, sooner than the original plan had called for, but events had dictated otherwise.

The moment had arrived.

***

Melchthal led the group through the dark forest with only his fiery torch and the moonlight to guide him. Behind him, Baumgarten matched his steps, and a hundred rebels followed their lead.

The familiar scents of the forest filled Melchthal's nostrils, but his mind wandered to a different scene – his father's agonized screams as Landenberg's men burned out his eyes. The memory burned hotter than any torch, driving him forward with each step. He glanced at the men behind him, catching glimpses of their hardened expressions. Some had lost homes, others family members, all victims of Austrian cruelty. Baumgarten, like Melchthal, was a fugitive, after slaying the Imperial Seneschal who'd attacked his wife.

The forest thinned ahead, revealing the first hints of morning light. Landenberg's Sarnen castle materialized from the darkness, its stone walls rising against the pale sky. Melchthal raised his fist, and the column halted instantly. They dropped low, concealing themselves behind fallen logs covered in moss.

'There,' Baumgarten said, pointing to the western wall where scaffolding still clung to the stone. 'Construction work on a new column.'

Melchthal studied the castle's outline, noting the positions of the sentries on the walls. He spotted movement near the gate – guards

191

changing shifts, their weapons glinting in the growing light. The castle's defences looked formidable, but he knew every fortress had its weaknesses. His father's unseeing eyes flashed in his mind again, priming his anger.

The rebels crouched silently, weapons ready, waiting for Melchthal's signal. Dawn painted the sky in shades of pink and gold, bringing their target into clearer detail.

Melchthal gathered his men close. 'We strike the guards first. No sound, no warning. Baumgarten, take the left tower. Hans, the right. I'll handle the gate. Once inside, torch everything wooden. The stone won't burn, but the smoke will create chaos.'

The men's heads bobbed in silent acknowledgment. These weren't trained soldiers, but farmers and craftsmen pushed too far by Austrian brutality, whose burning hearts outweighed their inexperience in battle.

Melchthal led them through the shadows.

At the castle wall, he raised his hand. The guards above maintained their lazy patrol, unaware of death waiting below. He caught Baumgarten's eye, then Hans's, and they quietly spread the word. Dozens of bows rose in unison.

Melchthal's finger tapped against his bow twice - the signal. Dozens of arrows whistled through the air. The guards crumpled without a sound, their bodies slumping against the battlements.

'Now!' Melchthal hissed. The rebels surged forward through the gate, spreading out across the courtyard. Torches touched thatch and timber, hungry flames leaping to life. The wooden scaffolding caught quickly, fire racing up its length. Storage sheds and stables blazed, casting wild shadows across stone walls.

The courtyard transformed into a furnace, smoke billowing into the lightening sky.

Melchthal burst through the wooden doors, sword ready, his pulse pounding in his ears. Smoke from the courtyard fires filtered through the castle's windows, casting an eerie haze through the corridors. Two of Landenberg's guards rushed at him, but Hans and Baumgarten cut them down with swift strikes.

'This way,' Melchthal called, leading his men up the winding stone staircase. His boots thundered against each step, the clash of steel on steel echoing from below as the rest of their force engaged the garrison.

They encountered three more guards at the top of the stairs. Melchthal parried a wild thrust, his blade finding its mark in his opponent's chest. Hans grappled with another guard, while Baumgarten's axe swung towards the third.

The corridor to Landenberg's chambers stretched before them. Melchthal knew the layout well. He'd delivered grain here in his younger days before the Austrians had shown their true nature. Before they'd taken his father's eyes.

Two more turns brought them to Landenberg's ornate door. Melchthal kicked it open, wood splintering under his boot. The chamber beyond was empty. No Landenberg.

'Damn him,' Melchthal growled, crossing to the window. The morning light revealed no sign of the governor in the courtyard below. He turned back to the room, scanning for any clue to Landenberg's destination. Scrolls lay across a desk, their wax seals broken, but nothing indicated where the tyrant had fled.

Melchthal strode from the empty chambers and descended to the courtyard. Flames still licked at the wooden structures, but the fires were dying.

His gaze swept over the faces of the ragtag group of warriors who'd claimed their first true victory. Some tended to minor wounds while others secured Austrian prisoners. Landenberg's seat of power had fallen.

A glint of light caught his eye. Melchthal turned toward the mountain ridges, where signal fires blazed against the dawn sky. Each flame lit by one of the messengers, alerting the people throughout the three cantons that the coordinated uprising had begun.

'Brothers,' Melchthal called out, his voice carrying across the courtyard. 'Today we've struck a mighty blow against Austrian tyranny. But this castle is just the beginning.'

The men raised their weapons, a cheer rising from their throats. Melchthal saw in their eyes the same fire that burned within him.

'Gather your strength,' he commanded. 'Tend to the wounded. We'll need every sword, every bow, every strong arm as we march through Unterwalden.'

The men voiced their agreement.

Melchthal then motioned to two of the men to follow him. 'Let's search the immediate area around the castle. I expect Landenberg is out there, cowering in the forest.'

***

The Austrian column wound its way through the narrow pass. Each hoofbeat echoed off the steep slopes that hemmed them in, the sound of chainmail and plate armour creating a steady rhythm. Their horses' breaths steamed in the cold air as they picked their way between the treacherous swamp on one side and the sheer rock face on the other.

Captain Friedrich von Kessler led the formation, his white plume stark against his burnished helmet. The knights behind him maintained perfect spacing, their shields emblazoned with the Habsburg double-headed eagle, their long swords ready at their sides. They had been forced to take this circuitous route after finding their intended path blocked by an avalanche, but their determination remained unshaken.

High above, concealed behind rocks and sparse mountain pines, confederate lookouts tracked the advancing column. One rebel counted under his breath – forty knights in the vanguard, and, too many to count, what appeared to be another several hundred, maybe close to a thousand, following. Their armour marked them as elite troops, veterans of campaigns across Europe.

'Go,' the lead scout said to young Niklaus, who slipped away through the rocks. The boy scrambled across hidden paths, as he raced to carry word to Altdorf. The remaining lookouts pressed themselves lower into their hiding spots, hardly daring to breathe as the column passed beneath them.

One of the older lookouts, watching from another vantage point, noted how the narrow path forced the knights to ride two abreast, stretching their column dangerously thin. He gripped the rock as he observed their steady advance, knowing that every detail would be vital to those preparing Altdorf's defence.

From his perch above the pass, Adam Glassier crouched beside the lookout, assessing the Austrian column. The morning mist had begun to lift, revealing the full extent of the advancing force.

'Their armour will be their undoing in these mountains,' Glassier said, noting how the knights struggled to maintain their balance on horseback along the treacherous path. 'They're trained for open battlefield charges, not this terrain.'

The lookout nodded, shifting his position behind a jutting boulder. 'The rear guard keeps glancing up at the slopes. They know they're vulnerable here.'

A loose stone clattered down the mountainside, causing several knights to jerk their heads upward. Glassier and the lookout froze, pressing themselves flat against the cold rock. The column continued its advance, metal creaking and horses' hooves crunching on loose gravel.

'We can only pray that Niklaus reaches Altdorf and that the Confederate leaders are warned before these knights reach open ground,' the lookout murmured, his breath forming small clouds in the chill air.

Glassier gripped the lookout's shoulder. 'Wait. Look there.' He pointed to where the path curved sharply around a massive boulder. 'That bend will force them to slow even further and there are many points like that along this route.'

'Yes, but will any of it slow their progress long enough before they surprise Furst's men in Altdorf?'

The lookout repositioned himself, careful not to dislodge any more stones. A flock of birds swooped overhead, their shrieks ringing out as though in warning.

'There's something else,' Glassier said as he studied the formation. 'Look at their supply train.'

The lookout peered where Glassier indicated. Behind the main column, wagons laden with provisions crawled along the path, their wooden wheels struggling against the uneven ground. Each cart required four horses to pull it, and the drivers fought to keep them from sliding toward the swamp's edge.

'They're carrying enough supplies for a long campaign,' the lookout said. 'They mean to stay.'

Glassier nodded, his weary face grim. 'And there, see how the knights near the rear keep looking back? They're protecting something valuable.'

Through gaps in the formation, they glimpsed a smaller group of riders clustered around what appeared to be a nobleman's carriage, its curtains open. There was no one inside but the sun glinted off something steely.

The lookout cursed under his breath. 'An arsenal. Extra swords and shields, I'd wager.'

A cold wind whipped around them, carrying with it the distant sound of the column's officers barking commands as the formation navigated another sharp bend in the path.

Chapter Twenty-Eight

Bertha jolted awake on the damp straw. The drip of water from the ceiling and the scurrying of rats had ceased, replaced by an unnatural stillness. She pushed herself to a sitting position.

The darkness of her cell seemed different. Heavier, more oppressive. She felt a creeping sense of dread. An inner sense, perhaps. She wondered, though, if that was simply due to her fear that soon men would come to torture and question her. She presumed, as she had not yet heard the sounds of construction on the rest of the prison outside that it was not yet day.

And then, suddenly, a distant cry pierced the silence, followed by shouts and the unmistakable ring of steel on steel. Bertha crawled to the cell door, pressing her ear against the oak. More shouts reached her, muffled but urgent, and the thunder of running feet from somewhere above. Her hands trembled as she gripped the door's edge.

What is happening?

The clash of weapons grew louder, accompanied by voices she couldn't quite distinguish. Her mind raced through possibilities. A prisoner revolt? An attack on the prison? The hope that had dimmed during her imprisonment came back to life, though she fought to temper it with caution.

Another crash echoed through the corridors, closer this time, followed by the acrid smell of smoke seeping under her door. How could this be? The prison was burning.

Bertha sprang to her feet, ignoring the ache in her muscles from days languishing in the cold dungeon. She slammed her fists against the oak door, the impact sending shockwaves through her bones.

'Help! Someone, please!' Her voice cracked from disuse. The smoke curled beneath the door in thicker tendrils now, stinging her eyes. 'I'm down here! In the dungeons!'

The sounds of battle intensified above – steel clashing, men shouting, the crackle of flames growing louder. A beam crashed somewhere overhead, sending slivers of dust under the door. Bertha pounded harder, her knuckles splitting against the rough wood.

She pressed her face to the gap she'd discovered a day earlier between door and frame, evidence of shoddy workmanship. The corridor beyond had filled with smoke, making it impossible to see more than a few feet. She fought down rising panic. The Austrian guards would never risk their lives to save a traitor. Her only hope lay with the attackers, if they even knew she was here.

'Ulrich!' She called his name without thinking, doubt gnawing at her resolve. What had happened to him since she'd been in here? What if he'd been captured too? The crack of splintering wood echoed through the stone passages, followed by screams that made her blood run cold.

Bertha forced herself to think clearly despite the chaos. The smoke was thickening, making each breath more difficult. She tore strips from her prison tunic, stuffing them into the gap under the door to buy precious minutes of cleaner air. Her mind raced through options. Could she signal her location somehow? Make enough noise to be heard over the fighting?

The heat was building now, and Bertha could hear the hungry roar of flames consuming the wooden structures above. She struck the door again and again, ignoring the pain that shot through her hands with each impact.

The smoke rolled in thicker waves now. Her throat burned with each ragged breath, and her eyes watered against the sting. The makeshift barrier of fabric beneath the door had bought her precious minutes, but those were slipping away fast.

'Help!' Her voice emerged as a raw croak. She struck the door again, her knuckles turning bloody. 'Down here! The dungeons!'

The cell's suffocating darkness pressed in closer as smoke filled the upper reaches. Bertha ran her hands along the walls, searching for loose stones. Her fingers caught on the empty iron brackets that were meant for the torch sconces, testing their strength. Too firmly mounted to wrench free.

She moved to the straw pallet, tearing it apart. The wooden slats beneath might serve as leverage against the door hinges. But the slats they'd used were old and rotten, crumbling at her touch. Her hands found only mouldy straw and rat droppings.

The coughing started then, in spasms that doubled her over. Bertha pressed her face into what remained of her tunic sleeve, trying to filter the toxic air. The smoke had grown so dense she could barely make out the door just feet away.

Still, she forced herself to continue the desperate search of her prison. The chamber pot was too fragile to use as a battering ram. The water bucket – empty now, and perhaps the metal handle could serve as a tool. She worked at the rusty rivets, trying to free the handle while fighting the urge to gulp the poisoned air.

The heat pressed against her skin, each breath now scorching her lungs. The roar of flames grew louder, drowning out the sounds of combat outside. Orange light flickered through the gaps in the door.

Her fingers clutched at her throat as another coughing fit seized her. The smoke burned her eyes, forcing them shut, but she forced them open again.

She staggered as the smoke made her head spin and she struck at the door again, ignoring the searing pain in her knuckles.

She pressed her face close to the floor, desperate for what little clean air remained. Her lungs heaved, trying to extract oxygen from the poisoned atmosphere and black spots danced at the edges of her vision, a different kind of darkness enveloping her.

With a surge of adrenaline, she used the bucket to strike the door's iron hinges with all her remaining strength. The metallic clang echoed through the stone corridors.

Sweat poured down her face, mixing with the tears that streamed from her smoke-irritated eyes. Her strikes became weaker, her arms tiring, but she refused to stop.

Bertha pressed her face against the gap between the floor and the door, her voice emerging as a hoarse whisper. 'Please... someone...' The words scraped her throat. Even the act of speaking sent her into another violent coughing fit that left her gasping. 'I don't want to die here.' The words emerged unbidden, barely audible even to her.

Her limbs felt leaden. Each breath burned more than the last, and the simple act of keeping her eyes open became a monumental struggle. The stone floor beckoned and she slumped to the floor, her cheek pressed against the now-heated stone.

Through half-closed eyes, she watched the orange glow dance across the ceiling. Memories flooded her mind of the sunlit gardens at her father's estate, her mother's smile, Ulrich's face the last time she'd seen him.

The roar of the flames grew distant as if heard through layers of thick wool. Bertha's eyes fluttered closed, her body going limp as her consciousness slipped away.

Chapter Twenty-Nine

Tell crouched behind a stone wall at the edge of Altdorf, watching the first rays of dawn paint the eastern sky. His muscles tensed as he counted the Austrian guards making their rounds, six at the prison gate, more patrolling the square. Beside him, Ulrich signalled to the rebels spread out in the shadows.

The mountain peaks caught fire one by one as signal beacons blazed to life. Tell's heart quickened at the sight. Across the valley, more flames appeared, a chain of light marking the spread of rebellion throughout the cantons.

The toll of church bells shattered the morning silence. The sound rolled across Altdorf, drawing startled shouts from the Austrian guards. Tell saw confusion ripple through their ranks as bells from neighbouring villages joined the chorus.

'Now,' Tell said, rising from his position. Ulrich echoed the command, and rebels emerged from doorways and lanes. They charged forward.

Tell nocked an arrow as he ran, his eyes fixed on the guards. The Austrians scrambled to form a defensive line, their swords glinting. Tell fired, his arrow striking one of the guards, driving him back.

More rebels poured into the square, their weapons ready. Farmers and craftsmen moving with the discipline of soldiers. They had trained in secret for months, preparing for this moment.

The church bells continued their urgent call. As the Confederates clashed with the town square soldiers, Tell advanced with his men, moving past the square and heading down the path to the prison. Behind the prison guards, the half-built fortress's stone walls were dark and forbidding.

As they drew closer, Tell watched as a rider galloped onto the grounds, his horse's hooves clattering against the newly laid cobblestones. 'Gessler is dead!' The Austrian messenger's voice cracked through the morning air. 'Struck down in the hollow pass!'

The effect on the Austrian guards was immediate. Their disciplined formation wavered, spears drooping as they exchanged uncertain glances. Tell saw fear replace the arrogance in their eyes. Without Gessler's iron grip, their resolve crumbled.

'Forward!' Ulrich's command rang out. The rebels surged ahead, their coordinated charge catching the demoralized guards off balance. Steel clashed against steel as the two forces met, with the Austrians rising to the defence. Tell's arrow struck one of the man's hands, dislodging his sword. Several threw down their weapons, backing away with raised arms.

Tell moved through the chaos beside Ulrich, both men focused on the prison's iron-bound door, Ulrich's eyes blazing with determination. Tell recognized the look, it was the same expression he'd worn when racing to check on Hedy and his sons.

'She's in there,' Ulrich said. 'Stauffacher's spy said she's in the lower level.'

Tell nodded, nocking another arrow as they approached. The remaining prison guards at the entrance shuffled nervously.

'Stand aside,' Tell commanded, his bow raised. 'Your governor is dead. There's no honour in dying for a corpse.'

His heart dropped as smoke billowed from the prison's eastern wing. Orange flames licked up the wooden scaffolding, consuming the half-finished construction with frightening speed. Local villagers cheered at the blaze, not realizing they'd trapped one lone prisoner inside.

'No!' Ulrich lurched forward but Tell grabbed his arm.

'Wait.' Tell's ears caught a rhythmic pounding beneath the roar of flames – metal or wood striking wood from somewhere within the prison.

Bertha.

But the fire had leaped across to the wooden facades of the front entrance, engulfing the door in flame, smoke billowing from behind it and from out of the window openings above it.

Tell spotted a way in – a section of scaffolding along the western wall was still untouched. The flames hadn't reached it yet, though smoke curled around its edges.

'There.' He pointed to the scaffold. 'We can climb to the upper level, step across to the window, then work our way down through the stone tower.' He studied the construction, mapping their route. The wooden planks would hold for a several minutes before the fire claimed them too.

The clanging sound grew more frantic. Tell shouldered his bow and gripped the nearest timber. 'Follow close. Step exactly where I step.' He didn't wait for Ulrich's response before starting his ascent.

Jakob Muller, who'd led one of the local village groups, charged into step beside them. 'I'm coming with you.'

It was too dangerous to risk the life of another man but Tell didn't argue. He and Ulrich were going to need all the help they could get.

Heat pressed against Tell's face as he climbed, the smoke thickening with each foot gained. Below, there was more of the banging. He tracked the fire's path, calculating how long they had before the scaffolding collapsed. Five minutes. Maybe a couple more.

A support beam groaned nearby. Tell quickened his pace, testing each handhold before trusting it. The prison's stone wall offered few crevices, but the scaffolding's cross-braces created a makeshift ladder. For now.

His muscles strained as he hauled himself up another level of the scaffolding, the wood creaking ominously beneath his grip. Heat pressed against his back where flames devoured the eastern section and sweat trickled down his neck. Below, Ulrich followed his exact path while Jakob Muller brought up the rear.

A burning timber crashed down mere feet away, showering them with sparks. Tell pressed himself flat against the scaffold's frame, feeling the structure sway. The smoke grew thicker, stinging his eyes and catching in his throat.

'The crossbeam's weakening,' Ulrich called out.

Tell reached for the next handhold, testing its strength before pulling himself higher. The window was just above. Another support beam groaned and splintered, sending tremors through the entire structure.

'Move!' Tell barked as he lunged for the window ledge. He swung himself through the narrow opening, landing in a crouch on the stone floor inside. Ulrich scrambled through next, followed by Muller just as the scaffold gave a final shudder.

Smoke pooled along the ceiling of the corridor, forcing them to stay low. Tell led them toward a spiral staircase, the banging growing louder beneath them.

The air grew thicker with smoke as they reached the bottom. Tell pressed forward, scanning the row of cell doors. The rhythmic striking of metal against metal guided them deeper into the prison's bowels.

'Here!' Ulrich's voice cut through the darkness as they rounded a corner. The pounding had stopped but Tell was certain Ulrich was right, and this was the cell it had been coming from. But the silence now was ominous.

'Bertha?' Ulrich called.

No answer.

Tell moved to the door's hinges while Ulrich and Muller positioned themselves to break it down. The smoke poured down the stairwell behind them, leaving them precious little time.

Tell examined the door, finding no weakness.

'Stand back,' he said, positioning himself alongside Ulrich and Muller. The three men lined up, shoulders pressed together. 'On my count. One... two... three!'

They slammed into the door as one. Pain shot through Tell's shoulder, but the door held firm. Smoke curled around their feet, spurring them to try again. Their second attempt produced a sharp crack from the frame.

'Again!' Tell drove forward with renewed force. The wood splintered near the hinges. There was a flaw in the workmanship, not unexpected given the slave labour used to build this monstrosity. Sweat dripped down his face as they reset their stance. His shoulder throbbed, but he ignored the pain. 'Again!'

This time the door burst inward with a thunderous crash. Tell stumbled through first, scanning the dark cell now lit by the fire's light. Bertha lay crumpled in the corner, a bucket still clasped in her hand – the source of the banging that had guided them.

Ulrich rushed past Tell with a strangled cry. He gathered Bertha in his arms, cradling her head against his chest. 'She's breathing,' he choked out, pressing his lips to her forehead.

Coughing from the thick smoke, Tell stepped into the corridor and squinted along it. There was a corner further along that he prayed might lead them to safety. He turned back to find Ulrich already on his feet, Bertha secure in his embrace, Muller adding extra support.

'This way,' he directed, pointing toward their escape route. 'The main stairwell will be blocked by now. We'll have to find another way up.'

The bend in the corridor led to stone steps that rose above them. Another tower, this one positioned at the rear of the prison, and only partway built. The unfinished opening several floors up enabled them to step out onto another timber rigging, that was also now burning. Tell's muscles screamed as he guided their descent, testing each wooden beam before signalling the others to follow. Smoke billowed, making it impossible to see more than a few steps beneath at a time.

'Step there.' He pointed Ulrich toward a crossbeam that looked sturdy enough to hold them. Bertha remained unconscious in Ulrich's arms, making his movements awkward and dangerous. Muller brought up the rear, ready to assist if either man lost their footing.

A sharp crack split the air. Tell's heart jumped as the scaffold swayed beneath them. 'Move!' He grabbed Ulrich's shoulder, steering him toward a lower platform. The wooden structure groaned, timbers splintering as flames leaped across from another section of rigging.

They were still twenty feet above the ground when the upper section gave way. Burning debris rained down around them as Tell shoved Ulrich and Bertha onto the platform below. The impact knocked the breath from his lungs, but he rolled immediately to his feet, pulling the others away from the edge.

The entire scaffold shuddered. Tell watched in horror as the upper levels collapsed, spewing a stream of flaming debris toward them. He threw himself over Bertha and Ulrich as Muller pressed against the wall. The platform held, barely, though Tell felt it list dangerously to one side.

'Down there!' Tell spotted a pile of hay bales stacked against the prison wall, meant for the guards' horses. It wasn't ideal, but it beat burning alive. He helped Ulrich secure his grip on Bertha, then positioned them at the platform's edge. Bertha jolted awake in shock.

The scaffold gave another warning creak. Tell didn't hesitate. 'Jump!' He pushed them forward, watching as they landed safely in the hay below. Muller followed immediately after. Tell took a final breath and leaped just as the platform collapsed behind him.

The hay softened their fall enough to prevent serious injury. Tell rolled to his feet, helping Ulrich extract a shaking and wheezing Bertha from the scattered bales.

He watched as she drew in deep breaths of air, her eyes gradually focusing on the faces around her. The smoke-filled haze lifted from her features, replaced by dawning recognition. Her hand trembled as she reached for Ulrich's face.

'You came for me.' Her voice was barely above a whisper. She looked to Tell and Muller. 'All of you.'

Tell nodded, noting how her noble bearing remained intact despite her ordeal. She straightened herself, though still leaning against Ulrich for support.

'The bells...' Bertha's eyes widened. 'I heard them through the walls. The people answered your call.'

'Swiss blood runs deeper than titles,' Tell said, meeting Ulrich's eyes. The young nobleman nodded. They were no longer divided by class or status but united in purpose.

Muller stepped forward, offering Bertha his water skin. The simple gesture spoke volumes, a peasant providing aid to a noblewoman without hesitation or deference.

Behind them, the prison's wooden scaffolding burned, sending sparks spiralling into the morning sky. The flames consumed Gessler's monument to oppression. Tell watched as sections of the unfinished walls crumbled, each falling stone another shackle broken.

Chapter Thirty

The Austrian column stretched like an iron serpent through the narrow passage. Tell watched from his elevated position as the knights guided their mounts between the steep slopes and treacherous swamp.

'More than five hundred men by the looks of it,' said villager Kaspar Ludwig, crouched beside Tell.

Tell nodded, studying the approaching force. These were no ordinary soldiers. Each rider wore full plate armour, carried a shield emblazoned with the Habsburg eagle, and wielded longswords.

Tell's mind drifted to their triumph in Altdorf the day before. The prison's smouldering ruins still sent wisps of smoke into the sky, a further signal of the Confederacy's growing strength, something he wished the old baron, Attinghausen, had lived to see. With Gessler dead and his men either captured or scattered, the rebels had secured a significant victory. The arrival of Melchthal and Baumgarten's forces had swelled their ranks considerably.

But celebration had been cut short when the first messenger arrived, breathless, with news of the advancing Austrian army. Tell had hoped that stymied by the avalanche, the army had retraced their steps and returned to Austria for further orders. No such luck. Tell, Ulrich, Stauffacher, and Furst had been forced to quickly formulate a new plan and organize their defences, positioning men along the ridges and preparing for battle.

Tell touched the crossbow at his side, its familiar surface always a comfort to his hunter's fingers. The Austrians may have numbers and training, but he believed the Confederates had something stronger. The fierce determination of men fighting for their homes and freedom.

He glanced at one of the halberds propped against the rocks beside them, appreciating the weapon's deadly elegance. The blacksmiths had worked day and night to forge thousands of these weapons.

'Our numbers may be fewer,' Tell said, 'but these will even the odds against mounted knights.'

Kaspar lifted one of the halberds, testing its balance. 'Fine work from the smiths. The pike head alone could punch through plate armour.'

'And that's just the start.' Tell's vision followed the curved edge of the axe blade. 'Six feet of reach keeps us safely away from the Austrian's swords while the pike unseats them. Once they're down...' He gestured to the axe head.

'The knights won't expect it.' Kaspar's eyes gleamed as he studied the weapon's design. 'They're used to peasants with pitchforks, not proper weapons purpose-built for dismounting cavalry.'

Tell nodded in agreement. The halberd's three-part head was a masterwork of engineering. The spear point for thrusting, the axe for cleaving, and the hook for pulling riders from their mounts. The long ash shaft provided the leverage needed to make each strike count.

He moved silently along the ridge, checking each group's position. Stauffacher's men crouched behind a cluster of boulders on the western slope, their halberds laid flat against the rocks to avoid catching any glint of sunlight. Through the morning mist, Tell could make out Ulrich's contingent spread across the eastern ridge, positioned to rain arrows down on the Austrian column.

Muller had positioned his group at the narrowest point of the pass, where a recent rockslide had created a natural bottleneck. His men had spent the night loosening more rocks, ready to trigger an avalanche that would split the Austrian column.

Tell touched the horn at his belt, knowing its blast would signal the start of their assault. The timing had to be perfect. They needed the bulk of the Austrian force to be committed to the pass before springing the trap.

He studied the terrain again, appreciating how the natural features would work to their advantage. The steep slopes would prevent the knights from spreading out into proper formation. The swampy ground along the eastern edge would bog down any who tried to flee in that direction. The narrowness of the pass itself would turn the Austrians' numbers against them, creating chaos as riders collided with each other once the attack began.

The Confederates had positioned themselves well. Each group knew their role. Stauffacher's men would use their halberds to unhorse the knights, Ulrich's archers would pick off any who tried to retreat, and Muller's barrier and rockslide would trap them in the killing zone.

Tell moved back to his elevated position, where he could observe the entire area. The morning air carried the sounds of the approaching column. He nocked an arrow to his crossbow, though he knew he would need to choose his targets carefully. Even Tell couldn't waste arrows on plate armour. He would focus on the officers, recognizable by their plumes and banners.

His nerves tensed as he watched the Austrian column halt before Muller's roadblock. The knights at the front dismounted to inspect the scattered boulders. Behind them, the rest of the column stirred, horses stamping in the confined space.

The Confederates held their positions, barely breathing. Tell could sense their anticipation. Hundreds of men waiting for his signal, their weapons ready.

He reached for the prepared arrow, its oil-soaked cloth wrapping catching the sunlight. He struck his flint, igniting the cloth. The flame caught quickly, dancing in the cool mountain air.

His crossbow raised, Tell took aim. The burning arrow needed to arc perfectly across the pass, high enough to be visible to all Confederate positions, but not so high as to lose its flame. He drew a steady breath, feeling the familiar pressure of the trigger against his fingers.

The arrow flew, trailing fire as it crossed the pass. Its bright path cut through the morning mist like a shooting star, landing with a spark among the rocks on the far slope.

Before the flame had even died, Stauffacher's men burst into action. Rocks of all sizes crashed down the western slope, bouncing and splitting as they fell.

The Austrian horses reared in panic, throwing several knights from their saddles. The tight formation dissolved into chaos as riders fought to control their mounts. More rocks rained down, striking armour with metallic clangs and causing horses to slam into each other in their desperation to escape.

Tell used his horn as a signal to Stauffacher's men, and they burst from their positions, halberds levelled. The long weapons caught the morning light as the Confederates charged down the slope, their war cries echoing off the rocks.

The Austrian knights struggled to form a defensive line, their horses still panicked from the rockfall. Tell watched as the first wave of Confederates struck home with halberds finding gaps between armour plates and hooks yanking riders from their mounts. The knights' superior armour meant little once they hit the ground, their heavy plate hindering movement in the confined space.

'Drive them back!' Tell's voice carried over the clash of steel and screams of wounded men. 'Keep them pinned against the rocks!'

The Confederates worked in pairs, one man using his halberd to unhorse a knight while his partner finished the fallen rider. The Austrian formation crumbled further as more riders were pulled from their mounts, creating a barrier of thrashing horses and fallen men that trapped those behind them.

Tell charged down to a lower ridge, calling out directions to groups of fighters to plug any gaps where the knights might break through. The halberds proved devastating – their long reach kept the Confederates safely beyond the knights' sword range while the weapon's specialized head found weak points in the expensive armour.

An Austrian captain rallied a group of knights for a counter-charge but Tell had anticipated this. He signalled to Ulrich's archers, who fired a volley into the gathering force. Arrows couldn't penetrate plate armour, but they spooked horses and found gaps in vizors, disrupting the attempted attack before it could begin.

The battle devolved into a series of brutal individual combats. Tell moved along the ridge, shouting encouragement and directing men to where they were most needed. Below, the rebels pressed their advantage, striking with their halberds. The knights' training counted for little in the chaos, their traditional battlefield tactics useless in the confined space against the ingenuity of the halberds and the determination of desperate men.

Tell's heart lurched as he caught sight of Muller through the chaos of battle. A knight's blade flashed in the morning light before plunging into Muller's chest.

Tell scrambled down the slope. He ducked beneath the swing of a knight's sword and shouldered past a rearing horse.

'Muller!' He dropped to his knees beside his fallen friend. Blood soaked through Muller's leather jerkin, spreading across his chest in a dark stain.

Muller's eyes flickered open, his hand clutching at Tell's sleeve, fingers leaving crimson marks on the rough fabric. 'The pass...we must hold it.'

'Save your strength.' Tell pressed his hand against the wound, knowing even as he did so that it was futile. The knight's blade had struck deep.

'Promise me...' Muller's voice grew weaker, barely audible above the clash of steel and screams of dying men. 'Promise our children will know freedom.'

Tell gripped Muller's hand tight, feeling the life ebbing from his friend's body. 'I swear it.'

A ghost of a smile crossed Muller's bloodied lips. His fingers went slack in Tell's grasp, his final breath carrying the word, 'Freedom.'

Tell bowed his head, grief and rage swirling through his body. Around him, the battle raged on, but for a moment all he could see was his friend's lifeless face, peaceful despite the violence that had claimed him.

He rose from Muller's body, his grief hardening into steely resolve. Around him, the tide of battle had turned decisively. The Austrian knights, their formation shattered and their mounted advantage nullified, began a disorganized retreat up the pass.

'Don't let them regroup!' Tell shouted.

The Confederates surged forward, their blood-stained halberds driving the knights back. Horses stumbled over fallen comrades, their riders struggling to maintain control on rough ground. The Austrian rear guard attempted to provide covering fire with crossbows, but Ulrich's archers picked them off with deadly accuracy.

Tell watched as the knights abandoned their wounded, fleeing in small groups rather than risk being caught in the narrowing pass. Their proud banners, torn and muddied, disappeared into the morning mist. The thunder of retreating hooves gradually faded, replaced by the groans of the dying and the ragged breathing of exhausted men.

Victory had come at a price. Tell moved among the fallen, his heart heavy as he recognized familiar faces. Besides Muller, at least fifty other Confederates lay dead or dying. Each loss struck him personally. These were not just rebels, but neighbours, friends, fellow hunters, and craftsmen who had answered the call to defend their homeland.

The surviving confederates gathered around Tell, their faces streaked with blood and dirt. Despite their triumph, there was no celebration. They had won the day, driven back the Austrian knights, but the cost weighed them down. Tell looked at their faces and saw his own pain reflected there, the bitter understanding that freedom demanded sacrifice.

'Tend to our wounded,' he said. 'And rest assured we will give our fallen brothers a proper burial. They died as free men defending their families. We'll honour them as such.'

Tell cradled Muller's head as Ulrich and Stauffacher knelt beside him in the blood-stained snow.

'He was the first to take up arms when we called,' Stauffacher said, his voice riddled with emotion. 'Abandoned his slavery at the prison knowing he'd be hunted, left his family…'He placed a weathered hand on Muller's still chest. 'Never hesitated, never wavered.'

Ulrich removed his cloak and draped it over Muller's body. 'He believed in the idea of a liberated land – Switzerland – more than he feared death. He gave others the courage to stand with us.'

Tell nodded, unable to speak past the tightness in his throat. He remembered Muller's help in rescuing Bertha the day before and then the long night planning today's strategy with Ulrich, Stauffacher, and Furst, sharing bread and hope around a dim fire.

'His children will know their father died a hero,' he managed finally. 'They'll grow up in the free land he helped create.'

Tell knew that the question now was how Emperor Albert would react. The news would have reached him by now that the governors he'd sent to rule over the Swiss cantons had been deposed and that the people had taken control. Soon he'd learn his armed reinforcements had been defeated.

Stauffacher and Furst would lead a group to meet with the Emperor in Vienna. They believed they could negotiate a peace treaty between the newly emerging Swiss Confederacy and the House of Habsburg. The emperor would be in a compromised position. A peace settlement was likely to be in his best interests in retaining support for his kingship over Austria and Germany and Tell hoped for their success. He never wanted to see such oppression over his countrymen ever again.

But in this moment, in respect for Muller and those fallen, Tell, Stauffacher, and Ulrich remained silent. Around them, the sounds of battle faded to a hollow quiet, broken only by the wind whistling through the pass. Liberty had come at the cost of so much blood.

Chapter Thirty-One

The morning sun glinted off the Reuss River, casting a golden sheen across the water as Emperor Albert's entourage approached the ferry crossing. Albert rode in the lead, his back straight and his chin held high, every inch the regal sovereign, despite the long-ago battle injury to one side of his face, the cause of one hollow eye socket and an expression in the form of a permanent snarl. His crimson cloak billowed behind him.

Behind him rode Duke John of Swabia, shoulders hunched beneath his dark hood despite the warmth of the sun. His nephews flanked him.

'Uncle,' one of his nephews, von Wart, said, leaning close, 'are you certain about this course of action?'

John held firm on the reins. 'We've come too far to falter now.'

'The ferry awaits, Your Majesty,' one of the imperial guards called out to Emperor Albert.

The Emperor raised his hand in acknowledgment, the gesture carrying all the casual confidence of unquestioned power.

Duke John's horse stirred beneath him, and his features twisted with grievance. His gaze took in the Habsburg castle, across the river. That stronghold should have been his birthright, his inheritance. Instead, it stood as a monument to his uncle's betrayal.

They reached the ferry, and the Emperor addressed the ferryman. 'Make haste, good man. I have urgent matters to attend.' With news of the revolt across the Swiss cantons came information that a similar uprising was brewing in the region of Swabia. The Emperor had already sent an army of elite knights to the Swiss cantons and now, with this

215

visit to Swabia, in the company of the region's Duke John, he would meet with his governors there to personally ensure the same did not occur in this land.

For a moment, doubt gnawed at John's resolve. Was the reckoning he'd planned the true path of justice?

The young lords – Duke John's nephews – altered their positions. Von Eschenbach's horse edged closer to the Emperor's left flank, while von Tegerfeld's mount blocked the path behind. Palm and von Wart spread out to either side. The imperial guards tensed, hands moving to their sword hilts as they registered the subtle change in formation, but then dismissing any concern. These men were, after all, members of Duke John's family.

The Duke pulled his horse forward, drawing even with the Emperor. His face emerged from the shadow of his hood, pale and drawn, but his eyes blazed with an inner fire. 'Uncle.' His voice cut through the morning air. The ferryman, who had been preparing to guide the first horses onto the wooden platform, froze mid-motion. 'Before we cross, I must speak with you. Alone.'

The Emperor turned in his saddle, his expression hardening as he took in the positioning of John's confederates. The rushing waters of the Reuss provided a constant backdrop to the sudden stillness that had fallen over the group.

'What matter requires such privacy, nephew?'

'One that has festered too long.' John's thin face was tight with barely contained fury. His black cloak hung on his slender frame, and his fingers worked restlessly at the reins.

On his tour of the Swiss cantons, John had witnessed Governor Hermann Gessler's brutal treatment of his workers at the Altdorf Prison and his treatment of the archer, Tell. Actions supported by Emperor Albert. Now the word from their messengers was that Tell had assassinated Gessler, sparking the people's revolt across the cantons. It struck John that power wasn't something you waited to have handed to you. Real power was something you took by force.

The conspirators subtly maneuvered their horses, guiding Emperor Albert's mount toward the ferry's wooden planks where the ferryman grasped the reins.

Albert demounted. 'We can speak during the crossing,' he said to John. 'But this isn't a trip that can be delayed, you know this.'

'It is a matter of inheritance, Your Grace. Of birthrights and promises broken. Surely you do not want such delicate matters aired before the common folk.'

Albert's expression hardened. 'You dare to question my decisions? Here, now, on the very banks of the Reuss? Now, with the Swiss rebelling, and word of unrest in your own region?'

'Yes, *I dare*, uncle…for the sake of justice.'

Albert took a deep breath, showing his annoyance. 'There is no time for this discussion now, John. A man of importance and intelligence would instinctively know that. We will speak of this later.'

The ferry rocked beneath the horses' hooves as they boarded. Von Eschenbach and von Palm positioned themselves so that no guards could follow and John snapped at the ferryman. 'As my uncle said, make haste. You can return for my uncle's guardsmen.' There was limited space on the ferry. The Reuss River churned below, its waters dark and choppy, slapping against the ferry's wooden sides.

Albert had moved to the bow where he was lost in thought, focused on the castle on the shore, distracted by the news of the Swiss rebellion, oblivious that he'd been separated from his guards and advisors.

Duke John's nephews exchanged silent glances as they maintained their positions, effectively isolating the Emperor from any potential aid. The Imperial guards were taken by surprise when the ferry pushed off at the insistence of the Duke, and they watched as the distance widened quickly between the ferry and the shore.

As the ferry cut through the waters, John's mind raced. The dagger concealed beneath his cloak seemed to grow heavier with every breath he took. He studied his uncle's profile, searching for any sign of the man who had once bounced him on his knee, who had promised him a future with endless possibilities.

But all he saw was a stranger, an usurper who had stolen his birthright.

Eventually, the ferry bumped against the far bank, and once he'd led his horse off the ferry, Emperor Albert mounted his steed again. Before him lay a freshly ploughed field, the loam releasing its earthy perfume into the air. Larks wheeled overhead.

John watched his uncle mount, and his lips twitched. The familiar rage rose in his chest as Albert settled into his saddle.

The Emperor glanced at John and the young lords and then his gaze wandered to his retinue on the far bank, and he addressed the ferryman. 'Make certain you bring my guardsmen across quickly. They can join me at the castle.'

'Yes, Your Grace.'

Albert then cantered his horse across the field, oblivious to the tension building behind him. Dark clods of earth turned beneath the horse's hooves.

'Uncle.' Duke John spurred his horse forward, drawing alongside Albert. This would be his uncle's last chance to listen to him, to take him seriously. 'We should speak now. You have denied me long enough.'

Albert turned, his one good eye narrowing at John's tone. 'What? Still you carry on with this nonsense?'

'You've held what is mine since my father's death,' John said. 'Treating me like a child rather than your brother's son. What of the promises you made to *him*?'

The Emperor snorted. 'Your father was a weak man.' He waved a dismissive hand. 'We must look to the future now, John. You're young, you still don't understand the complexities of power.'

'And what of my future? How long must I wait for what is rightfully mine?'

Anger flared across Albert's face. 'Enough! I am still your Emperor and you would do well to remember it.'

John felt the dagger at his side, his fingers itching to grasp its hilt. 'I remember everything,' he said, his voice low but the simmering rage beneath his breast ready to explode. 'Every promise, every betrayal.' The tension in the air snapped like a bowstring. In one fluid motion, John's

218

hand flew to his side, drawing the dagger. The blade flashed brilliantly in the sunlight, a brief, terrible glimmer before it plunged into the vulnerable spot between Albert's jaw and collar. Blood spurted across John's pale hand as he twisted the weapon.

Palm's lance struck next, the iron tip punching through the Emperor's back. Albert's body jerked forward, his remaining eye wide with shock. Eschenbach's sword completed the gruesome work, slashing across the Emperor's chest as the Habsburg ruler tumbled from his saddle.

John watched, his heart pounding, as his uncle hit the ground. The assassination, planned for so long, had unfolded in mere seconds. He felt a surge of triumph, quickly followed by a wave of nausea. 'It's done,' he murmured, more to himself than his co-conspirators. 'May God forgive us.'

Across the river, shouts of alarm erupted from the imperial party as they saw the horrific deed. Their cries echoed across the water. John turned to see their distant figures, gesticulating wildly. Their horses reared and pawed at the riverbank as the men drew their swords, helpless to intervene. The ferryman, returning for the guards, was less than halfway across.

'God save the Emperor!' The desperate cry echoed across the river, followed by more shouts of horror and rage. The guards could only watch as their sovereign's body crumpled into the freshly turned earth, his crimson cloak spreading around him like a pool of blood.

John dismounted and stood over his uncle's body, dagger still dripping, while his conspirators formed a protective circle around him. 'He left me no choice,' he said, trying to convince himself.

'We must go,' Palm urged.

John nodded numbly, casting one last glance at his uncle's body and the distraught figures across the river.

As he walked back to his horse, a sudden movement caught his eye. A peasant woman working in the nearby field dropped her hoe and rushed toward the fallen Emperor. John's breath caught in his throat as he watched her kneel beside Albert's body. Her slender hands, rough from years of labour, gently cradled Albert's head. Blood seeped into her rough wool skirt as she knelt beside him in the freshly turned earth.

'My Lord Emperor,' she said, her voice trembling. She wiped dirt from his face with her apron, an instinctive gesture of tenderness that transcended the boundaries of class and power, but Albert was gone.

'*We must go*,' Palm hissed.

John raised a hand to stay his companion. 'Wait,' he murmured, his eyes fixed on the scene before him.

The woman's actions stirred something within him. Here was a commoner, one of the very people Albert had oppressed, showing compassion to the man who had caused so much suffering in Swabia and the Swiss cantons. The contrast between her gentleness and the violence they had just committed was stark, almost unbearable.

'Your Grace,' Eschenbach urged, 'we must leave now. Every moment we linger increases the risk.'

John tore his gaze away from the peasant woman. 'You're right,' he said, his voice hoarse.

The Duke and his conspirators spurred their mounts into a gallop, the horses' powerful strides throwing dark sprays of soil into the air. The riders' cloaks streamed behind them as they rode hard toward the shelter of the distant mountains.

But the image of the peasant woman cradling Albert's head refused to leave John. 'Why would she show him such kindness?' he wondered aloud.

'It matters not,' Palm said. 'Our focus now is on finding refuge until the outrage dies down and you can return to claim the emperorship.'

Palm and von Eschenbach flanked the Duke as they rode, while von Tegerfeld and von Wart brought up the rear. The mountains loomed before them, promising sanctuary in their remote valleys and hidden passes.

Chapter Thirty-Two

Tell led the group back toward Altdorf. His arms ached from wielding the halberd, and the blood of both his enemies and his friends stained his sleeves. Behind him, the scattered conversations of his fellow rebels drifted on the cooling afternoon air.

'Did you see how those knights tumbled when our rocks hit?' A young fighter's voice rang out. 'Like tin toys knocked from a shelf.'

'Show some respect,' Stauffacher growled. 'Good men died today.'

Tell glanced back at their group. Some supported wounded comrades, arms draped over shoulders as they limped along. Others walked alone, faces drawn and distant.

Ulrich helped a rebel with a bandaged leg, while two men carried Muller's body wrapped in a cloak.

'We won though,' another rebel said softly. 'The Austrians won't forget this day.'

'Neither will we,' Tell muttered, his throat tight as he thought of Muller's final words about freedom.

The setting sun painted the mountain peaks in fierce oranges and reds. A cool wind swept down from the heights.

'The blacksmiths served us well,' Ulrich said, adjusting his grip on his wounded companion. 'These halberds turned the tide.'

'Yes,' Stauffacher agreed. 'But it was Muller's roadblock that gave us the advantage. He died giving us that chance.'

Tell's heart ached as they walked. The victory felt hollow without Muller's steady presence, without his quiet wisdom and unwavering loyalty. Yet the halberd in his hand and the crossbow slung from his shoulder, were proof that the Swiss people could win against impossible odds.

Tell watched the group continue their march toward Altdorf, and then, ever the loner, he slipped away unnoticed through a dense thicket of bushes. The branches scratched his face, but he pushed through without hesitation. His muscles throbbed from the day's battle, yet his steps quickened at the thought of reaching Hedy and the boys.

Twilight fell across the meadow as he emerged from the undergrowth. He paused, scanning the area for any signs of Austrian patrols that had not yet been rounded up by the rebel forces who had remained in Altdorf after the Confederate raid there. Satisfied they were long gone, he crossed the open ground.

The familiar shepherd's path appeared before him, barely visible in the fading light. He'd walked this route countless times and the path ahead held memories, casting his thoughts back to simpler times.

The path wound around the base of a rocky outcrop, then descended toward Bürglen. He moved with increased speed, knowing each step brought him closer to the Meier farm where Hedy and his sons waited.

A breeze carried the distant sound of sheep bells from the valley below. They belonged to Meier's flock. He was close now, and he pushed himself even harder.

He crested the final hill overlooking Meier's farm.

The farmhouse stood peaceful in the dying light, smoke rising from its chimney. His eyes caught movement – Meier himself, standing by the barn door.

Tell raised his crossbow high above his head, the gesture clear against the darkening sky. Meier's figure straightened, then disappeared into the barn with urgent steps.

The distance between Tell and the farm shortened. The wooden door swung wide again as Meier emerged, gesturing toward the hidden cellar entrance.

Hedy appeared first, her hair catching the last rays of sunlight. Walter and Tristan scrambled up behind her, their small faces turning toward where Tell stood on the hill. For a moment, they all froze –a family separated by war and circumstance, finally about to reunite.

Then Hedy broke into a run across the field, her skirts gathered in her hands. Walter and Tristan raced after her. Tell watched them come, his chest tight with emotion. Hedy's face shone with joy and relief, while the boys' excited shouts carried across the distance between them.

'Papa! Papa!'

Tell lowered his crossbow, his free arm already reaching for them as they drew near.

Hedy reached Tell first, throwing herself into his arms with such force he staggered back a step. He buried his face in her hair, relishing her closeness. His crossbow clattered forgotten to the ground as he wrapped both arms around her, holding her close against his chest.

'William,' Hedy breathed against his neck, her voice breaking. Her fingers clutched at his shoulders as she pressed herself closer.

Tell pulled back just enough to cup her face in his strong hands, his thumbs brushing away the tears that streaked her cheeks. Her eyes shone with a joy that matched the ache in his own heart. He bent down, capturing her lips in a desperate kiss that spoke of all the fear and longing of their separation.

Hedy's hands slid up to frame his face, her touch gentle against the scratches and bruises from battle. She kissed him back with equal fervour, pouring all her worry and relief into the connection between them.

Walter and Tristan crashed into their legs, breaking the moment. Tell laughed as he crouched down to gather his sons into his arms. Hedy's hands settled on his shoulders, unwilling to break contact even as he embraced the boys.

'We knew you'd come back,' Walter declared, his small arms tight around Tell's neck.

Tell pressed his forehead against Hedy's chest as she stroked his hair, overcome by being surrounded by his family again. The trauma of battle faded, replaced by the warmth of Hedy's touch and his sons' eager chatter.

***

In the royal castle of Buda in Hungary, Queen Agnes's face turned to stone as she received the news of her father's murder. The messenger knelt before her, telling her of the Austrian Emperor Albert's final moments. The queen's fingers pressed down on her throne's armrests until her knuckles whitened. She was a petite woman, a member of the House of Habsburg. She had married into Hungarian royalty and was widowed at a young age after the death of her husband, Andrew the Third.

'Bring me my generals,' Agnes said. 'And send word to every loyal Habsburg noble. These murderers will not find refuge anywhere in our lands.'

The Hungarian court watched in silence as their queen rose, her black dress rustling against the stone floor. 'My father's blood cries out for justice,' she declared, overcome with emotion. 'I swear by all that is holy, I will not rest until every man who played a part in this crime has been destroyed. Their families will be erased from memory, their lands salted, their very names forbidden to speak.'

Her words echoed through the great hall, and those present saw in her eyes the same iron will that had marked her father's rule.

***

Within hours, Hungarian troops began mustering outside Buda's walls, as they prepared to march west.

'Your Majesty.' General Kovács approached Agnes as she stood at the window of the castle. 'The first battalions are ready to march. We await your final orders.'

Agnes turned from the window. Her face bore the sharp features of her father. 'Send riders to every corner of the realm. I want the names of anyone who sheltered these murderers, anyone who fed them, anyone who failed to strike them down on sight.'

'It shall be done, my Queen.' The general bowed deeply.

'The Duke of Swabia and his conspirators think they can hide in the Swiss mountains until the coast is clear for them to assume power.' Agnes's voice cut through the chamber like a blade. 'But the coast will never be clear for them. I will tear down every stone, burn every forest, drain every lake until they are found.'

She crossed to a large map spread across an oak table, her fingers pointing out the territories where the assassins might seek refuge. 'Their families must learn that treachery carries a terrible price. Their names will be erased from every record, their homes stripped bare.'

The general watched as she marked positions on the map, her eyes blazing with an intensity that made him step back.

'Let it be known throughout the Habsburg lands,' she commanded, 'that any who aid these traitors share their fate. Their blood will answer for my father's blood.'

'Yes, my Queen.'

The following day, Agnes received reports from her general and the chief advisors of the court. She was told that word of her father's death had raced through the lands.

Town criers rang their bells in village squares, their voices cracking as they delivered the shocking news. Merchants abandoned their usual routes, seeking shelter behind city walls as fortress gates slammed shut across the realm.

Travellers found themselves turned away at checkpoints, while suspicious eyes watched from castle battlements. The Habsburg realm, once secure in its authority, descended into fearful chaos.

Throughout Austria and Germany, nobles barricaded themselves in their estates, unsure whether to declare loyalty to the crown or seek new alliances.

Markets emptied, taverns closed, and people huddled behind locked doors, whispering about the bloody deed that had shaken their world.

Finally, Agnes received reports from her general on the rebellion in the Swiss cantons, unrelated to her father's death, that had seen a confederacy of Swiss rebels take control of the cantons of Uri, Schwyz, and Unterwalden.

'That is where Duke John will seek refuge, believing himself to be beyond our reach,' Agnes told her general. 'Negotiate with this upstart Swiss Confederacy to find him and hand him over. If they will not, then we send an army of our own to find him, not to fight the Swiss, that is not my fight, but to capture my father's murderer and his co-conspirators.'

Chapter Thirty-Three

The villagers of Altdorf swarmed the town square, their voices raised in jubilant chatter and from there, many of them marched along the path to the blackened ruins of the prison. Armed with picks, shovels, and hammers, as they had for the past two days since reclaiming the town, they attacked the remaining stones of the prison, each strike a blow against the symbol of their former oppression.

Ruodi the fisherman leaned against a wooden post, his face lifted toward the mountaintops where beacon fires still blazed against the morning sky. Beside him, the Master Mason paused in his work, wiping sweat from his brow.

'Look there,' Ruodi pointed to the distant peaks. 'Fire signals from Unterwalden to Uri, and beyond to Schwyz. The whole confederation celebrates.'

A smile creased the mason's lined face. 'And listen to those bells. Every church in Uri rings out our victory.' He picked up his hammer again. 'Never thought I'd live to see the day when we'd tear down what I helped build.'

'Your hands were forced to build it,' Ruodi said. 'But now they're free to tear it down and build something to inspire.' He pushed himself away from the post, limping, his joints stiff from weeks of hiding in the cold forest. 'Like my hut. They burned it to the ground. But I'll rebuild it stronger than before.'

The church bells pealed across the valley, their joyous sound mixing with the rhythmic strikes of tools against stone. Children darted between the workers, gathering smaller pieces of rubble in their aprons and tossing them into waiting carts.

'Each canton's fire tells the same story,' the mason said. 'We are reclaiming our independence.'

The crowd surged back and forth, their collective energy crackling through the square and along the path to the prison. Pitchforks and hammers emerged from beneath cloaks, passed from hand to eager hand. A carpenter's apprentice hefted his axe high.

'Down with every stone!' The cry rippled through the masses.

Women pulled loose stones from the prison walls, their fingers bloodied but determined. A blacksmith swung his sledgehammer against the strips of iron strewn about the ground.

'For Tell!' someone shouted. 'For freedom!'

The crowd pressed closer to the prison's remains, tools raised high. But Daniel Furst pushed through the throng, his hands raised.

'Wait!' His voice carried above the din. 'You should conserve your strength and be vigilant, in case of any escaped troops of soldiers. The beacons burn, yes, but until we have further confirmation from Schwyz and Unterwalden—'

'The beacon fires mean victory!' A farmer interrupted, brandishing his pickaxe. 'What more confirmation do we need?'

Furst grabbed the man's arm. 'If we act too hastily and our brothers in the other cantons have not succeeded as much as we hope—'

'Look at the beacons, old man!' Another voice called out. 'They burn from peak to peak!'

'The Austrians could be testing us,' Furst persisted, his eyes scanning the eager faces around him. 'Drawing us out to crush us once and for all. We must wait for the messengers.'

But his words were drowned by the crash of stone against stone as the crowd surged forward, their patience exhausted. Furst stood amid the chaos, his warnings lost in the fervour but he understood the impassioned sentiment. He understood it all too well.

A commotion from the direction of the square drew the crowd's attention. Arnold of Melchthal strode through the parting masses, his red hair matted with sweat and dirt, Baumgarten at his side, both men leading their horses behind them.

'The beacons speak true!' Melchthal's voice boomed across the square. 'Landenberg's castle has been taken. The Austrian troops flee like rats from our lands.'

The crowd erupted in cheers. Baumgarten raised his bloodied halberd. 'Schwyz and Unterwalden stand free!'

'And Governor Landenberg?' someone called out. 'What fate for him?'

Melchthal's face darkened. He planted his feet wide, his broad shoulders tense. 'I found him cowering in the forest, begging for mercy. The same mercy he denied my father.' His voice cracked. 'I raised my blade, ready to strike but then I saw my father's face. Not as he was in his final moments – he died just a week ago – but as he was when raising me, teaching me to be a man of honour.'

The crowd fell silent.

'I spared him.' Melchthal's words carried across the hushed crowd. 'Stripped him of his fine cloak, took his sword, and drove him from our lands with nothing but the shirt on his back. Let him live with the shame of being shown mercy by those he called peasants.'

Baumgarten clasped Melchthal's shoulder. 'You honoured your father more with that decision than any act of vengeance could have done.'

The children began darting through the crowd again. A young girl with braided hair clutched a broken iron hinge to her chest, while her brother dragged a piece of scorched wood behind him. Their faces glowed with pride as they added their finds to growing piles back near the town square's edge.

'Look what I found!' A boy of ten held up a rusted chain. 'This held our people captive!'

His friend snatched up a chunk of blackened stone. 'And this one's from one of the cells!'

Their mothers watched with tear-filled eyes as the children transformed years of oppression into treasures of liberation.

Near the remains of the prison gate, a heated argument erupted over Gessler's hat, still mounted on its pole. Several men had already grabbed ropes, ready to pull down the one at the prison and the one back along the path in the town square.

'Burn it!' shouted a mason, his hammer raised. 'I'm not sure why we haven't already scorched the damned thing.'

'Feed it to the flames!' Another voice joined in.

Daniel Furst pushed through the crowd again, his aged frame straight with authority. 'Stop! I propose we keep it intact.'

'But it's his symbol of oppression!' The mason protested.

Furst placed his hand on the pole. 'Yes, but does it not today become something else? Let it stand as a reminder of what we overcame. Let future generations look upon it and remember the price we paid.' He turned to face the crowd. 'This cap no longer represents Gessler's power. It marks the spot where Swiss liberty was born.'

'Then it should not just be the cap that sits atop the pole,' Melchthal said, 'but also the arrow Tell used to shoot the apple from his boy's head.' There were raised voices of agreement. The men with axes slowly lowered them, nodding in understanding. A small girl approached the pole, laying her fragment of prison stone at its base.

'For William Tell,' she said, starting what would become a new tradition.

A commotion at the edge of the square drew further attention as a rider on a lathered horse pushed through the crowd. The man's Swabian dress and the dust of long travel marked him as a messenger from the neighbouring territory.

'Werner Stauffacher!' The rider called out, sliding from his mount. 'My name is Jorius. I bring news from the Reuss River crossing.'

Stauffacher stepped forward, Furst and Ulrich flanking him. 'Speak, friend. What word from beyond our borders?'

'Emperor Albert is dead.' Jorius paused to catch his breath. 'Murdered by his own nephew, Duke John, and a band of conspirators.'

A collective gasp rippled through the crowd. Stauffacher's face remained impassive, though his hands fidgeted.

'Tell us how this happened,' Ulrich said.

'They ambushed him at the ferry crossing,' Jorius said. 'Duke John confronted him about his denied inheritance. Before the Emperor's retinue could reach him, John's dagger found Albert's throat. The Duke's nephews struck next with lance and sword.'

Furst knitted his brows. 'Even a tyrant like Albert deserves better than betrayal by his own blood.'

The crowd shifted uneasily, their earlier jubilation dampened by this news. A woman crossed herself, murmuring a prayer.

'We'll not celebrate this death,' Stauffacher said, his voice carrying across the square. 'Though Albert denied our rights, we fought his troops openly, face to face, and our intention was to negotiate with him personally. This murder brings no honour to our cause.'

Daniel Furst raised his hands, commanding silence from the gathered crowd as he addressed them. 'Then let us all agree. It will be known throughout our cantons that we Swiss take no pleasure in Emperor Albert's death. Though he denied us our ancient rights, though his governors ruled with iron fists, we fought our battle in the light of day. Our victory comes from our own hands, our own courage, not from shadows and daggers in the dark.'

The crowd murmured in agreement as Furst kept speaking. 'Let other lands mark well how the Swiss won their freedom, not through murder of kin, but through the righteous struggle of a people united.'

Stauffacher, standing at the edge of the gathering, scanned the faces before him. He realized something was amiss. He touched Ulrich's arm. 'Where is William?'

The question rippled through the crowd. People turned, searching for the familiar figure of their hero. The celebration seemed suddenly incomplete, hollow without the presence of the man who had struck the first decisive blow for their liberty.

'Tell?' The word passed from mouth to mouth, growing more urgent with each repetition.

'He was with us after the battle,' Ulrich said, his voice carrying across the crowd. 'But I didn't see him enter Altdorf.'

'He's not a man who seeks glory, he'll join us when he is ready,' Ruodi assured those nearest him.

The mason's voice rose above the others. 'Every stone we tear down today echoes that shot in the hollow. The shot that felled Gessler and broke his power over us.'

The villagers began to gravitate toward the road to Tell's cottage in Bürglen. They clustered together, shoulders touching, eyes fixed on the path where they hoped to see Tell's familiar figure emerge.

A young boy tugged at his mother's sleeve, pointing toward the mountain path. 'Maybe he went home to his family first?'

'Yes,' Stauffacher, walking alongside them, nodded, his expression softening. 'Tell's first duty was always to his wife and sons.'

'Hedy and the boys were at the Meier farm,' Daniel Furst added. 'I had word from Meier that Tell met them there on his return.'

The villagers began sharing their own stories of reunion – wives embracing husbands who'd hidden in the mountains, children running to fathers they hadn't seen in weeks, sometimes months.

After a long trek, a smaller group reached Tell's home, and it was Ruodi who went forward, his hand raised and ready to knock on the door. But the voices of the group had carried inside and the door opened before he could knock.

It was Hedy Tell who emerged, young Walter clinging to her skirts, and little Tristan, thumb in mouth, watching wide-eyed from behind her.

'Hedy,' Ruodi breathed, relief washing over him. 'Is William here? The people... we all wish to honour him.'

Hedy's gaze swept over the small but expectant crowd before settling back on Ruodi. 'William is... he needs time,' she said softly. 'The events of the past days have weighed heavily on his spirit.'

Ruodi nodded, understanding dawning in his eyes. 'But he is well?' he pressed gently.

Hedy managed a small smile. 'He will be. He's up in the mountains, seeking solace in the wilds he knows so well.' She paused, her voice catching. 'I know he'll join you when he feels he can.'

'The people here in Bürglen are planning a street festival tonight, hopefully, if William's back, he can join us.' Ruodi turned to face the crowd, his voice ringing out clear and strong. 'Friends! William Tell may not be here in body right now, but his spirit is with us. Let us honour him by living up to the ideals for which he fought!'

A cheer rose. As Ruodi looked back at Hedy and Walter, he saw in their eyes a mixture of pride and longing. He waved as he and the others headed off, but he could not shake off a sense of unease. He was worried for his friend.

Chapter Thirty-Four

Tell moved like a shadow across the snow-dusted ridge. The mountain air bit at his exposed skin, but his focus remained on the subtle indentations in the snow. The distinct hoof prints of a chamois that had passed through less than a quarter-hour before.

A broken twig caught his eye, its fresh snap revealing the direction his quarry had taken. The bark had been stripped at precisely the height where a chamois would browse.

The wind changed direction, carrying the faint musk of his prey. Tell adjusted his path, moving upwind to prevent his scent from alerting the animal. His father had taught him this technique on his first hunt, showing him how to read the mountain's signs as clearly as footprints in fresh snow.

The memory of his father's steady hands guiding his own surfaced unbidden. They had stood on this same ridge years ago, his father's voice low and patient as he explained the way of the hunter. 'The mountain gives us what we need but we must approach with respect, take only what sustains us.'

The old man had been more than just a teacher of hunting craft. Each lesson carried deeper meaning, about standing firm in one's convictions. 'A man who bows his head to tyranny,' his father once told him, 'is no better than a wolf who preys on the weak.'

The last conversation they'd shared played in his thoughts. His father's face appeared before him, not as the strong figure who had taught him to hunt, but as the broken man who stumbled from that prison cell seven years ago.

An illness had taken his mother swiftly years before that, leaving Tell and his father to lean on each other. His father never complained, teaching Tell everything he knew about tracking game and tending herds. In their village of Bürglen, people sought his father's counsel, respecting his straightforward wisdom and unwavering integrity.

But that integrity cost him dearly. Tell could still hear his father's voice rising against the Austrian tax collectors, denouncing their cruel methods. 'We are free men,' he had declared, 'not slaves to be beaten and robbed.'

The guards dragged him away that night. Tell, only a young father himself, watched helplessly as they bound his father's hands and marched him to the prison. When they finally released him, his father's eyes had lost their spark, his shoulders permanently stooped.

'They wanted names,' his father had said later, his hands shaky as he gripped his cup. 'Names of others who spoke against them.' He never revealed what happened in that cell, but the bruises that marked his body told their own story.

Three days later, his father collapsed. Tell found him slumped on the floor by his chair. The village physician claimed it was his heart but Tell knew the truth – the recently-appointed Governor's men had killed him as surely as if they'd used their swords. After that, Gessler had spread his control over more and more of the Uri canton.

Tell blinked, the memories dissolving as he gazed across the vast expanse before him. Snow-capped peaks pierced the clouds like ancient spears, their jagged edges softened by the sunlight. Below, the valley stretched in shades of green and gold, dotted with grazing sheep. The sight stirred fierce pride in his chest.

'William! The hero of Uri!'

Kuoni's weathered face appeared over the ridge, his shepherd's crook marking steady progress up the slope. The shepherd moved with the sure-footed grace of one born to the mountains. His grey beard couldn't hide his broad smile, and his eyes sparkled with genuine warmth.

'The whole town speaks of nothing else,' Kuoni said, reaching Tell. He planted his staff in the snow and clasped Tell's shoulder. 'You should see it. They're tearing down the prison stone by stone. Children run through the streets with pieces of the rubble. And they call out your name.'

Tell shifted uncomfortably at the praise. 'I only did what any man would do.'

'Any man? No, my friend. We all dreamed of standing up to Gessler, but you – you acted upon it. They're calling you the father of Swiss freedom in the taverns. They're calling for the united cantons to be known as Switzerland.'

Tell set his jaw in a hard line as he turned away from Kuoni's praise. His crossbow felt heavy in his hands. 'This bow was meant for hunting, not killing men. I never wanted to be anyone's hero, only to protect my family, to live in peace.'

The memory of Gessler's final moments flashed through his mind. He had taken lives before that moment, but always of animals, always with purpose and respect. This was different.

'The blood on my hands...' Tell's voice trailed off.

Kuoni stepped closer, his wizened face serious. 'And what of the blood Gessler and his soldiers would have continued to spill? How many more fathers would he have imprisoned? How many more children would have gone hungry under his taxes? How many wives, like Baumgarten's, attacked by his men?' The shepherd's voice grew intense. 'I've seen mothers weeping over sons beaten by his soldiers, families driven from their homes. Your arrow didn't just end one life that day at Kussnacht, William, it saved countless others.'

Tell looked at his friend, seeing the conviction in his eyes. 'Perhaps. But that doesn't make it easier to bear.'

'Nor should it. A good man doesn't take life lightly, even when forced into a war like the one we've just endured. But sometimes the shepherd must kill the wolf to protect his flock.'

Tell's mind drifted back to that fateful moment in the ravine. Armgart Mechthild had thrown herself before Gessler's horse, her children clinging to her skirts. The governor's cold voice had cut through the air, ordering his men to trample them. In that instant, the choice became crystal clear, like the split second when a hunter must decide to fire his arrow or let his prey escape.

He'd known that taking a human life would stain his soul in ways that hunting never could. Yet the alternative – watching Gessler murder an innocent woman and her children – was unthinkable. As would allowing Gessler to walk away if Tell's arrow had killed his son.

The shepherd squeezed Tell's shoulder. 'You may not have chosen to be a hero, but sometimes the mountain chooses its path for us. What matters is that you had the courage to walk it.'

Tell said nothing.

'In spite of the celebrations, I'm afraid there is news that could cause greater calamity.'

'What news?' Tell asked.

Kuoni told him about the news of Emperor Albert's assassination by the Duke. Tell's face darkened in speculation as to what this would mean for Switzerland and for Stauffacher and Furst's aspirations to negotiate a permanent peace.

Tell watched Kuoni's figure disappear down the slope, the shepherd's words lingering in the crisp mountain air.

The wind whispered through the pines, carrying the scent of snow and distant woodsmoke. Tell resumed tracking the chamois, his boots crunching softly in the snow. Each step felt more grounded than the last, as if the mountain itself was lending him its strength. Perhaps Kuoni was right, sometimes the path chose the man, not the other way around.

The setting sun painted the peaks in shades of gold and purplish-reds. Tell paused to watch the light play across the landscape, struck by how the same mountains could hold both terrible beauty and deadly peril. Like the crossbow in his hands.

Today, he would abandon the hunt and let this chamois live. It was time for Tell to return to his family.

Chapter Thirty-Five

Hedy's hands trembled with excitement as she arranged fresh wildflowers in a clay vase, their sweet fragrance filling the cottage. The familiar sound of William's hunting horn echoed through the valley, making her heart leap.

'Walter! Tristan! Did you hear? Your father's almost home.' Hedy smoothed her apron and tucked a loose strand of hair behind her ear. The boys burst into the main room.

'I heard it too, Mother!' Walter's eyes sparkled with excitement. 'Right beyond the ridge, wasn't it?'

Hedy nodded, her smile tinged with worry. She knew the weight William carried. The pot of stew bubbled over the hearth as she stirred it mindfully, adding a pinch more salt.

'Mother, remember when Papa shot the apple?' Walter perched on a stool, his legs swinging. 'Everyone was so scared, but I knew he wouldn't miss. I stood as still as a tree trunk.'

Hedy's hand paused mid-stir, her throat tightening at the memory. 'You were very brave, my love.' She had long since come to an acceptance of what William had to do.

'I wanted to make Papa proud.' Walter puffed out his chest. 'He always says a steady hand and a steady heart go together. I didn't even blink when he raised his crossbow.'

'That's because you're just like him,' Hedy said softly, watching her son's face glow with pride at the comparison.

She wiped her hands on her apron as a dark shape filled the doorway, blocking the afternoon light. A monk stood there, his brown habit dusty from travel, the hood casting shadows across his face. Her initial wariness melted – after all, the church had been their ally in these troubled times.

'Welcome, Brother. Please, come in from the cold.' Hedy gestured toward the bench by the hearth. 'We have much to celebrate today.'

The monk bowed his head and shuffled inside.

'God's blessings upon this house,' he said, his accent distinctly foreign. 'I seek shelter for the night and wonder if you could help.'

Hedy ladled some stew into a bowl, noticing that the monk kept his face averted. Despite her rising unease, she said, 'Of course. Though I'm surprised you've come this way. Most travellers take the main road through Altdorf.'

'Ah yes, Altdorf.' The monk's head turned, scanning the cottage's interior. 'I heard there was... unrest there. Tell me, good woman, is this the path one would take to reach Küssnacht?'

Hedy's fingers tightened around the wooden spoon. Küssnacht – where Gessler's estate lay. Walter moved closer to her side.

'Many paths lead to Küssnacht,' she said. 'Though I'm but a simple housewife, not well-versed in giving directions.'

'Strange. I was told William Tell's wife would know these mountains well.' His shoulders hunched forward, and his hands twisted the rope belt of his habit.

Hedy wondered why this man was so nervous. Had one of the villagers told him this was William's home? Beneath his hood, she caught a glimpse of haunted eyes. 'Something worries you?' she asked.

The monk's voice cracked. 'There are those who will come for me and they'll search everywhere, including the monasteries.' He glanced toward the window as if expecting soldiers to materialize at any moment. 'Gessler's estate in Küssnacht is now in the hands of the rebels. I seek refuge with them.'

Before Hedy could respond, Walter let out a joyful cry. 'Papa!'

239

Tell burst through the doorway, his broad frame filling the space. Tristan bolted from his corner, and both boys crashed into their father's open arms. The monk stumbled back, pressing himself against the wall.

'My boys!' Tell's laugh echoed through the cottage as he lifted them both, spinning once before setting them down. His eyes found Hedy's, and the world seemed to stop. In three strides, he crossed the room and pulled her into his embrace.

But as he cupped her face and pressed his lips to hers, Hedy's head tilted, her eyes sending signals, and Tell turned his head, following her gaze.

***

Tell's sense of calm evaporated as his gaze took in the hooded figure. The monk's hands trembled as he pulled back his hood to reveal a gaunt face that Tell recognized instantly – Duke John of Swabia, whom he'd seen at the Altdorf prison weeks before.

The Emperor's assassin.

Hedy's sharp intake of breath broke the silence. She pulled Walter and Tristan behind her, backing away.

Tell's hand moved instinctively to his crossbow but stopped. The man before him did not exude the dangerous arrogance of the proud noble who had plotted against his uncle. Instead, Tell was looking at a broken shell of a man, desperation in every line of his face.

'You dare come here?' Tell's voice was tight with anger. 'After murdering your own blood?'

Duke John fell to his knees. 'I seek only shelter for the night. Then I'll be gone, I swear it.'

Tell's grip tightened on his crossbow. This man had committed the ultimate betrayal - killing not just his sovereign, but his own family member. Every part of Tell's being recoiled at the thought of offering sanctuary to such a man.

Yet something held him back. Tell had also assassinated a man – Gessler – though his act had been one borne of both justice and survival, not betrayal. Still, that decision had changed him. Tell was now looking at a man crushed by the consequences of his own actions. Something with which Tell could identify.

'You are the man who killed Gessler,' Duke John said. 'Surely you can understand my action and give me assistance.'

'You killed your uncle for power and personal gain,' Tell said. 'Not to protect the innocent in a time of war. We are not the same.'

'No,' Duke John said, his eyes downcast. 'We are not.'

Tell watched as Duke John pressed his palms together, pleading. 'I cannot sleep. His eyes haunt me. My uncle's eyes in that final moment. The betrayal, the shock...' His voice cracked. 'I thought killing him would bring me peace, would right the wrongs done to me. Instead, every shadow holds his face. Every night brings his dying gasps. The nephews who helped have deserted me, their confidence in me shattered.'

The Duke's shoulders shook as he sobbed. 'I was blind with ambition, drunk on dreams of power. Now I see the truth of what I've done. I'm begging for your help, Tell.'

Tell felt the tightness in his shoulders ease. Despite his disgust, he would not hold the Duke for the law enforcers but neither could he condone his actions or offer him sanctuary. 'I can offer you no assistance here. You must go.'

'Then there is nowhere for me, I'm better off dead.'

Tell could not help but feel some sympathy for this shallow man's plight. He pondered the situation. If there was to be any salvation for John, then Tell instinctively knew there was only one path that could offer the Duke a chance at redemption. 'Then perhaps your only recourse is to seek absolution for what you have done.'

'Yes, but how?'

'Go to Italy, to Rome and to Saint Peter's city. Throw yourself to the spiritual leader's mercy, confess your sin, and pray for salvation.'

'But His Holiness will hand me over to the Austrians.'

'Whatever the outcome, John, it will be God's decree.'

John raised his head, his haunted eyes fixed on Tell's. 'Redemption?'

'Not mine to give, John, but God's.'

241

The Duke shook his head despairingly. 'But I could not find my way there.'

'There is a route from here through the mountains,' Tell said, his voice firm but allowing a hint of compassion. 'Follow the shepherd's trail past the three crossed pines until you reach the glacier's edge. There you'll find a hidden pass between twin peaks. Locals call them the Devil's Horns. The path is treacherous, but it will lead you to a monastery in the valley beyond. The monks there can guide you to Rome.'

Tell stepped closer, his voice dropping. 'But understand this. The journey is a harsh one. You'll face steep cliffs, bitter winds, and the constant threat of avalanche. The path is barely wide enough for a single man in places, with drops that vanish into darkness.'

'Then that too is part of my penance.'

Tell nodded. 'But it's the only way you'll avoid the bailiffs that will be sent in search of you. And then your fate is in the hands of powers far above ours.'

Through the cottage windows, Tell heard the approaching sounds of celebration from Bürglen – singing, laughter, and the pealing of church bells carrying across the evening air.

He turned to Hedy. 'Give him bread and dried meat for his journey.' When she hesitated, he added softly, 'Enough for three days.'

Hedy moved to the pantry. Tell watched as she wrapped provisions in a clean cloth. She placed the bundle on the table without meeting the Duke's eyes.

'As I said, the path I described leads past treacherous drops,' Tell said. 'Tonight, wait at the foot of the mountain. And on the morrow, travel only by daylight.'

John gathered the provisions. 'Thank you.'

Tell moved to the window. This wasn't about forgiveness, some acts lay beyond that, but about allowing a man the chance to seek his own redemption. Outside, the voices of his fellow Swiss grew louder, celebrating their hard-won freedom.

The rear door of the cottage opened and closed softly and Tell knew without looking that the Duke had left to begin his journey of penance.

He stood at the window long after John was gone. He wondered if the Duke would ever be seen or heard of again. Hedy's hand slipped into his.

'You did the right thing,' she said.

The sound of approaching voices grew louder. Through the window, he saw torchlight bobbing along the path to their cottage – Stauffacher, his father-in-law Furst, and a crowd of people.

Walter joined him at the window. 'Papa, look! They're coming to get us for the festival!'

The burden of all Tell had endured seemed to fade as he watched his fellow Swiss approach, their joyful songs carrying on the evening breeze.

'Come,' Tell said, drawing Hedy and his sons close. 'It's time to join our people.'

The door burst open, filling their home with the glow from lighted torches. Stauffacher's booming voice carried over the threshold.

'William! You're here. Good! You can't hide from your own victory celebration!'

Tell stepped outside with his family, into the embrace of his fellow confederates and they began the walk toward Bürglen's centre, Tell and Hedy watching Walter and Tristan skip ahead with the other children.

Chapter Thirty-Six

The deep, resonant call of Alpine horns rolled across the valley.

Tell recognized so many faces in the crowd, farmers he'd known since childhood, craftsmen who'd forged the weapons for the rebellion, shepherds who'd helped guide rebels through mountain passes. Their joy was infectious, and he fought down the familiar urge to retreat from their attention. He could not deny any of them this moment.

As he walked, hands reached for him, and voices called his name. Tell found himself pulled into embraces; his shoulders clasped by rough hands that had wielded halberds beside him. Women pressed forward to kiss his cheek, and children tugged the hem of his coat.

'You gave us our freedom!' someone shouted, and the cry was taken up by others.

Tell acknowledged their gratitude with quiet nods. Hedy remained close beside him, her presence anchoring him as surely as the mountain at his back.

Conrad Baumgarten appeared beside him, with his wife, Anna, at his side. 'You gave us back our lives,' Baumgarten said. Anna leaned in, kissing his cheek.

They reached the Bürglen town centre and Tell watched as the crowd parted, making way for two figures moving purposefully toward him. Ulrich von Rudenz walked with a new bearing – gone was the proud nobleman who had once scorned his own people. In his place stood a man humbled by experience, his hand clasped firmly around Bertha von Bruneck's.

Bertha's face still showed bruises from her prison ordeal, but her eyes were bright with joy. Her fine dress was torn at the edges, yet she carried herself with dignity. Tell noted how the crowd's reaction altered from initial wariness to curiosity as the noble pair approached.

When they reached the centre of the gathering, Bertha stepped forward. Her voice rang out across the suddenly hushed gathering.

'My fellow Swiss,' she said, her gaze sweeping across the assembled faces. 'I stand before you not as an Austrian noblewoman, but as one who has seen the true spirit of your people. I ask now to be counted among you, to pledge my loyalty to this free land, and to find protection under your laws.'

Tell felt the crowd's collective intake of breath at her words. Here was something unprecedented, a noblewoman of Austrian birth choosing to cast her lot with the common people. He studied her face, seeing only sincerity there.

'Yours are the values I choose to embrace,' she said. 'Let me make my home among you, not as your better, but as your equal.'

Tell watched as hands reached out to clasp Bertha's shoulders, and women pressed close to embrace her. The acceptance was immediate and overwhelming, washing away the last vestiges of class distinction that had separated them.

'You stood against Gessler!' called out a farmer's wife. 'You risked everything for our cause!'

Tell felt a swell in his chest at the sight. Here was the proof that their struggle had achieved more than just throwing off Austrian rule. It was a major step in breaking down the ancient barriers between noble and common folk.

Bertha turned to Ulrich, her eyes bright with emotion and she extended her hand. Ulrich stepped forward to take it and Tell noted how different he looked from the proud young nobleman who had once strutted in Gessler's court.

'I choose you,' Bertha declared, her voice carrying across the hushed gathering, 'not as a noble choosing a noble, but as a free woman choosing a free man.'

Ulrich's fingers interlaced with hers, their joined hands raised high, a gesture that spoke louder than any proclamation.

The crowd erupted in more cheers

Tell watched as Ulrich stepped forward. The torchlight caught the determination in his eyes as he raised his hands for silence.

'My uncle's castle stands empty now,' Ulrich's voice carried across the crowd. 'Its walls were built on the labour of serfs bound to serve. But no more.' He pulled a rolled parchment from his coat. 'Here I hold the bonds of servitude that have chained families to my family's land for generations. Tonight, I break these chains.'

He tore the parchment in half, then quarters, letting the pieces scatter in the wind. Tell felt the collective gasp from those who understood the significance. Centuries of feudal tradition destroyed in a single gesture.

'From this day forward,' Ulrich declared, 'all who worked my family's lands shall be free to stay or to follow their own path.'

Tell observed the stunned faces of former serfs in the crowd. A middle-aged farmer fell to his knees, tears streaming down his face. Others stood frozen, as if unable to comprehend this sudden transformation in their status.

The silence broke when someone started playing a zither. Another joined with a shepherd's pipe, and soon the night air filled with music. Tell watched as people who had moments ago been servants and masters now joined hands in a traditional dance, their movements expressing what words could not. He wished his mother and his father could have lived to see this day.

He stood motionless, Hedy's warmth against his side and his sons pressed close, watching the dancers whirl beneath the torchlight.

His hand brushed the crossbow at his side. The weapon that had brought down a tyrant now felt lighter somehow, as if the burden of its purpose had lifted.

The music swelled, pipes and drums joining the horns in a melody that seemed to rise from the very mountains themselves. Tell recognized the tune, an old shepherd's song his mother had sung to him, now transformed into an anthem of freedom. Walter hummed along, his small fingers tapping against Tell's leg in time with the rhythm.

Hedy's hand found his. 'Look,' she said, pointing to where Tristan had joined the dancers, his small form weaving between the adults with uninhibited joy.

Tell watched his youngest son, remembering the fear that had gripped the child during his time in hiding. Now Tristan danced without looking over his shoulder, laughing with his brother, Walter, without listening for the heavy tread of soldiers' boots. This was the gift they had won, not just for themselves, but for all the children who would follow.

ABOUT THE LEGEND

The earliest known written account of the William Tell story appeared in the *White Book of Sarnen*, a collection of medieval manuscripts compiled around 1470 - some 160 years after the events it described. The *Song of the Origin of the Confederation* is a ballad version of the tale that appeared later, in 1477. These sources connect Tell's act of defiance to the wider revolt against Habsburg rule in the early fourteenth century. Told and retold across more than five centuries, the image of the defiant archer grew into a symbol of Swiss independence, occupying a unique place between history and mythology.

By the sixteenth century, scholars had begun to question whether the famous marksman had ever existed. As with tales of King Arthur and Robin Hood, the story of Tell was one that was shrouded in folklore.

Yet his cultural significance only continued to deepen. In the 1560s, the chronicles of Aegidius Tschudi gave the legend a detailed and authoritative historical framework. Then, in 1804, Friedrich Schiller's celebrated play, *Wilhelm Tell*, elevated the local folk hero into something far greater - a universal emblem of resistance against tyranny. Rossini's opera of 1829 carried that transformation even further, fixing Tell permanently in the international imagination.

In Switzerland today, Tell's presence remains woven into the fabric of national life and identity. His image has appeared on postage stamps, currency, and countless works of art. In Altdorf, the William Tell Monument, unveiled in 1895, draws tourists and locals alike, while each summer open-air theatrical performances re-enact his famous story in the meadows above Lake Lucerne.

And in the nearby village of Bürglen, the Tell Museum preserves and displays artefacts and documents connected to his legend, reflecting the universal human impulse to resist oppression.

ABOUT THE AUTHOR

Jensen Tanner has worked as a freelance writer for various publications. He has long had an interest in history, mythology, and folklore, which inspired his novel bringing the legend of William Tell to modern readers. He is currently working on another novel in the historical genre.

www.ingramcontent.com/pod-product-compliance
Lightning Source LLC
Chambersburg PA
CBHW022157260626
47155CB00019B/3060